CHILD LOST CHILD FOUND

BY
Patty Renfro-Wonderly

Edited by
Daja Terry

Cover and Interior Designed by
Jeannie Hart

Contents

Part One
The South of Eternity

Chapter One

When I arrived in Eternity, I was fresh, fully formed, innocent, just like all the other souls arriving without the marks of the world. Before opening my eyes, I felt a tickling sensation between my eyebrows. Focusing my attention on the sensation as it grew painful, whirling rainbow colors filled the space and a window to my thoughts opened up. "Find us," whispered a low rumbling voice.

Startled, I opened my eyes and reached for the tendrils of curly hair haloing a smiling face. Forest green eyes, crinkled at the sides with joy and wonder, invited me into her world. A sliver of recognition spiked deep inside. I took her hand, following her strong, silent guidance. Deep within my new self, I knew I'd been here before. Knew her.

"I'd know that face anywhere. She looks just like her mom." I knew this voice. Remembered his kind brown eyes that twinkled with delight as he looked directly into mine.

"Doesn't she? I wish I'd been able to live with you and my sisters on Earth." Her voice sounded full of regret.

"Me too, honey. But when they get here, we'll have eternity to get to know each other." Love, ocean blue and grass green, flowed from the center of his soul, blending with similar colors emanating from her.

"I'm glad I was here when she arrived. We weren't expecting her this soon." He sounded profoundly sad.

"Cheer up, Dad." She embraced me in a tight hug. Curls smelling of orange blossoms and Springtime fell against my face. I breathed in her scent.

"Who are you?" My voice cracked, sounding squeaky and new.

"I'm your Aunt Katy and this is your Great-Grandpa, my dad." She gestured to herself and then to the gray-haired soul next to her. The introduction helped me reconnect with this person as the first voice I'd heard faded.

"Come on, sweet one," she said. "Let's walk to my cottage. It isn't far and movement is what you need right now. This new body is your first."

"I think I'll go get Mom and bring her over in a while," he said. "Give her time to adjust to life." He embraced me, smelling of pine and winter, rivers and wildlife.

We walked, my legs feeling new, tingly, capable of running forever. I marveled at my long dark curls tickling the area between my shoulder blades, the bright purple mountains surrounding us, and the turquoise stream flowing past perfect little cottages housing other souls going about their day. Some greeted Aunt Katy. Others stared at me, a mix of emotions on their faces. The vivid colors, new sounds, and a multitude of scents made me feel uneasy in my new body.

"Looks like another one fresh from the hospital. I can smell the disinfectant from here. Hope you don't plan on keeping her here. I can't stand them."

I couldn't reconcile the hateful words with the beautiful soul who spoke. Aunt Katy tightened her grip on my hand, quickening her pace while giving the speaker a glare I hoped never to be on the receiving end of. The speaker crossed her arms and glared back, standing with feet planted firmly on the dark fertile soil in front of her cottage.

"Alice, if you ever speak to my niece or me again like that, I'll report you to Zadkiel. Her birth circumstances are none of your business."

"Whatever. Keep her away from me," the soul called after us as we quickened our pace.

A chill ran down my spine. I didn't like the feeling.

"Why don't we try out your new legs?" Aunt Katy suggested. "I bet you're itching to run. I felt like I could run forever when I first arrived here." She dropped my hand and started jogging.

I quickly outdistanced her as my new legs knew no fatigue, enjoying the surge of euphoria.

"Slow down, niece!" Aunt Katy laughed. "You have eternity to run! Let's get you settled into our cottage."

I stopped, allowing her to catch up and we walked together back toward the line of cottages on the outskirts of the village. The door and windows of her home were open, and small sunflowers lined the cobblestone walkway. I was surprised to see how spacious it was once we were inside and Aunt Katy closed the door. Peace permeated the space.

"Would you like to see your room?" she asked. "I remembered your favorites from before." She walked down a hallway lined with open and inviting doors. "What do you think?"

I stood speechless in the middle of the plush white carpet and gazed at myself in the full-length mirrors along one wall. My skin, tawny brown and flawless, was darker than Aunt Katy's. For the first time, I noticed that Aunt Katy was clothed in a short flowing skirt of sapphire blue with some sort of animal frolicking across the gathered folds and a halter top that showed her middle and back. I wore nothing.

She stood behind me with her hands on my shoulders. "Aren't you beautiful? You're just as I pictured you."

"I'm not like you," I said.

"No. You're you," she said.

"I don't have any clothes." I recalled the expression on the face of the girl who'd sounded so mean, realizing she'd seen me like this. Didn't understand why the thought made me so uncomfortable.

"Oh, right." She giggled. "No one arrives with clothes. It's normal." She moved toward a large white-washed wardrobe and pulled the doors open to reveal tops and bottoms of assorted lengths and patterns, every one of them appealing to my senses. "Pick something."

Each garment smelled of something from Earth and I insisted Aunt Katy tell me the names: lavender, roses, cinnamon, coffee, popcorn, babies. I relearned color names as we lingered near the wardrobe and she guided me in choosing items. Since they all dazzled my new eyes, I chose a halter top similar to hers with a rainbow of colors in wavy patterns she described as tie-dye and a matching short skirt.

Once clothed, we continued our tour of the cottage. A library filled with books floor to ceiling, a sitting room packed with plants, her bedroom—larger than mine but similarly furnished, and a great room near the back that opened on to the turquoise stream I'd seen earlier. Every inch was packed with her creations.

Vividly colored artwork adorned the walls. Shelves full of trinkets from Earth, bags of yarn, baskets with paints and brushes and pens sat next to stacks of canvases and drawing pads of every size.

"Eternity for me is all about creating beautiful things," she explained. "Since you have no Earth life, you'll have an opportunity to see what eternity means for you. You're actually going to have to attend some classes. Souls like yours, ones with only slight memories or none at all from their time on Earth need help assimilating here in the South."

"How come I don't have an Earth life?" I asked.

We sat in white wicker chairs placed on soft moss near the stream. I watched several emotions cross her face, her mouth opening and closing a few times. "You are an Aborted Child."

"I don't know what that means."

She furrowed her brow, anxiety dancing across her countenance. "Your mom, my niece, decided to remove you from the womb before you had a chance to fully form your Earth body."

"Why?" I asked.

"I wish I knew that answer, but even if I did, I wouldn't have permission to tell you. Creator will tell you if you ask Them." She paused, shifted in her chair as a large tortoiseshell cat walked into the clearing across the stream.

"Come here, Gypsy," she said.

The cat bounced across the stream on steppingstones and settled into her lap.

"We need to decide on your name since my niece didn't give you one." She settled Gypsy on her lap. "I have lists of family names from both sides and thought we could start there."

"Are you an Aborted Child?" I asked. "How did you get your name?"

Once again, her brows furrowed. "I'm not. I was named by Mom and Dad, your great-grandparents."

"That soul I just met?" I asked.

"Yes. That's Dad," answered Aunt Katy. "You'll meet Mom soon. She visits Creator often."

"How long did you live on Earth?"

"I only lived a day before I came here." She stroked Gypsy and the large cat purred.

"How long ago was that?"

"Nearly seventy years ago I was born with too many medical problems to survive outside the womb," she finally answered. Her eyes flitted from me to the stream and back, waiting for my reaction.

"But your parents, my great-grandparents, wanted you and mine didn't? Does that happen often?" I was confused. I thought about all the souls we'd passed on our way to the cottage. Their stories, their journeys, each one different. Were there any more like me? Was I the only unwanted one?

Chapter Two

When Aunt Katy hesitated to answer again, I grew impatient. I walked to the stream and waded in. The water tickled my legs and the smooth stones felt wonderful under my feet. Looking upstream and down, I noticed other souls wading in, sitting on its banks with books or throwing sticks and balls for dogs of every color, shape, and size. Caught a glimpse of the long-haired girl standing downstream and staring at me with malice in her eyes.

I wanted to run. Just as Aunt Katy had said, my new legs longed to be used. I crossed to the opposite side of the stream, the water reaching only to my knees before I stepped on to soft moss covering the gentle slope.

At the top, I discovered a large parklike clearing and souls enjoying the day. The pink sky was filled with kites. A group of souls sat near a small copse of white-barked trees listening to someone tell stories. Others were rolling down a grassy hill, giggling and bouncing into one another.

I ran. And shouted. And giggled. And cried. Oblivious to stares and comments, I ran. I reached the woods on the far side of the park. Ducking under low pines and cedars, weaving in and out of the smaller bushes, I ran faster, colors, scents, shapes, and sounds blurring into one. I leaped over more streams and climbed rocks and boulders as the terrain changed and drew me toward the tree line.

Bursting through the last of the scrubby lone pines, I stood on solid granite leading to the crest of the mountain. I wasn't breathless, just exhilarated at the sight of the snow reaching down into crevices unreached by the bright glow of sunshine. The pink sky of the park gave way to a vivid aqua blue that made me blink.

"And who might you be who ventures so near the top of my mountain?"

Startled by the deep rumbling voice behind me, I moved further away from the trees. When I turned to see who had spoken, I stopped breathing and stared at the huge white wolf holding me in his gaze.

"You're an animal," I said.

"And?" he asked, ears tweaking forward, a grin breaking out on his furry face.

"Animals can talk?"

"They can if the soul believes they can." He stepped closer to me, his great white paws silent on the granite outcrop.

"Wow. I don't know what I believe yet. I've never lived." I shook my head and the breeze at the top of the mountain whipped my long hair around my face.

He was nearly as tall as me, his thick gray-white fur rippling in the breeze along his back. I waited until his black snout was inches away from me. "Can I touch you?"

"Would you like to?" he asked."More than anything I've ever wanted in my life." My hand was already reaching toward the top of his head.

He chuffle-snorted. "You've only been alive for half a day."

Burying my hand in the fur along his neck, I sighed and moved closer. He allowed me to hug him, gently at first, and then I began to cry. Tears were a new sensation. I drew back a moment to feel the moisture on my face.

"Why are you crying?" he whispered near my ear.

"I don't know. I'm overcome. Everything is so new and you're so amazing and my aunt told me my parents didn't want me and you're so soft and big and . . ." I stopped to look into his amber eyes. Emotions I didn't know existed swam in those eyes. Black irises mirrored my tear-streaked face. He licked them away with his warm, wet tongue.

"Let's sit, dear child," he said. "Have you a name yet?"

"No. My aunt was just getting to that when I felt the urge to run." I felt embarrassed that I didn't have a name. I didn't know why having a name was so important, but I knew I wanted one.

He put his nose under my chin and lifted my head. "You have nothing to be ashamed of, little one. Many come here without them. Some change them once they've been here for a while." He waited until I was eye to eye with him before continuing. "I have always been here, so I was given my name by Creator. At first, I was just Fal. Now I am called Anfalmor." His breath smelled of the forest and ice on the wind.

"What does it mean?" I asked. "I don't know what to call myself. I don't even know where to begin. Yours and Aunt Katy's are the only two names I've heard since I arrived." I hoped Anfalmor would name me.

"Hmmm. I see. Well, others of your kind generally decide on a family name they like the sound of. Why don't you wait to talk to her?" His head lifted above mine and I turned to see what he was focusing on.

Aunt Katy stepped into view, silhouetted by the deep rose-colored sky, a lock of black curls coming loose from her headband to fall across her face. She nodded to Anfalmor. He grinned as she sat next to us.

"I'm glad she found you, Anfalmor." Loving, respectful familiarity filled her voice. "What have you two been talking about?"

"Names," he replied.

My aunt sighed. "Yes. We were getting to that when she ran."

I didn't like being talked about as if I wasn't there. As if not having a name made me less of a soul. Maybe it did. Unwanted and unnamed. So far, my existence wasn't making me feel very good about life here.

"It's okay, niece," said Aunt Katy. "I get why you ran. I should have anticipated your reaction. I've rehearsed how this day would go ever since Creator told me you were coming but forgot you would have your own will. I just want you to get off to the best start possible." She laid a hand on my arm and rubbed gently as she spoke. Anfalmor shifted to sit across from us, his eyes kind and wise.

"If my family didn't want me, then I don't want any of their names," I said. "I want Anfalmor to name me." It felt bold to say it out loud, as if speaking my thoughts was forbidden somehow. He chuckled and shook his huge white head. "I will help you decide, little one, but that's all."

"You said you were named by Creator. Can't I just go ask for a name?" I thought this was the best solution.

"When you choose a name, Creator knows it's right for you," said Anfalmor. "It will fit. It will help define you and that's especially important since you've no Earth-life."

"Well, let's get started then. What do they call souls like me on Earth?"

"They call you fetus, embryo, egg, growth." Anfalmor paused. "Help me out here, Katy."

I sensed some discomfort with the words he spoke. I didn't understand why he hesitated. I watched Aunt Katy look toward the mountain's peak, the snow, and deep purple crevices of shaded areas. She stared at me, her eyes narrowing, head cocked to one side in thought.

"I don't think she needs to know all the words from Earth. How about some other languages?" she offered. "There's *bambina*, *infans*, *kindje*, *usana* . . . do any of those sound good?"

"Why don't you want to tell me all the words?" I asked.

"Because some of them are really hurtful and demeaning and I don't want you to pick your identity from any of them." Aunt Katy's voice dripped with vehemence. "You arrived pure, just like every other soul here."

"Is that why that girl spoke to me the way she did earlier?" I asked. "She said something about a hospital. What does that mean?" "She doesn't know what she's talking about," Aunt Katy said. "And she's inferring something about your worth as a soul. She shouldn't have spoken." She and Anfalmor exchanged a glance I couldn't read.

"Did any of those words for baby give you good feelings, little one?" Anfalmor's furry ears flexed forward, fixing me with his full attention once again.

I asked them to say the words once again, more slowly so I could repeat them in a whisper to myself. My heart quickened at the word embryo. "What about Embry?" I asked. "Is that a good name? Will that work? I think it feels okay on my tongue. It feels light, like this place."

"I like it," said Aunt Katy. "Embry. Yeah. That's nice. What do you think Anfalmor?"

He licked me with his warm wet tongue, a smile on his wolfy face.

Aunt Katy and I giggled while Anfalmor chuffed his wolf laugh. "I'm going to take that as a yes." I sat for a minute feeling happy. Relieved. "What now?"

We laughed again.

Chapter Three

I learned to call Aunt Katy's Mom and Dad "Grandma and Grandpa" as we visited together in front of the fireplace that night. Grandma was soft and wonderful to hug, smelling of roses and ocean breezes. They laughed and shared stories of life here.

Darkness frightened me until Aunt Katy explained that it was a normal part of our existence and was meant to remind us of our time on Earth when it had signaled an end to the day. "We don't need to sleep, but it's nice to have a reminder that time is passing and that if we want, we can switch to calmer activities. Many ignore it and just go on with what they were in the middle of when darkness happens. I like it as it helps me take a break from whatever project I'm working on."

"Dad likes to find some of his buddies and go fishing by moonlight," Grandma said. "There's always a full moon and plenty of fish to catch."

"And Mom likes to play cards with some of her friends from high school," Grandpa added.

"What do you like to do, Aunt Katy?" I asked.

"Sometimes I go with either of them. Fishing's fun, right, Dad?" Aunt Katy winked at Grandpa.

"Always catch my limit." Grandpa chuckled.

"Mom's friend Amy is my favorite. She's got the best stories about her." Aunt Katy nudged Grandma in the ribs. "Sometimes I hang out with my cousins or friends I've made since I've been here. You'll meet them. You'll meet everyone."

"Why didn't my parents want me?" I asked when we'd been quiet for some time.

"You'll have to ask Creator, honey." Grandpa's voice was gentle. "I'm sure your mom thinks of you every day, probably your dad too."

"How do you know that?" I asked.

"Well, we never stopped thinking about Katy here after she died." Grandpa squeezed Aunt Katy as he spoke. "Right, Mom?"

"You know, we never did get money to buy her a grave marker," Grandma replied. "I took the girls to see her grave every year on her birthday." She wiped the tears away with the back of her hand.

Grandpa stood and reached for her hand. "Come on, let's let these two have some time before Embry has to go to class."

"Why do I have to go to classes and you don't?" I asked.

"Souls that don't get to learn what you're supposed to on Earth have to learn a little about what it would have been like. I think you're kind of lucky. Life on Earth can be pretty bad sometimes." Grandpa patted my back as we hugged. "Don't worry. You're going to have fun." Grandpa sounded sad. He ran a hand across his short hair and took Grandma's hand as they walked down the cobblestones away from our cottage.

"It's going to be fine, Embry," said Aunt Katy. "I promise." She led me to my room, hugged me tight before closing the door.

Alone for the first time since arriving, I sat perfectly still and looked at myself in the closet mirrors. I ran my hands through my wavy hair, wondering why my skin was so much darker than Aunt Katy's. I ran a finger down my nose, noticing its flatness and how my nostrils were wider than hers. I ran a hand down each arm, feeling the dark hairs and my long, slender fingers. I did the same with my legs and wiggled my short toes. Grandpa said I looked like my mom, but I guessed there was a lot of my dad in me too.

As strains of pleasant flute music filtered through the open window on river-scented breezes, I ran my hands along all the clothes in my closet. A seashell collection sat on a shelf under the window. I picked a large spiral-shaped one and lifted it to my nose. It smelled of Grandma. I smiled. So smooth inside. Rough and bumpy on the outside. Somehow, I knew to put it to my ear.

"Hello, Embry," the most perfect voice I'd ever heard whispered from within the shell.

"Who? What? Where'd that voice come from?" I looked inside the shell. Expected to see a tiny creature of some sort but there was no one.

"I'm over here."

Standing outside my window was a glowing presence. Every color in the world emanated from deep within Their center and radiated toward me. It felt perfect: healing, affirming, energetic, and peaceful, full of possibilities and only the highest expectations just for me. I felt like the only soul in existence gazing into the eyes of this massive powerful presence. Creator.

I couldn't speak.

"You are welcome here," Creator said. "We're sorry we weren't at your arrival, but we had others to attend to who didn't have anyone else to greet them. We knew you were in good hands with Katy and your great-grandpa."

I blinked and Creator was standing inside my room. Rainbow energy filled every inch, pummeling me and flowing through me at the same time. I felt like I was caught in a cyclone and floating on waves of a calm ocean. All the most pleasant smells imaginable assaulted my nostrils. Every perfect note ever heard hung in the air around us. I wanted to leap and swim, shout and be silent, laugh and cry, sing and be sung to forever. There was nothing I could think of that was better than the presence of Creator.

"Shall we sit and chat for a bit?" Creator reached for my hand as two chairs appeared next to the window. "Anfalmor told me of your naming. You chose well, Embry."

I was too awestruck to reply. Instead I openly stared at Creator. A kaleidoscope of color filled my room, filled me, filled the world.

They chuckled. "We know We're a lot to take in all at once, but you'll get used to Us. We used to have quite good chats when you were here before." They seared me with a penetrating glance, reading my mind. "Ask your question."

"Why didn't my parents want me?" I whispered, afraid to break the perfect spell of Creator's presence.

"Well, you were unexpected, a surprise," They started.

"Aren't surprises usually good things?" I asked.

"Yes and no." They spoke slowly, their eyes looking deep into mine. "When souls join with a body, they have no recollection of life here, so your parents had no way of knowing who you'd be or why they would have needed to let you live."

"But isn't that the same for everyone?" I asked.

They nodded. "It is. However, in some societies on Earth, a pregnancy at the wrong time can bring about such radical changes in someone's life that it's better in their eyes to end it. Your mom is very young. Your dad, well, he made a bad choice, and the result was you. He couldn't give your mom any help with you. When you were conceived, there was too much pressure from societal influences to consider having you. Your Mom went to a clinic and had you surgically removed, and you arrived here the same hour."

"So, my parents live in that kind of society?" I felt a little better knowing this, but it didn't dispel all the hurt. I still felt like they should have at least given me a chance to prove myself worthy. "Kind of a sucky society, right?"

"It's complicated." They shook their head. "You must reject self-pity, Embry. It has no place where Love dwells, so if you give those feelings a place in your heart, they will take root. Your eternal life is what counts now."

They stood to leave, filling the room with colorful energy. "In class tomorrow, you will meet others like you. They, too, are searching for answers. Trust your Instructor. Dina is an excellent nurturer."

Their vanishing, though not abrupt, left me feeling thoughtful, melancholic. I spent the remaining hours of my first day laying on my soft bed.

Chapter Four

As the sky brightened from deep sapphire to hues of pink and orange, Aunt Katy guided me past the rows of cottages to a meadow. I joined ten other souls sitting under an ancient evergreen tree, a light breeze bringing pine scents through the clearing, bending the petals of thousands of yellow narcissuses. A Light-Being, Dina, glowed soft with rainbow colors. She spoke of eternity's meaning for us because of how we were different than souls with knowledge from living on Earth. I watched a family of gray rabbits hop and nibble their way through the high grasses and yellow narcissuses, only half listening.

"Heard you met Creator your first night," whispered a voice from behind the evergreen. "Think you're all kinds of special don't you? You aren't. You were a mistake and your parents got rid of you."

"Alice," Dina said. "Either come out from behind the tree and speak or go away."

The female soul with the brassy aura who'd spoken to me the first day moved from behind the tree, hands on hips and swaggering. The tingling in the middle of my forehead started again as soon as she drew near. I rubbed the area, but the feeling lingered.

"Hello Dina. Such a waste of your time and talent teaching these know-nothing souls." Alice gestured at me. "Don't you just hate it?"

I watched, feeling shame and embarrassment. Unwanted. No Earth-life. My companions looked down at the grass beneath them, waiting for Dina to agree with Alice.

She didn't. Instead, she stood and walked to each one of us, tapping us on the head and erasing the feeling of shame before she took Alice none-too-gently away from our circle, out of earshot.

"What does she mean by know-nothing souls?" asked a smaller soul sitting across from me. He had enormous brown eyes, almost too big for his head. His gangly brown arms rested on crossed legs. "I'm Usan. My parents didn't want me."

"Mine didn't either," said the soul to his left, a larger soul with hair the color of early strawberries.

Each soul in turn repeated Usan's words, adding their names at the end as if to validate their existence until it was my turn. "I'm Embry. And my parents didn't want me either. But that doesn't make me any less of a soul than Alice. It just means she experienced things we didn't on Earth."

"Yeah, but we really don't remember anything since we didn't get a chance to live." Usan looked around the circle for agreement.

"We lived," I said. "We All started here before we got our chance to go to Earth. Don't you remember at least that?"

"Kind of?" said Isla, tilting her head and allowing her strawberry hair to fall away from her face.

Dina returned before I could continue, sat down on her log with a huff, her softened countenance gone, a possessive set to her mouth.

"Are you sorry you have to teach us what we don't know?" said a soul with skin darker than mine and tight ringlets sticking out from her scalp at odd angles, a tinge of defiance in her voice.

"Not at all," Dina answered. "It is, and always has been a privilege to be chosen to guide your kind back to who you are here. I chose each of you because I knew you Before. Every other soul of your kind was chosen by the other Beings in the same way. I loved you then. I love you now. I will love you always. You can't know how grief-stricken I was to learn you would return here so quickly." She paused. "Your circumstances are not your fault. Never forget that. Never listen to souls like Alice. Ever."

A red aura, the color of safety and protection, had replaced her soft rainbow glow, emanating out from the center of her Being to surround our small circle. It tinged the trees and air around us, looking like blood.

"Why are souls like Alice allowed here?" I asked. It seemed she might be better off in a part of Eternity that kept her out of contact with souls like us. I knew I'd be better off without her hate. The tingling in my forehead had stopped.

"All souls started here in Eternity, created by Creator," Dina answered. "All souls return to a part of Eternity after their life on Earth. We all have learning to do and eternity to do so. Alice learned jealousy, hatred, and anger there and arrived in Eternity with a broken heart. She was just finding out what love could be when she died in an accident. This is where she has the best chance to heal. But don't worry, her teachers will hear of her disruption today."

I pondered Dina's explanation and let it go. I vowed to steer clear of Alice.

———————————

My second day of class included a refresher on basic knowledge we might have forgotten: colors, shapes, numbers. Except for one soul, Isla, my class recalled this information quickly. Isla proved stubborn, asking why something was so every chance she got.

"Why is that color called pink? Are you sure? Why do we have to number things? Why did Creator make bugs? How did the rhinoceros get named that?" She asked about everything. At first, her curiosity was amusing, but later I grew tired of her questions and felt some degree of empathy for Alice.

When Dina dismissed us for the day, the sky was changing from pink to gentle lavender. Aunt Katy stood waiting for me on the edge of the copse of trees with other souls. I watched a yellow-clad soul with a red dot in the middle of her forehead greet Usan; a tall red-bearded soul wearing a black leather tunic over gray trousers grab Isla in a fierce hug; and was surprised to see even Dina was greeted by a Being glowing all the shades of the night with a large pale-yellow light in the center of his torso.

When they embraced, their colors blended together, love pouring into and through them to all the other souls close by. Noticing my gaze, Dina motioned for me to draw closer.

"This is Zadkiel." Tangible energy washed over and through me as I stood close to the couple.

Aunt Katy joined us, embracing first one Being and then the other. "How did Embry do today?"

I felt shy standing so close to Dina and Zadkiel. Wanted

to hide behind Aunt Katy. Didn't feel worthy to be anywhere near such power.

"She was one of my brightest students today, weren't you, Embry?" Dina replied.

"I was?"

Zadkiel laughed, the ground beneath us shaking a bit. "You need to let your students know how you feel while they're in class, Dina. This little one doesn't seem to believe you."

"Alice interrupted us today." Dina replied. "You need to speak to her tomorrow . . . and keep a closer eye on your own students. Embry, all of Zadkiel's students are products of a different type of unwanted existence during their lives on Earth."

Zadkiel nodded at Dina for a moment, shifted his feet, and addressed Aunt Katy and me. "I'm sorry, Embry. It won't happen again."

I wanted to believe him.

Chapter Five

As we walked toward our cottage, more souls smiled and waved than on the first day. Aunt Katy had been busy while I sat with Dina relearning the basics. Everyone knew my name.

"We're so glad you're here Embry," said a group of female souls standing together in front of a large cottage. Their soft energy matched the hugs I received from each one of them. "Isn't she just beautiful? I see her mother. And her father. She's a perfect blend of both." They all talked at once. It was bewildering.

Further up the hill, two male souls stood holding hands while they waved at us. "Katy. Bring her here. We've made something for her." Turning, they picked up a package colorfully wrapped and held it out for me to take.

"I hope she likes it," said the one with cropped black hair.

"She'll love it," answered the larger one wearing his blonde hair in a ponytail.

I set the box on a bench near the entrance to their cottage, gently pulling on the ribbon. As I did so, the wrapping disappeared and the lid flew up. Inside was a halter top and skirt much like the one I had chosen to wear that day. Tiny strands of the softest satin were woven into spirals and swirls covering their entirety. At once heavy and light, I lifted the garments from the box and held them up in the lavender sky. The two souls were crying as I draped them against my body, wanting more than anything to run home and change.

They spoke simultaneously, pride in their voices.

"Ty made the fabric," said the one with the ponytail.

"Martin designed the pieces," said the one with cropped black hair.

"They're perfect." I stepped closer to the couple. "I could never make anything so beautiful."

"Are you kidding me?" Ty spoke with a slightly different accent than everyone I'd met. "Your Aunt Katy made every garment that's in your closet. You come from a very talented family."

"Well, she collaborated with us on a few things," added Martin.

"It's true, Embry." Aunt Katy put her arm around my waist. "These two designed what you're wearing today. I told them about what you chose to put on when you first got here and they've been busy all day."

"You made these in a day?" I asked. "How?"

"Practice. Lots and lots of practice," answered Martin and Ty and the same time.

"I would love to learn. From all of you," I added.

"That's what we wanted to hear," said Martin. "You're welcome any time."

Aunt Katy and I stood arm in arm as they walked back to the entrance of their cottage.

"Why is everyone so kind here?" I asked. I folded the new clothing back into the box and we walked toward our cottage.

"Oh Embry. Everyone wants to show you the love you deserved but didn't get on Earth," Aunt Katy answered.

"What about Alice?" I asked.

"Alice, and others, are also learning what they didn't there. She arrived filled with jealousy, hate, anger, discouragement, shame." Aunt Katy hugged me tighter to her as we walked, our hips bumping against each other. "We try to keep those souls separate as much as we can, but part of their education is to try using what they learn about love, acceptance, compassion, and joy in everyday situations, so it gets difficult sometimes. Zadkiel is her teacher. He will have a talk with her about her behavior today."

"The others in my class are all unwanted souls. There's a lot of anger and shame in our group as well." I pulled away from Aunt Katy, feeling defensive of my classmates.

"I understand that, but yours comes from a completely different place and will dissipate sooner than Alice's will," said Aunt Katy. "She has to unlearn things, forgive, and relearn self-acceptance. You and your classmates have no reason to feel shame. It isn't something you learned as a result of experiences."

Once inside our cottage, Aunt Katy sat down at her potter's wheel to work with a large lump of light green clay, molding it and shaping it into a small water pitcher as I watched with fascination. Gentle flute music floated in through the open windows and I found myself drawn once again to the small porch near the stream. Sitting with my feet in the water, I allowed small golden fish spotted with white, black, and red patches to nibble at my toes. It tickled.

I closed my eyes, recalling the feelings of the day: wonder, joy, confusion, and shame. Shame rushed in to blot out the others, though I tried to find the green energy of the positive emotions. Breathing deeply of the floral and pine-scented air, I focused on joy. Find the joy. Forget the shame. Find the joy. Forget the shame. As I breathed, eyes closed, a presence made itself known to me. I heard the shiver of light fabric as the presence moved to sit nearby, saw yellow-orange energy through my closed eyelids, and a small splash as if it, too, had dropped its feet into the water.

"They tickle, don't they?" The voice was unexpectedly rough, as if the presence had come from somewhere the air wasn't as fine as here.

I felt afraid to open my eyes, though curiosity overcame fear and I did. Sitting next to me was a Light-Being similar to Zadkiel and Dina, yet far different. Where they were nearly too perfect to look upon, this Being bore jagged scars across his red-skinned face, arms and legs. Where they were shapely and groomed, this Being wore what looked like a bundle of rags around its torso. It allowed me to stare, staring back the whole time. No guile. No shame. No judgement. Just a steady stare.

"I can tell you have questions," he said in a rough, broken voice.

"What are you? Who are you?"

"I come from the Northern Side," It said.

"I don't know what that means," I replied.

"No, I guess you wouldn't. Yet." He shifted and yellow-orange energy pulsed into me with his movement. "The

Northern Side is reserved for souls who've much to unlearn from their time on Earth." Waves of sorrow, of muddied red and woeful energy blasted through me, blowing a hole in my soul.

I gasped, crossing my arms across my chest in protection against the onslaught.

"Some, most actually, never do," It continued. "In fact, as I've already said, I'm the only one from the North allowed to come and go."

"Why?" I whispered.

"Well, most souls arrive in the South wanting to learn and quickly embrace eternity. You grow in positive ways, emulating Creator. The souls placed in the North only have a glimmer of desire to grow and change left in them. Those that make the right choices, to learn, to grow, to change receive an opportunity to come South." He withdrew his feet from the stream to sit cross-legged facing me. "I come here to meet with other Light-Beings on high matters pertaining to the movement of souls and to renew my own Spirit."

I looked again at this ragged Light-Being. "What's your name?" I asked. Names were so important here, I'd come to realize.

"You can call me Dhororr," It replied.

"Does it have a special meaning? Did you choose your name?" I asked.

"Souls from Earth named me, though I would have chosen something similar," he answered. "I teach the ostracized."

"Who?" Words still confused me at times. It was only my third day.

"Souls who were shunned on Earth. Souls who've never known the compassion of Creator. Souls without any validation for existence on Earth and come here believing they don't deserve an Eternity."

"Like me?" I asked. "Shouldn't you be teaching me and the others in my class?"

"Not at all like you." His rough voice was a growl as he answered. "You accepted your Aunt's love immediately and without question. Your Grandpa and Grandma shared their lives with you the first night you were here and you never questioned their love." He pointed toward the cottage where Aunt Katy still worked with her clay. "The souls I teach were spat on, cursed at, misunderstood their entire lives and made to feel as if they never should have existed. Do you feel that way?"

"I feel unwanted," I admitted.

"These souls experienced it firsthand nearly every day of their existence on Earth. As far as you know, your life on Earth would have been filled with love and inclusion." He stood. "It's been a pleasure meeting you, Embry. Listen to your Aunt and release your shame." Yellow-orange energy pulsed through me once again and my heart felt gratitude for all those who loved me and had shown me love since my arrival. His words lingered even as he disappeared across the stream. Looking down, I noticed the golden fish with the red, black, and white speckles still nibbling at my feet.

Chapter Six

Aunt Katy determined I could find my own way to class the next day and waved from the end of the flower-lined walkway as I walked toward the meadow where I knew I'd find Dina. I was beginning to recognize souls along the way, smiling and waving back. Dhororr's words echoed in my mind: the ostracized so different than those of us who could receive love without question. For the first time, I felt lucky to have missed my learning on Earth.

"Hey, Embry." Usan surprised me from behind an ancient oak tree.

"Usan, I didn't see you. How long have you been standing there?" We continued toward the park.

"Not long," he replied. His large brown eyes, rimmed with long, straight lashes, made him look even smaller. "Some of us are going to hang out near the swings after class today. I was wondering if you wanted to come."

"Sounds fun." I was pleased to be asked, to be included. Usan surprised me again when he took my hand in his and swung them between us.

Instead of Dina, Creator greeted us in the meadow. Their rainbow energy engulfed Usan and me, love and light and acceptance pulsating into my soul.

"Today we will hear each other's stories," Creator said, Their voice resonating with joyful sounds. "We've sent Dina on an errand."

Isla and the others joined me and Usan on logs in a semicircle around Creator, eager to be near Them yet slightly awed of Their presence.

"We'll hear from Zach first." Creator sat down in front of us, pointing at a tall, sharp-haired boy with piercing, ice-blue eyes.

Zach jumped at his name, his mouth opening and closing like the fish I'd seen nibbling at my toes in the stream. "I don't know my story," he said. "I was hoping You were going to tell it."

Smiling, Creator shook Their head. "No. There's not much learning in that. You'll be surprised at what you know. I am only here to clarify and reassure."

"But can't you start with someone else?" Zach looked around, ice-blue eyes stopping when he got to me. "Embry, maybe?"

Thanks for that, Zach, I thought. *Why me? I don't know any more than you do, Zach with the ice-blue eyes and yellow hair sticking straight up from your head.*

As if They could read my thoughts, Creator smiled wider at the attention the other souls were giving me. They shifted Their rainbow energy into one single color, a vibrant emerald green, and once again, I was awash with love. "Zach, start at the beginning of your story. We will help you as you speak."

And so, Zach spoke, tentatively at first. "I think I was

going to be born to parents with too many children already and they didn't want me." He looked at Creator for confirmation and They nodded.

"I remember hearing many voices while I lay in my mother's womb before I arrived here. I think they were my brothers and sisters telling me they loved me."

"Exactly right, Zach. Anything else?" Creator prodded.

Zach shook his head. I noticed his energy changing to reflect the engulfing green love of Creator. I saw the healing in Zach's heart as he realized that he'd been loved and cherished even while the decision to end his life was being made. I cried silent tears.

The soul sitting next to Zach, a small girl with straight, coal-black hair and large wide eyes scooted closer to him and squeezed him tight as tears fell down her cheeks.

"Your story is similar to Kenja's," Creator said, Their energy shifting to aquamarine. "Her parents are deep in counseling over the decision to end her life."

"My parents had to get rid of me because of the law in my country," Kenja spoke. Her voice filled with sorrow, her chin lifting in defiance.

"My parents weren't married, but love each other even now," said a soul who had thick brown hair, a flat nose, and skin similar to mine with a reddish tone. He was surly, shoulders moving up and back as he looked at Creator. "They wanted me. They waited until it was almost too late to end my life, but their parents made them do it. My life was ended because of religious beliefs."

"That's right, Luis. Your grandparents still think it was Our will and that We are pleased with their decision." Creator's energy darkened, a fathomless green. "We are not."

At Their words, Luis's shoulders relaxed and his energy absorbed the healing green Creator speared him with.

"However, We understand," Creator added.

Each soul, encouraged now to share their stories as much as they could recall, spoke of how their lives had ended. I learned of Jordynn's mother, who would have faced parents disowning her if they'd learned she was pregnant, of Raiden's mom beaten by his dad so badly she faced death and how the doctors had had no choice but to end his life. Kris spoke of a father impregnating his mother while she worked in his office and how the father had paid for his mother to end his life. How she kept her job by agreeing.

Mia and Isla shared almost identical stories of moms trying to break out of a family legacy of underachievement and get college degrees. How they'd trusted in faulty birth control, gotten pregnant and ended their babies' lives early, before the pregnancy ended their dreams.

I sat with unfocused eyes as each of my classmates shared as much of their stories as they knew, receiving hints and encouragement from Creator. Glancing around the meadow, I saw other groups listening to their Light-Being instructors. Zadkiel gestured with one hand in the air as if he were describing something in the sky. I realized Alice wasn't among those seated at Zadkiel's feet. I sat up, searching the entire meadow for any sign of her and finding none. Where was she? Why wasn't she in class? I breathed more quickly, feeling the hair on the back of my neck rise with my anxiety.

When it was my turn, Creator, with energy returned to the vivid rainbow colors from earlier, smiled at me. "And Embry?"

"I learned from my Aunt Katy that my parents' union was sort of an accident, a mistake. My mom's parents would have disowned her. I don't think I was loved. I think they just saw me as a problem and wanted to get rid of me." I let my dark curls fall in front of my face. Looked at my brown skin and knew the mix had blended father and mother together.

I watched Creator rise from Their seat. "Are you mad at them?" I asked.

"Mad at who, Embry?" Creator's full attention, all the rainbow swirls of color, intensified.

"At our parents," I said. "They destroyed something You created. Aren't you angry?"

"They didn't destroy you," They said. "You're here. You don't look destroyed to us."

"But we didn't fulfill Your intentions for us, or for them," said Isla. "If someone messed up something I created, I'd be angry." Her freckled face grew redder.

To my surprise They smiled, brightening the air throughout the meadow. "Oh dear, what funny creatures you humans are. Even though We created you, We're still surprised at the things you do and say. No. I am not mad at your parents. I'm not mad at any of My creation. I'm disappointed, and that is something quite different than anger." They sat back down. "You see, all of creation has infinite chances to make good decisions. There's no limit. You're here sooner than we preferred, but we aren't going to condemn those responsible because we created them too. Their choices don't define Us. We could never be angry at our own creation just for making one decision that wasn't what We would have wanted for that soul."

They stood again and somehow grew large enough to engulf us in a group hug. "Your stories are your learning today. We're sorry your lives were cut short. We're equally pleased to have you back. Lies are in your making, but they are not in your future. Don't make them be your undoing." They vanished.

Chapter Seven

All but two of my classmates gathered near the swings on the other side of the meadow. Two rows of five swings were set in the ground exactly the right distance so that when we were all swinging as high as we could go, our feet touched. I giggled, then belly-laughed at the experience and challenge of meeting Usan's feet across from me. When Isla, swinging next to me and reached for my hand, I gladly took it and we joined our collective swinging force to connect with Usan and Zach. Our feet met theirs, knocking them off kilter.

Next to us were Kenja and Mia swinging to meet Kris and Luis. As we entered the twilight of the day, stars blinked into view.

"I'm swinging highest!" shouted Kenja from the end of our row.

"Not for long!" I shouted back, pumping my legs high into the star-studded, purple sky.

Mia and Isla joined the contest. Soon we were swinging in unison, with Isla gaining the advantage with her longer legs. And before I knew it, she swung all the way around the center pole shouting at the top of her lungs as she did so.

"That was crazy fun!" Isla yelled when she rejoined us. "Try it."

It was Kenja who achieved a full three-sixty next, her acrobatic skills helping her surpass me and Mia. Finally, all four of us were completing three-sixties with ease. Somehow, I caught a glimpse of Usan, Zach, Luis, and Kris completing their own sets as I flew through the air.

Dizzy from spinning, I slowed first. As my feet touched the grass, a scream pierced the night and Usan flew high above the swings. The others slowed and we watched in silent horror. Usan reached the apex of his arch across the purple sky and began to descend.

"Creator!" I screamed. "Dina! Zadkiel! Somebody! Help!" I knew I could do nothing to stop Usan from crashing to the grass, but I ran toward him anyway.

Just before he hit, I saw a white, furry flash streak by me as Anfalmor crouched on the ground where Usan landed. I knelt near the two of them as others joined in a circle around us. Anfalmor's eyes were closed, as were Usan's.

A chuffle-snort started as a low rumble from Anfalmor's snout before he opened his mouth in a wide wolf-grin and stood up, shaking Usan off of him. Usan was quick to follow his example, throwing his head back and laughing too. The sight of them alive and laughing filled me with relief.

"How?" I asked. "How are you alive? That fall. And Anfalmor, he flattened you."

"You forget where you are, little one." Anfalmor said. "This is Eternity. You can't die here." He nudged Usan with his nose, knocking him off-balance and into Luis who started laughing too. Luis shoved Usan toward Isla who caught him easily and shoved him back toward Anfalmor. Arms, legs, hands, and feet tumbled with his furry white body as we wrestled with one another on the grass, relieved no one was injured and happy to learn of the lack of limits to the bodies we occupied. No death. I should have known.

"Well, aren't you all just too cute."

I knew the voice immediately. Alice stood a few feet away from us, holding a large, heavy book in one hand as she sneered at us. She was flanked by four other souls who shared her expression. "Look at them. Creator's little favorites. You might not be able to die here, but there are other dangers."

My friends and I sat up, brushing grass and dirt off our clothes. Anfalmor stood, bristling white fur making him look even larger than he was. "Easy, Alice," he growled. "I thought Zadkiel spoke to you about your behavior."

"All she said was that you were cute." The boy who spoke was quite tall and quite beautiful to my new eyes. His black ringlets cascaded down to his shoulders, his green eyes flecked with gold. His full-lipped smile would have been beautiful if he wasn't drawing the corners up in a sneer. He held hands with Alice, their possession of each other clear in their body language.

"It's okay, Tay." Alice gripped his hand tighter though, despite her brave words. "Zadkiel spoke with all of us this morning. Another boring lecture about how we needed to allow these ignorant souls a chance."

"He wasn't clear on what kind of chances we should give them, though," said a girl with nearly translucent white skin and impossibly black hair. "I have some ideas."

"Go away," said Isla. "Go swing or something. It's crazy fun."

"Swing?" said the white-skinned girl. "Did she just say we should swing?" The others shook their heads, rolled their eyes. "You are ignorant. I'd even say stupid."

"Ronnie, watch your words," rumbled Anfalmor. He'd moved closer to them, placing his body between our two groups.

"What are you going to do?" Ronnie asked. "Bite me?"

Anfalmor's answering rumble made me think he might actually do it. "Not tonight." He lunged at her, catching her off guard. She grabbed the hands of the souls nearest her and ran toward the forest. Alice and Tay moved away as well.

"You're right, Anfalmor," Alice said. "We do have better things to do than swing." She and Tay turned and followed their friends into the forest, Alice clutching the large book to her chest.

"Why are they so mean?" asked Isla. "How are they even allowed here?"

"Every soul returns to a part of here when they're done living on Earth," answered Anfalmor.

"Even mean souls?" asked Kenja.

Anfalmor sat staring with his golden eyes growing wider, his energy forcing a strong green healing to flow toward us. "Alice and her friends have much to learn about forgiveness. Where better to learn than here?"

"It's complicated here. Why is it so complicated here?" asked Isla.

"Our complicated Creator made You in Their image." Anfalmor lifted his shoulders in an approximation of a shrug. "Animal souls are less complicated. If you ever find yourself weary of people souls, seek one of us out."

As quickly and silently as he had arrived, he vanished into the forest after Alice's group and I wondered if he would seek them out or go his own way.

"I'm glad you're safe, Usan," I said. "How in the world did you find yourself in the air in the first place?"

"I let go of the ropes," he said.

We all laughed at his simple explanation before hugging and going our separate ways.

I pondered all I'd learned as I walked up the path to my cottage. Martin and Ty sat on their porch, enjoying a glass of wine, raising them in silent salute as I passed. I had much to tell Aunt Katy.

Chapter Eight

"I heard from friends that Alice and her gang are still hassling you." Aunt Katy sat before an easel, paintbrush loaded with red paint, poised to add color to the tulips on the canvas. "Zadkiel needs to get them under control."

What can he do to them, though, really? I mean, now that we're all here, punishment seems like it isn't possible and they don't seem to be responding to his stern talks." I sat on a small cushion near her easel, tracing lines in the tapestried rug that covered the hardwood floor.

"There is something he can remind them of," Aunt Katy said. "If they continue to bother you and the others like you, I'll speak with Creator. It wouldn't be the first time we've moved souls from one part of Eternity to another,"

"What? That's possible? Doesn't Creator choose where we arrive?" I asked.

"They do." Aunt Katy dabbed small dots of red into impossibly small lines along the edges of each tulip.

"Then why didn't They put Alice and her friends in another part of Eternity? How did they end up here?" I asked.

"Creator sees opportunities for learning in every moment of Eternity. Billions of souls live here. Creator's wisdom is far greater than ours and They allow every individual's journey to evolve with as little interference as possible. Allowing the Light-Beings to gently guide, instruct, and mentor has always been Their preferred way." Aunt Katy swiveled on her stool to face me. "They see it all and monitor situations that cause us pain. Let's allow your learning to happen, shall we?" She leaned her elbows on her knees and stared at me.

"Don't really have a choice, do I?" I answered.

She shook her head. "Why don't you go see Grandma and Grandpa? Talking to them helps me when I don't get something here. I've always lived in Eternity, except for about twenty-four hours I don't remember. They lived to old age on Earth and have wisdom and insight I don't. As Creator likes to remind me, we're all on a journey toward enlightenment."

"Who is the most enlightened soul here?" I asked.

"Good question." She sucked on the end of her paintbrush for a moment. "The Light-Beings were here first and have the ability to visit Earth."

"I don't mean them. I mean souls, like me and you."

"Fourteen souls hold that distinction."

"Who are they and how did they get so wise?" I asked.

"Let me show you." She set her paintbrush down. "Follow me."

When we walked into the library, the lights flickered on, growing brighter as my bare feet burrowed into the plush, turquoise carpet. I watched Aunt Katy scan a shelf at eye level across from the door, select a thin volume with a golden spine and sit in one of two chairs near the window. "Sit here and I'll read you their stories."

Of the stories she shared with me, I was drawn mostly to the one named Hildegard of Bingen. She had been a German Benedictine abbess, writer, composer, philosopher, Christian mystic, visionary, and polymath. Socrates, Mahatma Gandhi, Jesus, Plato, Confucius, Gautama Buddha, Solomon, and Hypatia, Anne Conway, Themistoclea, Gargi Vachaknavi, and Mary Wollstonecraft were fascinating, but Saint Hildegard of Bingen was amazing. I wanted to meet her. Wanted to ask her about her life.

"Do you think I could meet her?" I asked. "Have you met any of these souls?"

"I've seen all of them but met only three. They spend much of their time discussing philosophy with each other, greeting wise souls arriving daily, and sometimes communicating with the Originals." Aunt Katy closed the book and hugged it to her chest.

"Who are the Originals?" I asked.

"I shouldn't have said anything. You're not supposed to know about them." Aunt Katy stood and started toward the door.

"It sucks being a soul who didn't live," I said.

"Why do you say that?" she asked.

"Never mind." I left the library. I didn't want to hear about anyone else who knew more than me. I wanted to throw rocks. I wanted to run and sit and cry and scream at the top of my lungs all at the same time, which made me angry because I was pretty sure that wasn't how I was supposed to feel. It hadn't been like that in the beginning. It had been peaceful and exciting at the same time. We had looked forward to our time on Earth, imagining the learning, the excitement, the tastes, sounds, sights, and smells we would have the chance to experience. I'd been robbed of all of that.

How was that fair? Could I get another chance? Go to some other parents who wanted me and raised me and let me do all the things? Why was it a rule that we only got one chance?

I found myself in a new section of the South. Buildings with tall white marble pillars and multiple sets of steps lined both sides of the area. Souls glowing with clear pure colors moved up and down the steps and into the buildings, seeming self-aware and brimming with confidence. I went unnoticed by them, my energy glowing dimly in comparison. It was obvious these were souls with an advanced degree of wisdom or knowingness and I wondered if any Aunt Katy had mentioned were among them.

I had mixed feelings about talking to them. Going un- noticed felt more comfortable. I reached the end of the row of impressive buildings as the sky became the darkest purple. This was becoming my favorite time here as there were fewer souls about. A natural rhythm of doing less seemed to per- meate the time. Water babbled over rocks nearby, the stream near my cottage rejoining the path I walked along. I chose a granite-striped rock with a rounded-out top to sit down near the stream and gazed at the billions of stars.

Occasionally souls walked past, though none noticed me in the camouflage of night and foliage near the stream. After a time of contemplation, I calmed, my mind slowing to feel the warmth of my breath on my upper lip. My shoulders released from being scrunched near my ears and I closed my eyes. Sounds of animal souls moved in the grasses across from me, splashes of water souls in the stream, even laughter and snippets of conversation reached my ears the longer I stayed still. I realized I hadn't really been still since my arrival. My focus had been on learning, on fitting in, on thoughts and feelings of my inability to fit in.

The longer I sat with my eyes closed, the more I heard and felt. Behind my eyelids, colors appeared, purple like the sky at first, then moving through the spectrum. I became aware of the area just above my eyes and focused my attention. The sensation was gentle, not painful. As if I'd willed it, my vision switched from what I could see behind my eyelids to what felt like another's eyes. I saw Anfalmor walk by. He looked into the deepest part of me before moving on, several wolves smaller than him trotting across my inner vision.

I waited, breathing in the deep night scents of forest, stream, and sky. Cozy, comfortable on top of the granite rock, I lost myself inside the world in my head. Each of my friends appeared, surrounded by families or engaged in activities suited to their interests. Isla was learning an intricate folk dance with a male soul who looked like her. Aunt Katy was painting, Usan reclined on a multi-colored pillow reading a book with a boy on the cover, Jordynn played a game with several other souls on the wooden floor of her cottage. Even Alice and her friends appeared inside my head, their teasing laughter causing me to scrunch my eyes at the invasive sounds.

After a time, the familiar scenes ended, replaced by an awareness of places I had yet to visit. Watching in wonder, I focused my inner attention on an area with no human souls. The ground was strewn with glittering crystals, sapphire blue and yellow, ruby red, emerald green, tiger's eye striped, and clear crystals. Mountains rose abruptly from the flat ground, jagged against the dark purple sky. From one of them rose a great red flame that spewed more crystals to the ground.

Then a large violet eye filled the entire space inside my head, blinked, and continued to stare into me. I gasped, almost opening my eyes but resisting the urge. The rest of the face came into view as the soul withdrew from my brain and I saw its scaly purple face with its long snout and huge nostrils. It continued to stare into me as it withdrew so I could see it clearly. When it beat its large, leathery wings and lifted from the crystal-strewn ground, I saw it fully. A dragon. My jaw dropped but I continued to scrunch my eyes closed and steady my breathing. It joined a thunder of eight other dragons in the purple sky and flew toward the fire-spewing mountain. The violet-eyed dragon looked back once and breathed, "Find us." This had been the voice who spoke in the first minutes of my arrival in Eternity.

Chapter Nine

I couldn't wait to tell Aunt Katy. Couldn't wait to tell the others and ask Dina how to find the dragons. Jogging easily through the streets lined with marble-pillared buildings and back up to my cottage, I rehearsed the scenes my inner vision had shown me. Like a dream fading away when awakening, I lost details as I ran. I ran faster. Rehearsed harder.

"There are dragons here!" My arrival caused Aunt Katy to draw a red stripe across the field of green she'd painted underneath her tulips.

"What on earth are you talking about?" She pressed her hand to her heart, turning to face me. "Dragons? Where? There aren't any dragons. I've never seen any dragons."

"No, Aunt Katy. Seriously. I just saw them." I gestured toward the marble-pillared buildings I'd wandered through. "Well, I saw them in my mind's eye. I think. It was weird."

A warm glow of bluish light caught my attention as Zadkiel materialized in the room. For the first time I saw he had wings that he folded quickly before they disappeared behind his back. "I saw you running past me just now through the streets of Cheshiphon. Are you okay?"

"I'm fantastic. I was just telling Aunt Katy about my inner vision. I saw dragons." I anticipated excitement in his reaction. Instead, a slight furrow creased his brow before he moved closer to us.

"Inner vision is a curious thing. Can you tell me any more about what you saw?" His velvet voice hypnotized me a bit.

"It had a purple eye. It looked into me like nothing else has. I think it spoke." I struggled. I doubted. "I know I saw it. It flew away with eight others." The last bit had been an effort. I was no longer sure it had happened. The smell of orange blossoms and lavender emanated from the energy around Zadkiel. I drooped to the floor near Aunt Katy, suddenly fascinated with the patterns in the carpet. "They said, 'Find us.'" My voice was dull and I slumped across Aunt Katy's feet.

Though I hadn't really been asleep, I later awakened in bed. Grandma and Grandpa sat in cozy chairs that hadn't been in my room before. "How'd I get here? Why'd I lose consciousness?"

Grandpa moved to the side of my bed, took my hand, and patted it. "Oh, honey," he said, "you've so much to learn. Sometimes the air here makes us lose consciousness and Katy said you'd been running when you burst in to tell her you'd had a vision. She said you collapsed at her feet and she brought you in here. We wanted to be here when you came back to us so you weren't frightened."

"It's almost time for classes with Dina and you've been doing so well," Grandma added. "Dina brags about her new souls all the time."

I changed clothes and grabbed some savory croissants, freshly baked and warm, as I followed Grandma and Grandpa through the kitchen and out the door. They walked on either side of me, taking my hands. We swung them back and forth and chatted about inconsequential things before they left me at the edge of the clearing, where Dina sat waiting while my friends arrived.

"I hear you found Cheshiphon, Embry." Dina's voice held something of a promise, making me uneasy though I couldn't recall why. At the mention of the city, I recalled all the details of its white marbled pillars but not the reason I'd visited it. All I could do was nod as she turned to greet the others.

As we sat down on logs arranged in a semicircle facing Dina, I saw Zadkiel move across the clearing. He looked at me with a slight knowing smile.

"Embry has discovered our City of Knowledge, Cheshiphon," Dina said. "Several other Light-Beings and I have decided on a field trip to the City. We may even see Creator as They often visit the wise souls who tend to occupy it." She rose and beckoned us to follow her.

I took Isla's hand as we walked along in a curious huddle.

Usan sidled up next to us. "How did you find it, Embry?"

"I really didn't know where I was going," I started. "I was just sort of done with it all, you know?"

They nodded.

"I get overwhelmed with being an unwanted child. When that happens, I can't sort my emotions and I run. I just started running in a direction I hadn't gone before and the next thing I knew, I was there. I didn't know where I was. There were very few souls or Light-Beings walking around, but I still wanted to hide from everyone. Somehow I don't feel worthy here." Usan grabbed my other hand and we followed Dina toward the City. "I climbed up on this huge boulder, shut my eyes, and tried to breathe more slowly."

"I've done that too," Usan said. "It's supposed to be perfect here, but I haven't found it to be that for me."

Isla and I nodded.

"Have you guys had any visions?" I asked. "Like dreams but not?"

"No," Isla replied. "My family keeps me super busy. I'm hardly ever left to myself." She sounded envious of my ability to get away by myself.

"Me neither," added Usan.

"Well I have. Like behind my eyes, in my forehead, I see things there." I pointed to the area I remembered feeling as if my third eye had opened. "It happened last night."

"What did you see?" asked Isla.

"That's just it," I said. "I know I saw something amazing. I just can't remember what it was."

"Weird," said Kenja. She'd been listening from behind us.

"Right?" I turned back to acknowledge her. "I get snippets of what happened last night, like, I ran home to tell Aunt Katy and she ruined her painting when I walked in."

"That sucks. Maybe she smacked you and that's why you don't remember." Kenja pretended to smack the back of my head.

"We're here, Kenja," said Usan. "People don't smack people silly here."

"How do you know they don't?" asked Kenja.

"Okay guys. Nobody smacked me. Especially my Aunt Katy." I laughed at the absurd notion. "I remember Zadkiel showed up in Aunt Katy's studio right when I was telling her of my vision. I don't remember much after that. I woke up today with my Grandma and Grandpa sitting in my bedroom."

"Zadkiel?" asked Usan. "Isn't that the Light-Being that teaches Alice and her gang?"

"Yup. Weird, huh?" I turned my attention to Dina, who was slowing to draw us close as we entered Cheshiphon, the City of Knowledge.

The buildings were so tall their tops disappeared into the pink sky. I'd missed that detail the night before. Souls and Light-Beings floated, flew, and glided in and out of them, appearing to be on very important business. I felt as though this was the most important place here. As if all the big decisions of the Universe were made here. Ethereal music emanated from above our heads. Scents from a thousand different plants blended together, creating such a pleasure to my senses I nearly swooned. Isla squeezed my hand and we beamed at each other as we gawked at our surroundings.

Kenja stood next to Usan with her hands to her face as she spun around taking it all in. The others exhibited various reactions of awe as well. I hadn't felt any of this the night before. It made me slightly suspicious, but the pleasure the City brought to me pushed all troubles aside.

"Welcome to Cheshiphon, my children." Creator appeared before us clothed in a flowing cape of pastel rainbow colors. I could see through Them to the buildings behind. "We'll float together to one of my favorite lookouts."

I didn't notice when we left the ground, but the feeling of weightlessness coupled with all the beautiful music and the wonderful scents in the air was exhilarating. I wanted it to go on forever.

"Check out Usan!" yelled Isla.

He was pretending to swim through the air. Next to him, Kenja imitated a dolphin as she lifted herself to dive into an imaginary wave. All around me, others were doing their own acrobatic feats as we floated alongside Creator. They laughed at us. Even Dina did a few backflips. I tilted my head back and with a simple wave of my arms found myself backflipping through the air and bumping into Isla, who floated away belly-laughing the whole time.

Other souls pushed off from the ground and joined us in the bright pink air. Light-Beings swooped out of nowhere to show off their expertise, flipping, swirling in tight loops, diving toward the ground, and pulling up at the last minute. Without warning, the Light-Beings surrounded us. Herding us together, they joined hands and pulled each other around us, causing a whirlpool effect in the sky. Had we been in fragile human bodies, we would have been squashed or trampled by the power of the Light-Beings and the force they created.

Creator, in the center of our soul storm, was motionless, a serene smile lighting up Their face. I couldn't take my eyes off Them and wished this feeling of perfection could last forever. For a while, I thought it would. This was the best I'd ever felt in the whole of my existence. I snuck a look at my friends and could see the sheer joy reflected in their expressions as well. My feeling of abandonment vanished. I knew I belonged. I knew I was loved.

One by one, the Light-Beings slipped away and the whirlpool slowed to a stop. We stood next to Creator on the top of the highest building in Cheshiphon. I was breathless, smiling, still holding Isla's hand. She squeezed it again and we shared another giggle as we took in the dazzling view from the top of the city.

At first everything was out of focus, too far away. Creator talked with each of my friends, pointing and leaning over the edge of our lookout. When it was my turn, They pointed toward the direction of my cottage as I followed the line of the stream that trickled and tripped its way down the hill. I saw Aunt Katy outside, sitting in one of the chairs by the stream with Gypsy on her lap.

Creator pointed in another direction and I watched as Anfalmor led a large pack of wolves across the snow into a group of pines along the edge of a meadow. They pointed one more time and I saw the clearing where we normally had class. Zadkiel stood in front of Alice and her classmates, gesturing toward us as if he knew we were looking at him.

I looked away, suddenly feeling like a voyeur, as if I shouldn't be able to spy on others. I felt uneasy then. Something about seeing Zadkiel had caused me to momentarily remember having a vision. The urge to ask Creator about it weighed heavily in the back of my mind, but the words just wouldn't form. The moment slipped away as They moved on to another classmate, giving them a moment of Their precious time and leaving me feeling deflated.

Chapter Ten

Creator left us at some point, Their departure causing a momentary dimming of the surrounding light before Dina called our attention to another class of souls moving toward us.

"We should move along, dear ones. I've much to show you." She descended a flight of stairs and we followed, Isla finding my hand again and Usan close by.

"What did Creator show you guys?" I asked.

"They showed me my cottage, my family," Dina replied. "It feels amazing up here, being able to see so much. We have to come back some time. Do you think we're allowed?"

"Pretty sure we wouldn't get in trouble anywhere here," I answered.

"They showed me a group of souls I haven't met yet, but they all looked like me," Usan said excitedly. "You know, my brown skin and thick, black hair. They were singing and making music on these weird instruments. They said I should seek them out when I get done with classes today.

They thought I'd be good at that sort of thing. What did They show you?"

I told them of seeing my Aunt Katy, of Anfalmor in the snow, and of seeing Zadkiel's class in the clearing. "I remembered something, you guys. Something I need to tell you before I forget again. Do you think we could sneak away somewhere and talk?"

"Follow me," Isla whispered.

As we continued to descend the stairs, we noticed doors opening off of long corridors. Dina talked to those closest to her and we slowed our pace to draw near the back of the pack. Several floors later, Isla tightened her grip on my hand, reached for Usan, and we darted through the door closest to us.

Pausing on the other side to listen for any reaction from our classmates, we stared into the room we'd entered. It held artifacts from Earth on floor-to-ceiling shelves. Ancient-looking books lined one wall while skeletons of every kind of animal found on Earth crowded each other for space along another. In the middle were plants occupying pots sized to keep each plant small. Yet someone had neatly labelled the species of each and I knew in the wild, many of these would be trees towering over us. It was some kind of Earth museum and I wondered what purpose it could possibly serve to anyone living here.

Hearing nothing from the other side of the door, we ventured into the room, pausing at items we found most interesting. Usan was drawn to the skeletons, Isla to the plants, and I wandered along the book-lined wall, turning my head sideways to read titles. I could easily read every word, though I could tell there were many languages represented. My friends' *oohs* and *ahhs* were the only sounds in the room.

I smiled. Wondered why we didn't have classes here where it seemed everything we needed to know about Earth was preserved.

Ten minutes passed before any of us spoke. I took a few books from the shelves to read the backs and inside flaps. I was afraid of getting caught doing something I wasn't supposed to, being somewhere I wasn't allowed.

"You guys. Come here," I said in an urgent whisper, causing Isla and Usan to join me where I stood looking at a book I'd taken from the highest shelf. "I remember what I wanted to tell you."

The book, *Do Dragons Exist Here*, brought the vision to my mind in its entirety. I wanted to leave right then with the book, but at that moment, before we got caught, before we were interrupted by a well-meaning Dina or anyone else, I needed to tell Isla and Usan what I'd seen.

I left no detail out as I spoke of the third-eye vision I'd experienced while hiding in the dark the night before. How I'd seen each of them and our other classmates. How I'd even seen Alice and her friends gathered together. I described the crystal-strewn ground of the uninhabited area, the mountains rising straight from the ground spewing fire and fumes and more crystals as I watched.

"Sounds like a volcano," said Usan. "At least I think that's what it's called."

I nodded. "I think so. But that's not the coolest part. What does this title say?" I held the book in front of them.

"*Do Dragons Exist Here*," answered Isla.

"I know for a fact that they do."

"How?"

"I saw them."

"Wait, what? Where? Let's go," Usan blurted.

"No, I saw them in my vision. One of them just appeared in my third-eye's field of vision. Completely, though all I saw at first was a big violet eye." I demonstrated with my hands making a big eye shape where my third eye would be in the middle of my forehead.

"Wow. Cool. What did it look like?" asked Isla.

"Never mind that. Take us to where they are." Usan reached for my hand as if to pull me out of the room. I nearly dropped the large book.

"I don't know where they are," I said. "I think this book might hold some answers. But that's not the weirdest part."

"Well, tell us." Isla sounded nearly as impatient as Usan.

"The purple dragon backed up and I could see others in the air. Before he turned to join them, he said 'Find us.' Then he flew away."

"Let's go." Usan was even more urgent to leave.

"Wait, Usan. I don't know where they are. I don't know why he said that. I don't even know if I want to find them. And I don't know if it was just an imagination thing. I mean, have you guys had any visions? Why did it appear to me?"

Usan let go of my hand and reached for the book. Before I could take it back from him, the door opened and we froze. The light in the room changed from dull browns to bright, crisp yellow and orange as the soul drew near. His appearance surprised me. His light was renewing, young, fresh, but his long gray hair and even longer beard flowing over a dark purple tunic and floral-patterned leggings showed him to be an ancient soul.

"Ha. Three fresh souls have found my lair." The tone of his voice was filled with amused delight, but his body language told me he was suspicious of our presence. He was a contradiction in every way.

We stood, speechless. Caught in the act of we knew not what.

"Which book has caught your interest?" He glided toward us, not moving his feet. "Ah, a tome written by one of my very good friends, Zeno, the man known for his subtle paradoxes. A good choice, but not one I think you fresh souls are ready for." With a flick of his hand, the book returned to the top shelf and that part of the room darkened, hiding all the titles from our view.

"We're sorry." I felt the need to apologize. This soul was obviously the primary keeper and occupant of this room in Cheshiphon. We were trespassing.

"Not at all, not at all." He turned to float toward the windows overlooking the marbled city. "I don't get the fresh souls in here very often. The Light-Beings have much else to show you about your lives here. Although, I don't know why they don't bring you to places where you will see what you would have learned about on Earth." His voice filled with a wistful regret. Straightening his shoulders, he looked each of us in the eye. "Welcome to the Terra Museum. I am its keeper."

For the next half an hour, we listened with fascination as we followed the keeper through the stacks. He named every skeleton, every plant, and described what we could find in the books in what seemed like a very short time. I wondered if he was doing something to our brains to speed up the process as we learned of millions of species.

"Keeper, may I ask a question?" asked Usan.

"Call me Parmenides, if you please."

"Parmenides, can we come back here?" Usan asked.

"On one condition."

"What's that?" I asked.

"You must promise to ask before you take any book from the shelf."

"We promise," we said together. It was too easy a task not to agree to.

"Very well. I shall speak to your instructor, Dina. You won't want to get into trouble with that one, I assure you. She seems sweet enough, but she won't like that you've wandered away from her field trip. You'd best catch up before she finds a way to assign you homework." Parmenides's eyes twinkled as if we shared a secret joke.

"I have a question," I blurted. "Before we go, can you tell me if your friend Zeno ever decided that dragons exist here?"

"Hm. Why do you need to know?"

"Because I've seen them." I spoke before the risk of speaking reached my brain. The light around Parmenides shifted, darkened slightly toward brown.

"I'm quite sure that is impossible." Parmenides crossed his arms. "Zeno was a friend. But he was a fool. Dragons do not exist here. And not on Earth. Now I think you'd better go, but feel free to visit soon."

I was first out the door and as Usan turned to shut it I saw someone duck into a doorway down the hall. I wondered if other students had decided to detour from Dina's tour and go adventuring. Isla bumped into me, sandwiched between the two of us. "Move, Embry," she said.

"Sorry. Just thought I saw someone down the hall." I continued looking.

"Well, I'm feeling a little stuck back here," Usan's unamused, muffled voice said, "so either step aside or get shoved."

With one last look, I stepped out of the way and followed them toward the stairs. Just before taking the first step, I caught a glimpse of someone sliding along the wall toward the Terra Museum. They had long, dark hair.

We found Dina only a few floors down on a landing where each of our classmates took turns on a giant swing that took us in a wide arch over the marbled city. Giggles and whoops of joy filled the air. We joined the line with silent nods to each other in acknowledgement of the secrets we shared.

My turn came and I kicked away from the landing out over the city. Leaning back in the swing, I let my legs fly toward the fluffy clouds floating in a multi-colored sky. Let go of every dark emotion, every feeling of unworthiness, every thought of visions and enjoyed the moment. As I floated back toward the landing I scanned the horizon, wondering if Parmenides had spoken the truth. Hoped he was wrong. Wondered if I'd seen Alice sneaking down the hall. Knew I would have to answer these questions myself. Knew I now had a quest, a reason for being here.

Chapter Eleven

Our tour of Cheshiphon ended where it had begun, at the edge of the city where the sculptured landscapes gave way to the clearing and the woods at the other end. Before Dina dismissed us, she drew Isla, Usan, and me aside. "I know you snuck away from class. I don't mind at all. You would have eventually met Parminedes and I'm glad that was the room you wandered into. However, there are reasons we do things in a certain order. You might not have been so lucky in your wanderings. There is nothing to fear here. Nothing will harm you, but there are some things you are not ready for as new souls who've never lived on Earth." She paused. Her gaze piercing my heart. "Next time, ask."

We watched her join Zadkiel and waited until they'd disappeared from the clearing before we turned to each other and giggled a bit nervously.

"Oh my gosh," Isla said. "I think she might be really mad at us."

"You can't get in trouble here," said Usan. "I mean, really what can they do to us? You can't die here. And we already feel as much shame as anyone can feel here. I'm not worried."

I didn't know what to think. I was too busy trying to think of a way to get that book away from the Terra Museum without Parmenides knowing about it. Too busy trying to decide if my vision had been anything more than imagination. Too busy wondering who had been hiding from us while at the same time deciding to keep what I'd seen to myself.

"You guys believe me, though, right? That I saw what I saw?" I asked.

"What did you see?" It was Alice.

Why did she have to appear in my life all the time? How did she have the knack of knocking me off-center? If she didn't like me or my friends, why was she always around?

"None of your business," answered Isla.

"Wasn't talking to you," said Alice.

"Isla's right, though," I replied. "It's none of your business since I wasn't talking to you either."

"Whatever. I'm sure you saw nothing important anyway." Alice tossed her long, glossy, black hair over her shoulder and jogged toward Tay, who stood near the trees with her gang. He put his arm around her shoulders and whispered something in her ear. She looked back at us and laughed.

"What is it with Alice?" I asked. "What is her problem? How does she always turn up in our lives? I wonder if there's someplace we can go where she can't bother us."

"I ignore her," answered Isla. "I think it bugs her that Creator shows us more attention than They do her and her group. I think she's jealous."

Usan said nothing. Being small of stature, he seemed more easily bothered by the possibilities of making enemies here.

"Jealous?" I said. "Seriously? Of me? Of us? No, I don't think that's it. I don't know what it is, but that can't be it." I shook my head emphatically. "No. There's something else going on and I'm going to figure out what it is."

The three of us hugged and went our separate ways, me to the woods to find Anfalmor.

The crisp iridescent air of the woods cooled my skin, cleared my thoughts, caused the vision to clarify. I pondered my ability to see through my third eye, focusing attention to the area on my forehead as I found a granite outcropping near the tree line to watch the sky turn to shades of night; lavender, violet, indigo. Evening scents of jasmine, pine, and cedar wafted my way on breezes blowing my hair across my face.

As soon as I shut my eyes, my third eye opened. At first, I only saw the evening colors, though they were sharper inside my head. In moments, I was back in that crystal-strewn landscape. I searched for anything living among the vividly colored rocks and along the horizon, but there was nothing moving. Nothing in the air. Nothing around me. I turned in a circle in my mind, the crystals crunching under my feet.

A ray of fiery blue light bounced off a crystal near me, drawing me closer. I picked up the egg-shaped stone and examined its smooth, cold texture. It was heavier than I expected. I felt calm almost at once, as if the crystal emanated tranquility while absorbing my tension. I continued to stare at the stone, enjoying the feeling of freedom, love, and acceptance coming over me.

"It's a fire opal." Anfalmor's voice rumbled deep from behind me.

I opened my eyes to see him standing before me. The stone was still in my hand, though I no longer stood in the crystal-strewn and barren land of the dragons. How had it manifested from my third-eye vision to reality on this mountain?

Anfalmor sat, tongue lolling to the side of his great, grinning mouth, looking much more like a great dog rather than the ferocious king of wolves I knew him to be. "I felt your heart seeking mine. What is troubling you, Embry? It isn't every soul who can draw something from their third-eye vision like that. You must want something very badly."

"I do. But no one will listen to me and it feels like everyone wants me to just be happy and get on with life without asking questions. When I ask questions, I feel like I'm a bad soul." I shifted to sit in front of him, holding the fire opal with both hands in my lap.

"You aren't a bad soul, Embry. Far from it." He licked a tear from my check. His tongue scratchy and warm on my face. "You wouldn't have come to the South if you were a bad soul."

"What? Then there really are other parts of Eternity that hold bad souls?" I'd begun to doubt it since I'd not heard or seen anything of the Light-Being named Dhororr after our one encounter. "Is that where the dragons live?"

"No. No, that's not where the dragons live." Anfalmor shifted his ears back slightly. The word *dragons* sounding a bit sharper as he spoke.

"Then you admit there are dragons here? Nobody else will talk to me about them, Anfalmor, and I know I saw them. The fact that I'm holding this fire opal confirms that they're real." I hefted the gem in my hand.

"Yes. But they are banished from here. I don't know how you saw them with your third eye. I've never known a soul to know of their existence without Creator's permission." Anfalmor spoke with sadness.

"Why?"

"Why are they banished or why must Creator give Their permission?"

"Both."

"Dragons have the power to open portals to Earth and between districts here. They use the crystals and gems they cultivate in their land to alter the energy. If human souls had access to dragons, the temptation to revisit Earth would be too great. Creator used to allow the dragons to transport souls between here and Earth on special occasions until something went horribly wrong. The dragons remain here on one condition: they never have contact with anyone other than the Original souls again. The dragons love human souls, but they honor Creator's orders."

"What happened?" I asked.

"I can't tell you. We are forbidden to speak of it. Creator mourns to this day over the tragedy."

"Then why did they appear in my vision?" I was becoming angry again, even as the stone's calming energy tried to stifle the emotion. "What is wrong with me, Anfalmor? Why can't I just be less curious and accept my life? Why didn't they just leave me alone?"

"When we first met, I sensed there was more to you than other souls here." Anfalmor shifted his weight so his eyes were level with mine. "It's one of the reasons I've stayed in this part of the forest for so long and not moved on with much of my pack to the other side of the mountain to see our friends there. I feel connected to you, Embry. And the fact that you seek me when you're troubled confirms my instinct to protect you."

As we talked, stars in wonderful shapes and constellations filled the night sky behind him. Overcome with love, I hugged him. When he stiffened in my arms and stood abruptly, I backed away, rebuffed.

"Be still," he ordered. Before I could reply, he moved in silence off the granite outcropping and disappeared into the trees.

The air had stilled, bringing no scents or sounds to me other than the occasional owl hooting and frog croaking. Stiff from sitting in one position for so long, I shifted to a low crouch so I could be ready to spring into action. I placed the fire opal in a pocket of the loose pants I wore. Scanning the sky, the tree line, and the top of the mountain, I saw nothing to give me a clue as to what action I should take, if any. Was Anfalmor coming back? Was he all right? Should I follow him? Did he need my help? He'd ordered me to be still, but I could no longer do that.

The yelp of pain came as I silently slid off the granite outcropping onto the pine-strewn forest floor. I sprinted in the direction of the sound, pine needles pricking my skin as I passed through the forest. Bathed in a spotlight of moon-beams, Anfalmor lay bleeding in a clearing, his eyes open and filled with pain and fear. Someone had shot him full of arrows and though his thick fur had protected him from some of them, the ones sticking out from his neck told me he was in danger.

"Creator!" I screamed. "Aunt Katy! Dina! Someone, come—"

Before I could pull Anfalmor into my lap, someone shoved a sack over my head and wrenched my arms behind me. Pulling me to my feet by my arms caused me to stumble forward and another set of arms, stronger than the ones holding me, caught my fall and laughed.

"I got her," said a laughing voice. "Pull the ropes tight."

Before I could speak or yell again through the sack, someone knocked me over the head and I went limp.

Chapter Twelve

I lay on my side, the sack still over my head and my hands tied too tight behind my back. Voices nearby echoed against the walls where I was being held. I wanted to rub my aching head. Needed a drink of water. The memory of Anfalmor lying on the ground with arrows sticking out of his body imprinted itself inside my eyelids. I groaned, wriggling to find a more comfortable position on the hard surface of my prison.

My captors giggled. "It lives," said a male voice I recognized as Tay's.

"Wonder if it's awake?"

I recognized Alice's taunting tone. Pictured her and Tay standing over me with gleeful expressions.

"Can we just do this already? Where's Steve? He's supposed to be back by now with the final crystal." The high-pitched male voice came from farther away. I tried to put a face to the voice from those I'd seen hanging around Alice and recalled a thin boy with tight curly hair who always seemed to be rocking back and forth as he stood in the shadows with Alice's other followers.

"How did Creator make a soul so whiny, Devin?" Alice asked. "No one ever comes to this part of Cheshiphon. We've got plenty of time. He'll be here."

"Leave him alone, Alice," said another female nearby. "Can we cut her hair or something while we wait? Maybe she's not tied tight enough. I'm going to check."

"Ronnie, leave her alone. She's fine. We're not going to cut her hair. Get away from her." The other girl moved away from me even as she mumbled something under her breath.

Ronnie was another girl in Alice's gang, the one with straight, black hair and translucent, white skin. I wondered what her Earth life had been like if she thought cutting my hair and tightening my bonds sounded fun.

"Hey, what was that about a second death Zadkiel was talking about the other day?" asked Tay. "Do you think it's true? Wouldn't it be cool to go back to Earth and tell everybody they're going to be okay? I could see Bryan. Tell him about us."

"We're not going to send her to Earth, Tay, remember?" Alice answered. "This monument is to that one soul who died a second death because of their return to Earth and it somehow going wrong. No way do I want that on my conscience. I just want to get rid of her. The book shows exactly how to open a portal to another part of Eternity. Once we have all the crystals, we'll do it. Besides, we'd need to have dragons to send her to Earth. Zadkiel says they no longer exist."

I stayed as still as possible, hoping they'd believe I'd lost consciousness again. Pictured that day in the Terra Museum and was sure it had been Alice sneaking down the hallway toward its door. She must have either stolen a book about portals or somehow talked Parmenides into loaning it to her. I was sure it was the former.

The one she called Devin continued to whine until Tay threatened to send him through too. His complaints were replaced by heavy sighs and he seemed to decide that tapping an annoying beat on the ground nearby was okay. Alice and Tay left him alone then, their voices withdrawing to whispers too low to hear.

I took a chance that no one was paying any attention to me and tested the strength of my restraints, but they held fast, cutting off the circulation in my hands and feet. Straightening my legs caused sharp pains to shoot up through my back, so I drew them back up into a fetal position next to my bent arms. I searched my third eye for any help from beyond the dark hood covering my head, but all was silent.

When I could no longer take the pain in my head, hands, and feet, I decided I'd have to speak. I had so many unanswered questions, the biggest one being why.

"Hey!" I yelled. "Get this thing off of my head!"

"Alice, she's awake," said Devin.

"So?"

"So, what should I do?"

"Come over here and untie me for starters," I answered.

"Alice?" whined Devin.

"Hey, mates, look what I've got." The new voice sounded friendly, boisterous and came from just in front of me. "Whoa, she's still out? How hard did I hit her?" I listened while this new person inspected me, poking and prodding my head through the hood.

I changed my mind about his friendliness after hearing him confess to knocking me out. If I could have kicked, bitten, or scratched him, I would have. Instead I yelled again.

"Get this hood off me! I know I can't die here, but it sure feels as though I'm going to." I tossed my head in the direction I'd last heard the new voice but didn't connect with anything. He'd already stood up.

"What took you so long, Steve?" asked Tay. "Thought you knew right where that crystal was. Devin's been whining since we got here, and Ronnie wants to torture her."

I kicked and wiggled and screamed, though I was so parched there wasn't much sound coming out of my mouth. I felt someone kneel next to me and rip off the hood. I blinked, trying to focus on the face in front of me and those standing near.

"Why are you doing this to me?" I asked. "What have I done to you?"

Alice's expression, hatred and disgust, stopped me for a moment. I scooted myself to an upright position on the concrete floor of the memorial stones. She stood in front of the other five, so obviously in charge and in command. Ronnie held her head to one side, looking a bit bored. Devin's mouth was open, waiting for something to happen. Tay, a superior gleam to his gorgeous green eyes, stood on Alice's right, as if he was her personal guard.

"They even smell like hospitals," said Steve from behind the other four. He was almost two heads taller than the others. He shook his black ringlets out of his eyes and held a large red stone up so I could see it. "This should send you to the North. And when we're done with her, let's do it to the others."

Alice turned away from me. "Steve, we're doing this to her and only her. Got it?"

"Whatever," Steve said. He lowered the stone. "Let's do it then."

"Wait," I pleaded. "What are you going to do with me? Why? Answer me."

"Not exactly in a position to be making demands, Embry." Ronnie stepped toward me.

"Gag her," Alice said. "And let's get on with it."

Steve stepped forward and shoved a piece of cloth into my mouth. Its acrid smell burned my eyes. I tried to hold my breath. Tried to bite him, but he succeeded at last in shoving it between my lips. Woozy, I tried to brace myself before I lost consciousness.

Part Two
The North

Chapter Thirteen

Light flooded into my half-open eyes as someone lifted the sack from my head. A wide, ugly grin filled with crooked teeth greeted me.

"Well, whatdowehavehere?"

Someone lifted me from the dirty floor to a seated position and I felt a knife slice the ropes binding me, cutting the edge of my wrists at the same time. I could barely bring my arms around to the front they were so stiff. I groaned. They laughed. Two men sat on either side of me with hands on their knees, watching my every move. I looked around, trying to find a familiar face. Finding none, I kept my mouth shut.

"She ain't too talkative, is she Argon?" The man still held the sack that had covered my head. There appeared to be blood or some other sticky substance on his skin and he reeked of something sour.

"Look how she wrinkles her nose at you, Kristoff," said Argon. "Think she's not used to the smells of real human souls."

"Or the company we keep, eh?" added Kristoff. He moved toward me with the sack and I ducked away from him. "Hold on, hold on." He held my chin in a pinching grip and wiped my face with the rough sackcloth. "You got a bit of mess on your face. Must be from crying and snotting while you was in the sack." Sitting back on his knees, he scanned my face, assessing his cleaning job. "Any idea how someone like you got here?"

"Where am I?" I asked.

They laughed and slapped their knees as if I'd told the funniest joke ever.

"Why, you're here," said Kristoff. "You're in Paradise itself." He pronounced Paradise 'Pair-ee-dice' as he gestured around him. It didn't look anything like my Eternity.

We were in a dark, dusty room filled with broken furniture, discarded and unwanted cast-offs. My skin, where I'd been lying on the floor, was covered with dirt and I felt hot and grimy. Toxic, orange light filtered through gaps in the wood-sided walls of the building. After the clean pink sky I'd grown used to, this color made me fearful. I crossed my arms in front of me, warding off the feeling, these men, and whatever might be outside.

"No way. This can't be Paradise." Unfamiliar with how the world worked, I only knew of one way Paradise should be. Though I'd met Dhororr, the Light-Being in charge of souls somewhere else, I hadn't imagined it to be this dark and threatening.

"Well, Argon and me are a lot of things, but we ain't liars." Kristoff shifted on the crate he used as a chair. "What was you on Earth, Argon? You was a thief, right? Stole from all those old retirees down there in the Unightie States?"

"Hedge fund manager, Kristoff. Hedge fund manager." Argon's tone of disdain showed he wasn't entirely happy with his companion's lack of decorum either.

"You heard 'im. Me, I gave my Da a hard whack on the back of his head with my hoe while he was beating my Ma," Kristoff bragged.

I scooted across the dirty floor away from my captors. "Why did you kidnap me? How did you get into the South?"

"You think we had anything to do with that?" asked Argon. "We're not in the South." He stood next to Kristoff, shaking his head. "We were simply completing a business deal here out of sight of the Enforcers when we nearly stumbled over you."

"Then how? Who? Why? Anfalmor! I have to get back to Anfalmor! He's been shot! He's dying!" My voice rose with every word. Panic set in. I scrambled up out of the dust, searching for an exit. The blood rushing to my head as I stood brought all the memories back. Alice. She'd somehow succeeded in sending me out of the South. I groaned and rubbed my head, sitting again in the dirt.

"Hold on, there, little miss." Kristoff grabbed me by the shoulders. "Don't know what yer talkin' 'bout, but don't know no Anfermore. If he's shot full o' errors, we don't want to be anywhere near him."

"Not *Anfermore*. Anfalmor. He's King of the Wolves here." I spat words in his face like bullets. "And he's my friend." At last, I sobbed. I couldn't imagine that Alice could hate me this much, and these two souls were far different than any I'd encountered in my short life.

Kristoff laughed at my tears. "Aw. Dry up, little miss. You been hallucinatin'. Ain't no wolves here. Aneemals don't come here. They jes' die and go back to the earth."

I cried harder. Couldn't absorb the new reality. "I was kidnapped and sent here. Why?"

Argon took me from Kristoff's grip, guided me to another overturned crate before pressing me to sit. "Someone doesn't like you very much. What did you do?"

"I didn't do anything. I just arrived, like, a couple of days ago." I wiped my eyes and nose with my dirty hand. "I never lived on Earth," I sounded pathetic and hopeless even to myself.

"She's one of them been ripped from the womb," Kristoff said, grimacing in disgust. "Creator likes them especial. Always showin' 'em around and givin' 'em extra attention. S'why They're never in the North. Even gives 'em those special Light-Beings as teachers."

"Really, Kristoff. You are a Barbarian. The soul can't help what her parents did. She's obviously an Innocent." Argon's words, meant to comfort, only served to make me feel even more foolish and ignorant. He knelt in front of me. "Now then. What shall we do with you?"

"Take me back. I have to tell Aunt Katy what happened. Have to get help for An . . ." I hesitated. "For my friend."

"We aren't allowed out of the North," said Argon. "We've no idea how you got here, either. I honestly don't think it's ever happened before, at least, not in my time and I've been here for twenty years."

"Hell, I been in the North for over sixty years and I ain't never seen someone arrive here without deservin' it. Everybody here got some work to do. Everybody here was criminals of some sort or other." He pointed at me. "All yer guilty of is, well, you ain't guilty of nothin'." He shook his head, obviously confused.

"Well, you made a powerful enemy so you must deserve to be here," reasoned Argon.

"I didn't, though," I argued.

"Musta done," said Kristoff.

"You need to help me get back." It was honestly all I could think of. They'd mentioned Creator wasn't around much and that didn't seem right. If I could find Them, talk to Them, They'd help me. I knew it. They'd punish Alice.

"Don't know 'bout that, but you can't stay in here. We ain't inclined that way, but there are those who'd love to get their hands on fresh meat like you, if you know what I mean." Kristoff raised his brows, the gesture making me feel as though I wasn't wearing enough clothes.

"True, Kristoff. Hadn't thought of that." Argon lifted me to my feet. "Come, girl. What's your name?"

"Embry," I answered.

"Embry, come with us." Argon dragged me forward toward a dark corner of the building. I hesitated. "It's all right. That's the way out."

The toxic orange light outside the warehouse cast a sickly glow. I couldn't imagine what had turned the crisp pink sky this horrid color. I didn't want to know. I could only accept this as a reality because of the single encounter I'd had with Dhororr. He'd spoken of a different place in Eternity. This had to be the place he'd described where souls needing more 'teaching' went when they died. I was beginning to understand what that meant.

Argon guided me none-too-gently across an open square paved with cobblestones along a muddy gray river. Dilapidated buildings lined one side of the square. Kristoff walked behind me as if to cut off any escape attempts, but I wasn't inclined to try anything. I knew I needed to know more of my situation.

Nothing looked familiar. The souls had different energy signatures from the residents of my part of Eternity. They were dirtied, as if mixed with black paint. I drew stares from everyone we passed, mostly male souls, though an occasional female soul looked at me with fear in their eyes. As if I was a threat. As if I could do them harm. I couldn't fathom what might cause such a reaction. Most souls were larger than me, since I'd not been given a chance to grow on Earth. I was supposed to do my growing here. If I stayed in the North for very long, I doubted very much that I'd do much growing.

I realized all of these souls had far more knowledge than I'd received. And that it was probably the wrong kind of knowledge. Argon's tight grip on the flesh on back of my elbow began to hurt as he guided me away from the muddy water, up between narrow buildings leaning against each other as if they were too tired to stand up on their own.

As we progressed to some unknown destination, the slumping structures gave way to more open spaces and grander buildings. It was into one of these that we turned. Argon rapped three times on the wooden gate barring our entrance. I hadn't seen anywhere in Eternity that needed permission to enter. This was new to me too.

The door opened inward and Kristoff shoved me through, closing the gate quickly once we were all inside. I stood in a small courtyard with scrappy plants attempting to thrive in the awful light. Someone had shaped them into points and hedges, though the scruffy looking greenery mostly showed bare branches.

"Welcome Master Argon, Kristoff," said a voice somewhere in the corridor in front of us.

"Take her to the maid and find her some more clothes. It won't do to have her walking about in those." Argon shoved me forward, gesturing at my clothing as if I were somehow not dressed properly.

I fell into the waiting hands of a sturdy female soul wearing a longer skirt and cotton blouse. Wiry brown hair escaped a swath of cloth wrapped around her head and tied in the front. Deep frown lines from the sides of her lips downward defined her aged face. Her critical small eyes scanned me top to toe and she *hmphed*.

Her grip was stronger than Argon's. She pulled me along several hallways and down a flight of steps before we found the maid.

"Master brought this home with him. Him and that Kristoff," she said.

"Kristoff's here?" replied the maid.

"Never you mind about that Kristoff. You're to get this one some decent clothes and find someplace to put her for now." The frowning woman looked at me one more time before leaving the room.

"Ethel's a bitch to everyone. Stop looking so scared." I was scanned up and down yet again while this new soul took her measure of me. "You're from the South then?"

"Um, I guess?" I answered.

"Yeah, well, this is the North, and nobody dresses like that here. Especially females."

"Okay?"

"Yeah, okay? Is that all you can say for yourself? Who are you?"

"I'm Embry."

"Embry. Hmm. Okay, Embry. You live her now. You do as I say. Follow me."

At least this time I was allowed to walk on my own as I followed her into the next room where she fumbled through what appeared to be barrels full of cast-off clothes. She had something specific in mind as she held up then threw aside numerous blouses, skirts, and loose pants.

"Put this on," she ordered.

It was, or it had been, a fern-colored tunic with a simple opening at the top that came down to my knees. The scratchy fabric chafed as I slid it over my head and I was thankful for the smooth halter and skirt I wore.

"And these," she added.

The garment thrown at me this time was a pair of stretchy hose, thick and darker green than the tunic. I stopped myself from wondering who else had worn them as I pulled them on underneath my skirt.

"Is this Argon's house?" I asked after I was dressed.

"Master Argon," she replied.

"Why is he your master?" I asked.

"'Cause that's the way it is in the North," she replied.

"Why does Creator allow it?" I asked.

She put her hands on her hips. "Next time I see Them, I'll ask. Like that's going to happen," she added more quietly. "Come on. I gotta report to him about you, so let's you and me solve the mysteries of life later."

Again, I followed her. This time up several flights of stairs to a hallway with closed doors on either side. She paused for a moment before proceeding to the third door on the right. "This'll do," she said more to herself than me. She took a large ring of keys from a pocket in her own tunic and unlocked the door. "In you go."

Not knowing what else to do, I entered the room. The door slammed behind me and I heard the lock click, her footsteps echoing away to silence. Having never been locked in anywhere in my life before, the sensation caused a new feeling. Panic. Tears welled up. My heartrate increased, and I took short, shallow breaths, trying to determine what I was expected to do. There was only a low cot in front of me, a stained sink to one side and a narrow-barred window allowing very little of the toxic orange light into the room. I sank onto the cot, covered my eyes with dirty hands, and wept. Great heaving sobs came next. This wasn't supposed to happen in Eternity. These feelings were not supposed to be felt here. It was supposed to be an enlightened place where only the highest thoughts, feelings, and actions occurred.

Chapter Fourteen

ours passed and I heard nothing but the sound of my own breathing and an occasional sniffle. I'd not known fatigue in the South but felt it now as hope began to fade. I thought of Aunt Katy searching for me and asking questions of everyone, Grandma and Grandpa probably at her side. Of Anfalmor filled with arrows—was he dead? Of Dina and Creator—did they know where I was? Did they care? Would I be rescued or was I stuck? And why didn't Creator make this part of here better? Weren't They all-powerful? Omniscient? Omnipresent? What the heck were They doing about my situation? And the biggest question of all, why did Alice hate me so much?

I grew thirsty. Another new feeling. I waited, thinking that someone would come. Finally, I tried the faucet in the sink near my cot and slurped at the trickle of lukewarm water. In the South, I'd enjoyed eating and drinking only for the taste and flavors that brought pleasure. The taste of this water made me spew it back out. Better to be thirsty.

I knocked on the door, tentatively at first, but growing in urgency. I knocked on all the walls, adding my cries for help to the noise. I shook the bars on the window. Tried to see beyond them to the outside, but tall, sickly trees blocked my view. Was I destined to live eternally inside these walls? Forgotten? I repeated the knocking along walls and door, harder, yelling louder. Still no response. Panic gave way to despair, another new feeling. I was all out of tears and they hadn't helped anyway. I hugged my knees to my chest as I sat at the end of the cot and buried my face in my arms. The rocking came next as I tried to comfort myself. I even sucked on my fingers, something I remembered doing while in the womb. Some part of me recalled the comfort I'd known in that safe environment. Wished I'd never been born or removed from that perfection.

My thoughts continued to descend, spiraling into a pattern of self-pity and finally, silence. I felt nothing. Darkness inside and outside my soul became my new reality. There was no comfort in anything and I wanted to be dead. Eternity like this was unthinkable. Even my third-eye vision couldn't pierce through the despair.

Though the sky never changed color to show the end of the day, I was aware of time passing. Occasionally I looked up, saw nothing, and returned to my self-created womb and sucked on my fingers. No one was coming for me. No one cared. Creator had forgotten me. Aunt Katy, my friends, Dina, all had moved on with their lives and I was fading into a distant memory, to be forgotten forever. Alice would be happy I was gone, though I'd not understood why my very existence had angered her so.

At some point, memories of every encounter with Alice paraded across my consciousness. I knew for certain she'd followed me, or had one of her friends do so. I examined every word we'd exchanged but could find nothing to indicate the depth of her loathing nor the reason behind it. I should have been more insistent about getting help from Dina, from Zadkiel, from Aunt Katy. Even Grandma and Grandpa had dismissed me. I hadn't even thought to seek out Creator. I had trusted everyone in the South to take care of me. They'd let me down. Now, I was on my own and knew little to nothing about survival. I was going to have to rely on whatever instincts I'd inherited from my parents.

I forced myself back out of the darkness. Forced myself to create a plan. I had to find the dragons. That much was clear. They'd come to me in a vision, spoken the words, "Find us." And that was exactly what I was going to do. But first I needed to survive here in the North. And to do that, I needed to get out of this cell.

"Argon! Let me outta here!" I allowed fear and panic, despair, and every blackened thought to feed my anger. I kicked the door. Kicked it again and dust flew from the thick, wooden planks. "Argon! Ethel! Maid! I'm going to scream for eternity till you let me out!"

In between my screaming, I heard footsteps grow louder outside my cell.

"Quit yer hollerin'," said Ethel. "You'll raise the dead."

As soon as she pulled the door open, I used its momentum to shove her aside and ran down the corridor toward the stairs.

"Here, then! Come back here, you ungrateful little bitch." Ethel, though sturdy, was not fast enough to stop me from descending each flight.

I remembered to turn into an alcove I'd seen on the way up and as she hurried past, still calling me an ungrateful bitch, I stuck my foot out and tripped her. The idea had entered my mind without prior planning, and I wondered which parent had blessed me with mean thoughts. I whispered a thank you to each of them as I stepped over Ethel, through the kitchen, and out the door.

Her hollering had raised the other occupants in the house and I heard them shouting. I thought I recognized Argon's, and perhaps the maid's voices joined by several male voices. I knew I couldn't stick around to be captured again. I had to find the warehouse I'd first awakened in. Hoped there were clues to how I might get back.

The drab, green hosiery and tunic scraped against my skin as I sprinted away from Argon's home, hoping I'd chosen the right direction. Souls dressed in drab clothes from every era of history observed me with only mild interest. No one tried to stop me. Souls running from other souls must have been normal for them. They looked away and continued on their business, even as I heard my name called.

Rounding a corner a block down from Argon's house, I caught a glimpse of the muddy river ahead, but the cobbled road between me and my destination was filled with souls. Shrinking against the side of the building, I tried to stay in the shadows as shouts grew louder. Several souls looked up at my pursuers. For the first time, I was thankful for the drab colors of my new clothes and the smallness of my stature. Even my long, curly hair was a blessing as I allowed it to cover part of my dirty face.

Dead trees in oversized concrete planters ran along this side of the street and I managed to edge along the building and hide behind one of them as Argon came into view.

"Have you seen a young soul run by here?" he asked the first soul he came to. Ethel, the maid, and two male souls I didn't recognize drew up beside him, breathless.

The soul shook his head, clearly afraid of Argon.

Argon grabbed the front of the soul's shirt, "Are you sure?"

"Seen nuffin'," answered the frightened soul.

Argon shoved him away and continued into the street. "Anyone seen a young soul run by here?" he shouted. "She's mine, if anyone sees her. There's a reward!" he added, louder.

At the word *reward*, other souls looked up with mild interest and I knew it wasn't long before my hiding place was discovered. Even now, I could see that Ethel and the others were moving along my side of the street. If I moved away from the shadow of the large planter, the souls in the street would see me. If I moved back to the shadows of the building, I'd be caught by Ethel and the others. Did I take my chances with the unknown souls in the street or be captured and thrown in a cell again by Argon? Fear pulsed through my heart. Panic threatened to immobilize me. And then my third-eye opened. All emotions focused into anger, into independence. I could solve my own problems and was in charge of myself. Nobody needed to take care of me.

"I'm here, but I'm not going back with you if you're going to lock me up again!" I stepped into the street.

Every soul turned their attention to me. Argon stepped into the street toward me.

"Stay where you are," I ordered. "All of you just listen. I don't know where I am. I don't know how I got here. If any of you can help me get back to the South, I'll find a way to repay you." I hesitated, as nothing worth anything to any of them came to mind. This was the basest part of Eternity. Souls arriving from Earth without learning kindness, compassion, caring, integrity, and honesty apparently occupied the North. What was I really facing? What could these souls do?

I continued. "I'll speak to Creator on your behalf."

Ethel snorted. "Well, that changes everything now, doesn't it?"

All the souls moved toward me in unison.

Chapter Fifteen

We sat in a parlor filled with dingy, overstuffed furniture, too much of it crowding the small room. Argon had succeeded in dragging me out from the grasping arms of the souls in the street. Ethel had even thrown a few punches to ensure I was released. Argon sipped from a silver flask and I had already drained my glass of its contents, a sweet dark concoction with bubbles that tickled my nose.

"You have to take me back to the warehouse," I said.

"It isn't safe there."

"What is going to happen? This is Eternity? You can't die here."

"In the North, things can happen that are worse than death."

"Like what? Where's Dhororr then? Let me talk to him."

"We've sent for him, but in the meantime, let me assure you that your young soul is not ready to ask about the kinds of things that go on here." He sipped from his flask.

"You were going to leave me in that cell forever," I accused. "Just leave me there and forget about me? Is that what you're about? Is that what you do here? Find innocent souls and just lock them up till nobody remembers they even existed? You're a sick soul."

"I left instructions with the maid to check on you. I had business." Argon waved his hand as if to excuse himself for my mistreatment. I noticed he didn't apologize. I shook my head, anger again welling inside. He didn't deny my accusations either. Was he a jailor? Some kind of law soul? Deputy to Dhororr?

"I need to get back to the South." I crossed my arms. "Nothing else matters."

"I can't let you out on the street by yourself."

"Then take me to the border or the wall or the portal or whatever it is that will allow me to make my own way to the South," I said. Why was he being so dense? I didn't think my request was so hard.

"The portal to the South is closed," he said. "Sealed on the other side. That's what I went to check on."

"What? Well, find another one."

"They don't open from our side without Dhororr and Creator's approval." He sipped from his flask. "Dhororr has Enforcers all over the North and when he hears of changes of heart in the populace, there is an inquiry. If Dhororr discerns you're ready, he can open a portal to allow you to move to the South. It seldom happens," he added.

"Then let's go see him. Now." I stood. Strong arms shoved me back to my seat. I batted at them. They held me down anyway.

"I'm not in a good position to ask Dhororr for favors at this particular time." Argon set his flask aside, leaned forward, waited till I stopped struggling with those holding me down. "I have souls watching Dhororr. Souls seeking to get to the South like you. Dhororr only opens a portal when a Northern soul exhibits their worthiness to enter the South. Impossible to slip by him."

I stared at him, weighing my options.

"I will harbor you here," he said, "in this home, and try to help you through a portal if you agree to my terms."

Argon's tone sent a chill up my spine. Unfamiliar with the ways of the world, I couldn't imagine what I would be required to do. Arriving in Eternity feeling less than whole was bad enough. That I should find myself in the North, where souls existed without trying to make the heart changes that would lead them to a life in the South was too terrible to contemplate. Why didn't they learn to be better? Why were souls so bent on continuing their wicked ways when I was sure Dhororr was showing them a better life?

Argon squinted his eyes and whispered, "You must serve me while we watch Dhororr, do anything I ask you to do, prove your worth to me, and I will do my best to get you through a portal back to the South."

"Serve you? What does that mean, serve you?"

Ethel snickered and elbowed one of the men now standing beside my chair. "I can imagine a lot of ways she can serve."

The man grabbed his crotch and rubbed himself.

Argon leaned back again, took a sip from his flask, and cocked his head before he continued. "I have many uses for a soul of your stature."

My third-eye vision went black and fuzzy as if urging me not to agree to his terms. "My stature?"

"You're small and . . . female."

"So?"

"So, do you accept my terms or not?"

"I don't even know what I'm agreeing to. How do I know you'll help me? Why can't I just go to Dhororr and ask him to open a portal? I met him once in the South. He knows I'm not from here." I crossed my arms.

"Because I won't let you," said Argon.

"You're such a liar!" I tried to stand and was forced down again. "You said you'd sent for Dhororr and now you're telling me you won't let me talk to him? No. I don't agree to your terms. I'll take my chances out there." I waved in the direction of the muddy river.

Argon sighed. "Lock her up again. But, maid, make sure to check on her once in a while."

The two men lifted me easily between them and no amount of kicking and struggle loosened their grip. "Let me go! Argon!"

They threw me onto the floor of the cell I'd been in before, laughed when I cried in pain, and slammed the heavy wooden door shut. I rubbed my hip and shoulder. Great. Just freaking wonderful. I'd escaped, gotten caught, negotiated with my captor to no avail, and was back in this Creator-forsaken cell. My third-eye vision continued its fuzziness. No ideas or information there. I pondered Argon's offer. Something insidious invaded my thoughts. There was no doubt in my mind he wanted me to do unthinkable things. Wanted me to dirty my soul with learning from the North.

The maid brought me a glass of the dark, bubbly liquid I'd tasted before and some limp, green vegetables in a bowl.

Hovering behind her was one of the male souls in Argon's service. She was taking no chances this time.

"Master said to check on you, so here I am." She stood waiting for me to take the food from her. "I don't have all day. Got things to do for the master."

I stared at her a little longer before taking the glass and bowl from her hands.

"Don't I get a thank you? You could starve for all I care." She put her hands on her hips.

"I didn't need food in the South," I said.

"Well, isn't that just fine. Need it in the North or you'll waste away." She turned and shoved her way past the tall male soul. "Come on, Hersh." He hesitated, leering at me before slamming the door.

"Creator!" I yelled. "Dhororr! I need to see you! If you're anywhere around, please, get me out of here!"

The dark bubbly liquid was terribly sweet, but I drank it. I couldn't get past a mouthful of the limp, green vegetables before I gagged and everything came up out of my stomach into the sink next to my cot. The maid came three more times to bring me food, taunt me, and ask if I was ready to leave my cell and agree to Argon's terms. Each time, she was accompanied by Hersh. On the third visit, Ethel entered first. Her agitated energy shone a sickly green around her tall, gangly body. My third-eye vision sensed a decision had been made.

I sat against the wall on my cot while she stared at me. "Master Argon wants to see you again," she said. "Says we can't let you waste away up here if we're ever going to earn our way to the South."

Ethel led the way down the stairs as the maid and Hersh followed. I thought about giving her a good shove and attempting to escape again but wasn't sure I'd be able to get past her and away from the maid and Hersh. Instead of the musty parlor we'd met in earlier, Ethel led me to a room filled with file cabinets on one side and reddish-brown, covered books on shelves along the other. Hersh stepped forward to shove me into a chair across from Argon seated at a large mahogany desk.

"Leave us," ordered Argon. As soon as the door shut, he set his pen down. "I've been thinking of the best way to use you while we wait for Dhororr to open a portal. I've decided to make you my assistant."

"I don't want to be your assistant," I declared.

"Nevertheless, after much pondering, I've realized that if I misuse you in any way, I will never reach the South. I have been in the North for twenty years and in all that time I've not been presented with such a perfect opportunity to prove to Dhororr that I am worthy of a portal myself."

I waited. A glimmer of hope sparked purple in my third-eye vision. With Argon watching for a portal for himself, or trying to earn one on his own, I stood a better chance of getting back. Maybe he'd realized misusing me in any way would certainly ruin his chances.

"Why haven't you made someone else your assistant?" I asked. "Why me? Why now? I don't know anything other than the good of the South. I'm pretty sure I'd be a lousy assistant."

"Did they teach you to ask so many questions there?"

"No." I thought the question rude and didn't feel like elaborating. "You don't answer any of them very well so I'm just going to keep asking."

He sighed. "I haven't ever trusted anyone to assist me. I have leverage over everyone in my employ, but I don't trust any of them. Each soul here in the North is trying to learn what they need to so they can get to the South. Unfortunately, we arrive with so many bad habits, so much baggage, that we fall back on them to survive.'"

"Then what's Dhororr doing about it? How is he helping you get better?" I was exhausted from my lack of knowledge of how this world worked. I'd just begun learning how to live in the South. The North was just a dark buzz of confusion for me.

"Dhororr creates situations for us to choose the right path. He cannot influence how we act, cannot lead us to goodness. We must see the right choice and make it." Argon, for the first time since I'd met him, sounded almost kind. "When the light of Creator takes seed in our hearts, Dhororr is able to create a portal to the South."

"Sounds easy enough." I didn't see the problem.

"Oh, you innocent soul." Argon shook his head. Didn't say anything for several moments. Looked around at his file cabinets, books. Sighed. "So much to learn."

"I don't want to learn how to be bad. Not from you. Not from anybody."

"Well, you're stuck in the North. For now. So that's what you'll experience while you're here. I didn't bring you here, but you need to show me your gratitude for finding you before someone with less noble habits did." My third-eye vision was becoming clearer as I watched his energy changed. It was now a sinister-looking grayish red. "If Kristoff had found you by himself, well, you'd already be learning some bad habits."

After I promised not to run away again, Ethel escorted me to a small bedroom appointed with more of the musty old furniture I'd come to expect. A real bed, covered with a faded floral comforter stood in the center, a round rug covering a portion of the wooden floor. Near one of the two windows stood a washbasin and a pitcher of water. My reflection shocked me as I rinsed the dust and dirt off my face and arms. Knots of my hair tangled into single locks, sticking out in all directions from my head. Purple bruises ringed my eyes and along my arms. I hated it here. But I began to see a way out. A way back. Argon was giving me a bigger gift then he realized. I would watch. I would listen. I would store all my questions. And I would hope that Creator would appear before I became bad.

Chapter Sixteen

Our first venture out of the house was to visit what Argon called his accounts. I carried a large leather satchel filled with contracts and papers as I ran to keep up with his long strides. He'd insisted Ethel find clothes more reflective of his status in this community, so I wore tight black pants and a stiff, white shirt tucked in. Flat, shapeless, black shoes kept the cobbles from bruising my feet. I'd combed through the painful tangles and knots in my hair and tied it back with a piece of black ribbon, a long curly ponytail winding down my back. I couldn't stop gawking at the orange-tinted, gray buildings we passed, unable to tell where one ended and another began.

I learned little from the first few stops, as papers were taken from the satchel, reviewed, stamped or signed, and returned to their resting place in its folds. Few words were spoken between Argon and those behind desks doing the stamping and signing. It was all droll, tedious. I simply served as a pack animal and didn't see why he'd chosen me when anyone could have walked beside him carrying the satchel.

He exchanged some coins for two squatty, vegetable-filled pies from a vendor on a street corner. There were more souls than I'd ever seen in the South scurrying up and down the asphalt streets, some even pedaling two- or three-wheeled contraptions he called bikes.

"Eat. You look like you're going to blow away." Argon shoved one of the pies at me and I juggled the satchel to rest behind my back as I took the pie.

It was much better than anything Ethel had prepared for me. I finished it off and licked my fingers. Argon laughed.

He pulled out his flask and thrust it at me. "Drink."

"What is it?" I asked.

"I only drink water during the day, unless . . ." he answered.

"Unless what?" I asked, swallowing a large gulp of slightly stale water.

"Unless the occasion calls for something stronger." He looked at me with an expression I'm sure had meaning but was lost on me.

We hurried down more streets, turning corners and winding our way through the city. Fewer souls occupied the area. Those we encountered had harsh words to say if we got in their way.

"Never mind them," said Argon.

"Everyone's so mean here. Mad. Angry. Does anyone ever get to go South?" I hadn't meant to ask any questions, but they just kept spilling out.

"It happens," Argon replied.

"Are you making the right choices, Argon?" I asked. "Are you close to getting your own portal?"

He turned and slapped me. I staggered backward on the sidewalk, staring at his hand. My cheek throbbed, heat flowing through me with the pain. My third-eye vision saw nothing but red. A bystander laughed and pointed, adding to the mix of new feelings of shame.

Argon watched my reaction for a moment before moving toward me to grab my hand. "Never question my actions, Embry. I will not be judged by the likes of you." His breath smelled of bitterness, metallic and sour. "Nod if you understand."

I nodded.

He turned and continued down the street, moving even faster than before and I ran to keep up. Pondered escaping from him again but remembered what he'd said about my chances of falling into worse hands. Something about Argon could be trusted, though I'd learned the valuable lesson of thinking before I spoke.

I barely reacted quickly enough when he turned a corner and disappeared down an alley. Dim light filled with dust motes disturbed by our passage. Though Argon strode with purpose, apparently unaffected by the sudden darkness, I moved more tentatively into the unknown. I looked up to see only a small, ineffective crack of daylight between the tall buildings leaning in toward each other at the top.

"Over 'ere, Argon. This way."

I recognized Kristoff's voice at the end of the alley. We paused before entering a warehouse similar to the one I'd awakened in and I wondered if another soul from the South had been kidnapped and brought North.

"Ah, here we are," said Argon. "How many this time?"

"Three." Kristoff gestured toward a heap of dirty rags grouped together. "Here. Stand up and let him see you."

The heap separated itself into three male souls barely recognizable as such. They stood shaking and slumped with frightened eyes and sickly auras.

"Them don't look like much, but they all come to thievin' honest-like, so they tell me. Just arrived. Got into a brawl in jail with some tough-uns down there on Earth. All of 'em got some family 'ere."

"Anyone else bid on them yet?" asked Argon.

"Got one offer from Sid, but he was low-ballin' so I told him he could go fuck 'imself." Kristoff saw me and winked. "S'cuse the French."

"Embry," Agron said, "look inside the zippered part of my satchel. You'll find some coins. Take out the three largest ones."

I was glad for the diversion as the three souls standing there hadn't stopped gawking at me while Kristoff and Argon talked. Finding the three largest coins with my fingers, I handed them to Argon.

"Will this do?" he asked.

"More than fair, more than fair," answered Kristoff.

"Good. Find them appropriate clothes and clean them up before bringing them to the house." Argon brushed past me.

I followed him at a trot, wanting to blurt all the questions in my head. My cheek still stung from the slap and I sealed my lips shut. Who were those souls? What was he going to do with them? Shouldn't we take them to their families? What were those coins? My feet ached from the miles we'd walked. A slight ache was building up behind the area of my third eye.

My starched-stiff white blouse hung limp on my body and had come untucked in the back.

Argon marched up the front steps of his home with me dragging along behind him. Without a word, he took the satchel from me and disappeared into his study and closed the doors. The maid glanced my way, wrinkled her nose at my appearance, and continued to dust the vases in the foyer. Ethel hollered from somewhere in the back of the house for me to go upstairs, that I was to stay in my room until she called for me and I went willingly to the only place I'd experienced a reprieve from the constant barrage of new and unwanted feelings and experiences.

A Light-Being I hadn't met before glowed neon green light into my dim and dusty bedroom.

"Come in," she whispered in a low gruff voice. "Close the door."

I stared at her presence, waiting.

"Don't be afraid," she said. "Dhororr sent me."

As soon as she spoke, fear lifted from my heart. The dust in the room disappeared. Items scattered on the mantel and around the room straightened themselves. Even the faded floral comforter brightened with fresh hues of lilac and purple. I stepped away from the door toward this new Light-Being in wonder, hoping she was my savior.

"I am not," she said. "But I bring you news. Please, sit." She gestured toward one of the now-cozy chairs sitting in front of a cheery fire.

She sat across from me as I settled into the cushions, pulling my feet up underneath me. "News of your disappearance from the South has traveled North and Light-Beings are working together to get you back to where you belong."

"Let's go," I stood, all fatigue vanishing.

She laughed. "Not so fast, Embry. There are things that have to happen first."

"Like what? Why is it so hard to get me back to where I belong?" I lowered again to the cozy chair, but it wasn't as comforting as it had been.

"When Creator made the rules at the beginning, They agreed to follow the same rules when it came to Their Creation," she explained. "Situations like yours are so rare that the wise souls, Light-Beings, and Creator must meet to determine how best to move in and around Their rules. The portal you came through has been sealed forever and the magic used to create it has weakened the protections on all the portals everywhere in Eternity. We can't just pop you back through without further weakening them."

"What about the dragons?" I asked.

"No." She shook her head and her aura dimmed for a moment. "We cannot trust the dragons with portal magic anymore. They love your kind too much. They don't know how to say no to you."

"I think I'd like to live with the dragons," I asked. "Can you tell me what they did that was so terrible?"

"The dragons caused a second death, a final one. The death of an eternal soul. Creator banished them to the Crystal Mountains." The Light-Being's aura dimmed so completely I could barely see her. "Ask me no more about the dragons. I can only stay a little longer. Dhororr wants you to know he remembers you. He will open a portal for you as soon as he can. Be ready."

"I'm ready now," I said. "I don't want to stay here. Argon's making me do things with him."

The Light-Being didn't respond right away. I watched her green aura whirl and flow as if reflecting her thoughts. "Argon isn't what you think he is. We are content to let you stay with him for now. Dhororr knows of his dealings with new souls and is working hard to design situations for Argon to make the right choices."

"He slapped me today." I turned my cheek to show the puffy redness growing there.

"That is unfortunate, and our treatment of Argon will reflect our displeasure. However, there are souls here that would have done much worse to you by now. The rules are different in the North because every soul created in the beginning must be treated with patience and given the opportunity to choose to return to the very best version of themselves. It sometimes takes decades, centuries even, for some to rediscover their light.

"In the South, souls arrive either as innocents, like yourself, or as enlightened souls ready to enjoy eternity, adding to enlightenment," she continued. "Argon arrived very dark. He has made tremendous progress in a few short decades. Much light has been restored in him."

"Then how is Alice in the South?" I asked. "She doesn't seem very enlightened. Maybe she needs to be here instead of me."

"That's exactly the kind of thinking that will keep you here a little longer." The Light-Being rose and stood with her hands on her hips. "I won't explain Alice to you. I only urge you to find pity and compassion in your heart for her. Only then can your heart stay pure."

She faded as she spoke until her presence was no longer in my room, taking the light with her. Colors faded to their former noxious-orange hue. I pulled the ribbon from my hair and shook it out along my back. I wanted to shut my eyes and awaken from this nightmare. Wanted to step into the stream behind Aunt Katy's house and submerge myself in its cool, soothing flow.

I thought about Alice, trying to find pity and compassion for her. It was hard to shake my resentment and anger.

Chapter Seventeen

Not trusting to the pipes in the old house to deliver hot water, I heated some in a bucket on the stove while the maid and Ethel fumed over me with stares and growls of disapproval. I ignored them. It took me five trips up and down the stairs to fill the old clawfoot tub with boiling water before I added just enough cold to achieve the right temperature. Stripping, I dropped into the tub and sighed. Holding my breath and dunking under, I shook my hair out around me and blew bubbles. I spluttered back up, took a big breath, and went under again to stay still, listening to the silence. Not quite as soothing as my own stream in the South, but I felt somewhat better.

I leaned my head against the chipped porcelain edge. With eyes closed, my third-eye vision showed Aunt Katy sitting with Gypsy in her lap by our little cottage, a look of distress on her face. Next, I saw Grandma and Grandpa walking along the streets of Cheshiphon with purposeful strides, holding hands, and I wondered if they were on their way to see Creator. Usan, Isla, and Kenja appeared next, talking to Dina with urgent gestures and pointing toward the forest. I didn't know if what I was seeing what was real, or what I wished was real. I dared to hope they were discussing me. I leaned into the feeling of trust that the right things were happening, that my return was of utmost importance in their minds. But was it selfish of me to think I was that important?

I scrunched my forehead, and my third-eye vision blurred. A sapphire-blue light replaced my friends and family, piercing into the center of my brain. It was followed by ultraviolet before giving way to ripples of rich, deep purple. The dragon eye appeared again, filling up my vision without blinking. The water in the tub vibrated with the ripples of purple inside my head.

"Hello, little one." The voice surged through my mind, low and ancient.

My eyes popped open, but I was blind to everything but the purple eye.

"You're closer to us than you were before," the voice continued. "I can sense the presence of the crystal you took from our lands. You must be in the North."

I nodded.

"We feel you. We hear your questions. If you find us, we can help." The eye shrunk and more of the dragon came into view. His thick, scaly neck curved in a high arc as he turned his head to face me. Between his small, oval ears were three sets of spikes growing in size down his back. His wings were closed against his thick muscular body, but I could see the ten-inch claws curled at their ends.

"What's your name? Why do you come to me? Why do you want to help me so much?"

"I am Archeladon. I come to you because of the song in your blood. I knew of you as soon as you arrived," he rumbled. "As an innocent, you walk in questions, your blood calls to us. When you were able to secure a crystal from our land, we knew you were special."

"What the heck does that mean?" I sat up, rippling the water over the sides of the tub. Noticed the tepidness of the water and shivered. As soon as Archeladon became aware of my discomfort, he breathed through the opening of my third-eye into the water and warmed it almost to the point of boiling. "Not too hot," I urged.

He smiled, frightening me with a mouth full of sharp teeth and three tongues licked out and around his leathery lips.

"What's special about my blood?" I settled back into the newly warmed water.

"Both of your parents carried ancient blood, origin blood. As centuries have passed, origin blood is almost completely diluted. When your parents made you, and your soul entered your physical body, the blend strengthened. It was a good combination," he added. "We wept many crystals when they dismantled you before you'd had a chance to live."

He withdrew from my third-eye vision so that now I could see other dragons nearby, standing as if listening with great interest to our conversation. Sorrow filled me as I thought about their crystal tears falling for me. These huge, majestic creatures knew me. Wanted me. Wanted to help me. I had to find them.

"Can you tell me how to find you?" I asked.

"I am forbidden to tell any soul where we are, but I can tell you how to get close. The rest is going to be up to you. When you're close, we will feel you and I will be able to appear here, in your third-eye vision. Keep the fire opal close."

"Embry!" It was Ethel's voice accompanied by loud, urgent pounding on the locked door of the bathroom. "Been in there too damned long! Now get out of there and get dressed! Master wants to talk to you!"

I almost lost contact with the dragons, but sent urgent energy toward my third-eye. "Quickly. Tell me how to get close."

"Embry! I'm going to have Hersh break the door down if you don't answer!" Ethel sounded angry and gleeful at the same time.

"Come to the west end of town. Alone." Archeladon's voice faded as something like a sledgehammer hit the bathroom door.

"I hear you! I'm coming! Stop pounding the door!" I splashed out of the bath, grabbed a towel to wrap around me, and opened the door just as Hersh took another swing. It barely missed my head as I ducked away, and my towel dropped. Hersh stood looking my naked body up and down, his eyes widening with something in them I didn't like.

"Get out of here!" I shoved him back into Ethel, slammed the door, and ran to the other door that opened up to my bedroom, and shoved a chair underneath the knob. Wrapping the towel around my wet hair, I pulled on some fresh leggings and a tunic before descending with loud steps to the study.

Chapter Eighteen

"Tonight, we go to the homes of those new souls I bought from Kristoff." Argon sat behind his mahogany desk, a sly expression on his face. "Returning souls to their families helps me earn favor with Creator."

"I doubt it." I pressed my lips together so I'd not add my condemning thoughts.

"Watch your tone," he warned. "Meet me in the foyer in an hour." He waved for me to leave.

I hesitated, frowning at him. I didn't want to go. Didn't want to be associated with the actions of this soul. Didn't want to look into the faces of families as Argon made his deals. When he didn't look up again, I turned and walked back up the stairs. Just before I reached the landing, Ethel hollered for me to come eat dinner. I resented having to feed this body as hunger pangs reminded me of the difference between eating in the North and eating in the South. The sweet and savory tastes I'd enjoyed with Aunt Katy had given way to unappetizing lumps of greenish vegetables with no flavor. Yet, I had to feed this body while in the North, so I forced a few swallows before my stomach rebelled and I excused myself to go change into my so-called professional clothes.

Hersh accompanied Argon and me as we trotted back across the city in the dusk of the dusty afternoon. The three souls, cleaned up somewhat and still subdued, were linked together with rough rope, and stumbled behind Hersh. I felt their eyes on my back and longed to comfort them as my family had when I'd arrived in the South. Each time I turned in an attempt to catch their eye, Hersh cuffed me on the shoulder or shoved me forward so that I finally gave up and paid attention to my surroundings once again.

Argon opened a squeaky gate that had once been painted white but now stood askew on its hinges in front of a small, gray house. Light from a single bulb atop a lamp with no shade tried to brighten the window it sat in front of, but the effect was neither cheery nor welcoming. I didn't want to follow Argon into that house but with Hersh bringing one of the souls with him behind me, I was forced to move forward. The other two souls stood quiet, tied to the fence like animals.

After Argon knocked hard a few times, a tall, bearded man in a dingy, white undershirt opened the door.

"Whaddya want?" The bearded man moved to block the entrance, but Argon stepped into the room as if he had some sort of legal right.

"I think you might know this soul," said Argon. He gestured past me to the soul Hersh held by the shoulders.

"Zachary? Is it really you?" The bearded man's voice softened as tears streamed down his face. "You're here? You're too young to be here." He moved with his arms outstretched toward the soul named Zachary, but Hersh blocked him.

"Not so fast, you damned Scot." Argon grabbed me by the arm and rifled through the satchel I carried for a folder.

"I own your young Zachary. If you want him, you'll have to pay for him. Deed of sale right here."

"What? Are you serious? I don't have to pay for my own damned son." The bearded man drew up to his full size as if he would fight Argon, but Hersh hit him hard in the stomach. The bearded man doubled over, unable to breathe.

"Dad? Dad, are you okay?" Zachary reached for his dad with his bound hands but got slapped across the mouth for his trouble.

"Shut up, kid," said Hersh.

I wanted to vomit. Wanted to kick Hersh and Argon, comfort the bearded man and his son. The gentle, loving, and joyful reception I'd received upon my arrival was the way it was supposed to be. Argon was doing so much damage to these fresh souls. How could anything on Earth have prepared them for this kind of ill treatment? What was Earth like if this was what souls received after their deaths? Why weren't they learning all the good and enlightened things Creator wanted them to learn? I began to appreciate how I'd been spared a life on Earth. What would I have learned? What would I have chosen? Would my reception in this life have been different had I chosen to do bad or evil things? I realized this was the case.

I watched as the transaction between Argon and the bearded man concluded with coins exchanged for the soul named Zachary. As we left the house, I caught Zachary's eye to communicate my sorrow for being involved in his capture and release but was met with only mild interest as he looked me up and down as Hersh had when I'd come out of the bath naked. It left me feeling exposed, a creepy chill running up my spine.

"That went well," said Argon. Hersh grunted as he untied the other two and we continued up the street. "Zachary seemed a bit interested in you, Embry. What do you think?"

I didn't understand the insinuation in his voice, but I didn't like it. The creepy feeling returned.

He and Hersh laughed. The two remaining souls chuckled as well.

Similar scenes occurred when we sold the other two to their families, with only one highlight happening at the third house. The two female souls who greeted us at the door appeared to be sisters and wept at the sight of the young male soul Hersh held captive. As Argon began to explain what he needed in return for their family member, they shushed him as they reached for a brown crockery jar at the end of a bookshelf piled with memorabilia from Earth.

"We know what you do, Argon. We've been preparing and saving for Julia and her son for when they arrived. Didn't think Hakim would arrive first, though." The smaller of the two female souls held the coins out for Argon while Hersh untied him and shoved him into their arms.

As we left, their sobs increased as Hakim broke down as well. I couldn't help thinking they would probably all go to the South soon. Something in their energy told me they were making the right decisions.

Hersh disappeared soon after we'd left the third house and Argon slowed his pace so that I could walk comfortably beside him. He was thoughtful, quiet, so I looked around. Thought about the dragons. Wondered if we were near the west side of town. Wondered if I should ask Argon. During our travels, I'd noticed street signs, but they hadn't meant anything to me as they'd mostly been numbers or people's names. None had included directional indicators and only now did I know to even search for the West.

I bumped into Argon as we crossed a street, thinking we'd proceed home the way we'd come.

"Not going home, Embry. I need to see about a portal that might be opening soon." Argon grabbed me by the arm and firmly tugged me as we rounded the corner. "It appears you might know your way home, but I don't want you out of my sight. For several reasons," he added.

I knew a few of those reasons, not the least of which was the chance of meeting some of the unsavory occupants of the North, so I stayed close. This part of the city had low buildings with signs in the windows advertising what could be purchased inside. Souls scurried or sauntered on planked sidewalks, their steps causing the surface to squeak and groan. I watched a gathering of souls on a corner listen to a shiny soul tell them of hope and a better life in the South if they would stop sinning.

"What's sinning?" I asked.

Argon laughed. "Oh, the innocence." He stopped walking and looked at the rusty sky for a moment. "Something you will never do."

His wistful tone confused me. I couldn't tell if he wished I could experience sinning, was sad that I hadn't, or sad that he knew what it was and I didn't. I watched him look at me with brown eyes full of something other than disdain for once, as if he was considering his words carefully. He took a breath, started to speak, stopped. Looked at me harder with his head cocked to one side as if listening to someone I couldn't see.

"Sin is what souls do when they forget where they came from while they inhabit human bodies. Sin is the name of all the selfishness, narcissism and dysfunctional choices people make on Earth." His words were slow, careful, coming out after considerable thought.

He continued down the walkway without waiting for me to respond.

"Are souls sinning here? In the North?"

"What you see here is the memory of sin there. If habits aren't overcome, choices become ingrained inside souls before they die and follow us to this side of Eternity." Argon gestured up and down as if that helped me understand.

"If you know that, why don't you just stop making selfish choices long enough for Dhororr to open a portal for you? Why do you continue to . . . sin?" I asked before I considered the impertinence of my question. I stepped away from him before he could slap me again. He didn't even try.

"I haven't decided if that's what I want," he answered.

"Seriously? You'd rather stay here? It's gross here. It's scary, and everyone is angry and dangerous and dirty and mean. The air stinks and it's never nighttime and you can't mean you think this is better than living in the South." I dared to place a hand on his elbow.

"Since you're the first soul I've ever met that has lived in the South, I'll have to take your word for it." He pulled his arm away from my touch but didn't strike me as I'd expected. "This world is all I've known of Eternity, and I do quite well. How do I know it's better in the South?"

I knew I was close to the end of his patience, but it didn't stop me. This was the most information I'd received from Argon or anyone since I'd arrived and I wasn't going to miss an opportunity to ask. "Are we near the west side of Eternity?"

"What? Why do you ask?" He stopped, this time violence once again emanating from his eyes.

"Oh, I just heard Hersh talking with the maid about something on the west side." I lied. It was my first lie and I felt my heart darken, cloud over with the selfishness of my words. No one was going to benefit from this line of thought except me, but I knew I couldn't just ask to be taken to the west side of here. I don't know how I knew, but I did. "I want to make sure we're not going there because they were talking about some awful things that could be done there. souls paying for things to do with other souls and stuff." My second lie came easier. It was frightening. He chuckled.

"They're referring to the Flesh District," he said. "Exactly where we're going."

Chapter Nineteen

I didn't know whether I was frightened or ecstatic as both emotions caused my heart to race and thoughts to slow. I hadn't noticed the souls around us as we walked, but now I realized there were numerous barely clothed individuals dallying on corners and down alleys. I couldn't distinguish sexes. Everyone was engaged in pawing at each other and making strange noises. It was darker here, the sky an oxidized, dirty red. Souls winked at Argon and I, made comments about us I didn't understand. He only smiled, but drew me closer to him, keeping a hand on the small of my back. I didn't move away, feeling safer with him than the souls all around us.

He shoved me forward into a darkened doorway where beads hung across the entrance, soft, wordless music coming from somewhere inside. A soul at the door spoke his name in recognition and guided us through a room where souls wriggled and writhed in front of other souls watching.

I lowered my eyes, following the soul to a warm, well-lit room at the back of the building.

"Sit there," ordered Argon, pointing to a chair in the corner, away from the beautiful soul sitting at a desk.

She wasn't like any soul I'd seen in the North. She belonged in the South. Her clothes, a cut similar to Aunt Katy's daily wear but with sparkly gems and sequins, hugged her beautiful dark skin. Her hair haloed her head like a black, curly wreath and she had slender, graceful fingers that held a file folder up for Argon.

"Who is she?" asked the soul in a honeyed voice.

"A soul I'm brokering," answered Argon.

"Not like any soul I've seen before." She stood and leaned over her desk to stare at me. "She's unmarked. Shiny. How is she in the North?"

"I'm—"

Argon crossed the room and held his hand up, ready to slap me again.

"Come now, Argon. There's no need for that kind of behavior. How are you ever going to get to the South if you slap innocent souls like that one?" She stood and glided toward us on bare feet. I was drawn to her like a moth to a flame as she moved between us, so close to Argon I saw him shudder. I didn't know if it was out of fear or pleasure at her nearness. Ignoring him, she turned her back to face me. "What were you going to say?"

"I was kidnapped and shoved through an illegal portal from the South," I blurted. "Argon found me. Him and Kristoff."

"I see. Fascinating. I've heard of it happening." She took my arm and moved me into the middle of the room, away from Argon. She held my hands and examined me as if she were considering whether to buy me or not. "Not in my lifetime, but . . . What are you going to do with her, Argon? Do you know how much she's worth here?" She continued to stare at me while addressing her questions to him.

"I do, Hamisi. And I haven't decided, yet." Argon sounded like the calculating broker I'd followed all day. A deal was in the making, and I was the subject.

Her clear green eyes sparkled with anticipation and I tried to wriggle my hands out of hers. She gripped them hard. Here was a soul more deceitful than Argon. I had to get away from her. I was finally realizing how fortunate I'd been to have fallen into Argon's care.

"He promised to find a portal for me to return to the South," I said.

Hamisi laughed at my defiance. "Oh, he did, did he? How nice of him. Trying to prove to Dhororr you need a portal of your own, Argon? Is she your ticket out of here? Going to go through together?"

I glanced at Argon and saw him struggle with an answer. His conflicted allegiances showed on his face.

"Haven't decided yet, have you? Well, let me have her. I'll give you a good price and save you having to make such a hard decision." Hamisi ran her fingers across my cheek as she spoke, a sensuous smile forming on her full lips.

I twisted my hand but couldn't break her grip, succeeding only in knocking a frame off her desk. She caught me before I fell to the floor and held me close against her body.

"Oh, she's fabulous," she cooed. "I must have her."

Argon reached for me and I tried to free myself from Hamisi's grasp. I was caught in a tug-of-war between them as they nearly pulled me in two. For a moment, Hamisi fought both of us off, finally letting me go with a shove. Argon caught me and only our nearness to the wall saved us from toppling onto the floor in a heap. I scrambled toward the door with no idea where I'd go but knowing I needed to escape from her, from him, from everyone. It was locked.

"Sit down, girl," ordered Hamisi. "Let the adults negotiate."

I turned to face both of these horrid souls who wanted to keep me and do Creator-knew-what with me. I'd started to trusted Argon. I didn't now. Hamisi shimmered with false beauty. I'd been taken in by it. Dhororr was moving too slowly, the other Light-Beings either couldn't or didn't care enough to get me back to the South, and Creator had forbidden anyone to open portals unless they'd earned it. How Alice had opened the portal was beyond me and in this moment, I knew finding the dragons was my only hope. Even if it meant going to Earth. Even if I had to die a second death, I was not going to spend Eternity with these selfish souls.

"Fine, stand at the door then, Embry." Argon pushed off the wall and stood in front of Hamisi's desk. She sat and adjusted herself as if nothing had happened, focusing her attention on him for a moment, somehow still sending me uncomfortable signals. My third-eye vision filled with cloudy rainbow-colored static, as if it didn't know what to block out and what to allow in.

"Embry is not for sale." Argon leaned toward Hamisi, threatening further physical violence, though I now knew him to be the weaker one. "At any price," he added. "The souls Hersh delivered to you the other night should see your profits rise quite nicely. And I need to get paid. Since you won't give anyone but me the money, here I am."

Hamisi sat so still, I don't think I saw her breathe. I held my breath as well, and the moans and sighs of the souls on the other side of the door could be heard above the tuneless music still weaving its way into my brain. Her eyes and lips narrowed to slits. Argon shifted his weight from one foot to the other while we waited for Hamisi to reply. A hearty giggle echoed through the walls from behind Hamisi's desk, followed by footsteps and a loud thud. More giggles and then rhythmic thumping and muffled moans right behind Hamisi's head. The invisible souls on the other side of the wall didn't distract her from her continued assessment of Argon, though her lips relaxed into a sly grin.

"I will have her," she finally said. "But . . . I can see we're going to need to negotiate without her in the room. I'm too distracted by her lovely innocence."

When I fell under her scrutiny again, I tried to give her what I thought was my most defiant look, but she laughed and returned her gaze to Argon. Pulling a side drawer out without looking, she removed a small pouch, emptied a few coins into her hand, and held them out for Argon.

"Since you've put me to so much trouble tonight, I'm doubling my price." Argon reached for the pouch, turned to grab my arm, and pounded on the door. "We're done here," he shouted.

The door opened and we pushed past the soul who'd been holding it closed. His eyes were rimmed with something dark, and sweat glistened off a well-muscled torso. He patted my bottom as I followed Argon back down the hall and into the dark-red day.

Chapter Twenty

I paid close attention to every turn and street name on the way back to Argon's home. His angry energy was palpable, darkened indigo waves pounding me as I trotted along a step behind him. We brushed past souls without so much as a glance or acknowledgement. My third-eye vision was now static of a different kind, causing the area to ache. It was an internal pain, unlike that which had erupted when he slapped me. I felt dirty, too. Dirtier than I'd felt in the warehouse when he and Kristoff had first discovered me. It, too, was an internal dirt.

As we walked, I began to plan. I had to escape. Dhororr was unlikely to open up a portal for Argon any time soon, and he was probably lying about getting me through one opened for someone else. I couldn't wait any longer for the Light-Beings and Creator to decide how they were going to return me to my rightful place in the South. I believed They were willing to let me earn my way back, but that didn't seem possible either. Every day I got dirtier, inside and out. Every day I felt it more and more difficult to make good choices since my life was not my own. I had to get away.

I clomped up the steps after Argon and didn't wait to see if he needed me for anything else before I ran to my bedroom and slammed the door. The house was quiet, the maid, Ethel, Hersh, and other members of the household off on their own business. I slid a side table in front of the door, hoping it was heavy enough to keep everyone out. Too late I remembered there wouldn't be hot water for another bath unless I heated it and carried it up myself. Facing anyone and having to explain why I needed another one was too much to contemplate so I used the water in the porcelain basin to rinse off. It did little to assuage the dirtiness gathering around my soul.

I held my breath and plunged my face in the remaining water. Colors behind my eyelids grew clearer the longer I stayed under until the rich rainbow colors I associated with Creator returned to memory, erasing the soiled colors of the North. I dunked a few more times; each time, my head grew clearer. Even my third-eye vision cleared. No static at all.

I sighed, sinking onto my side on the faded comforter with my knees drawn up to my chest. My sore muscles relaxed. My insides stopped churning, the unsettled heaviness and filth that had caused my own light to dim finally lifted. Sleep called to me and though I knew my physical body didn't need it, I felt weary of living.

But I had plans to make.

After searching through several drawers of the desk in my room, I found some scraps of paper and a pencil, barely sharp enough to write. Eschewing the dark corner where the desk was, I sat cross-legged on the hardwood floor near the window and shut my eyes. Scents of food mixed with odors of filth filtered into the room, but I was growing accustomed to the assault on my senses here. No wonder it was so hard to make good choices in a land filled with offensive sights, sounds, and scents. I would never understand how this worked. Didn't want to.

Wrinkling my forehead, I concentrated on my third-eye vision, recalling street names, corners, turns, and the way to the West became clear. I drew a faint outline of the route I needed to take. Once there, I needed to find a place to hide until Archeladon and the other dragons found me. I had no clear idea how to plan for any part of my future. Some instinct compelled me to take my life in my own hands, to do this thing, to move forward without anyone's help. There was no one to trust. I should have felt forlorn and abandoned, but something red and orange burned in my chest. Some feeling of independence grew, fostered by instincts and experiences.

I listened to the house. Listened for movement, voices, activities. Assuming Argon was still behind closed doors in his office, the others either away or busy, I heard only sounds of other souls going about their business in the neighborhood. Looking around the room, I decided there really was nothing in it I needed. I took only the clothes I'd arrived in from the closet where they'd been hung after someone washed them. Rolling them tight, I stuffed them into a pillowcase and tied a knot in the end. In the calming breaths before I exited, something made me pause and take stock of my chances of success. Realizing I could fail, end up back in this room, I scanned it for something I could use as a weapon. Not to take with me. I planned to be too stealthy for that. But something to defend myself with if I failed.

The spindly chair next to the desk offered a solution if I could unscrew one of the legs. As hard as I tried though, it held fast. Desperate, I lifted the chair by the back and whacked it against the desk. Once, twice, three times and it splintered. I stopped. Held my breath as long as I could. Let it out and took another. Nothing. My third-eye vision stayed closed, but I felt guided to give the chair another whack. This time, the leg splintered off and clattered to the floor. Again, I held still with the chair poised above my head. Nothing. No one burst into my room demanding to know what the hell was going on.

With the chair propped against the desk so it wouldn't fall over and give me away, I scanned the room for a hiding place for my weapon. Somewhere they wouldn't find it, but where another hopeless future soul might be able to put it to some use. Hopefully not me. I remembered a dingy spot at the back of the clawfoot tub that the maid hadn't cleaned for decades, grime and dust congealing into a gray ooze where the bathwater had spilled. In plain sight to me, it was obviously not a place anyone thought to look. Placing it there, I whispered to Creator to keep me safe and help whoever came after me.

Moving slowly, listening every few steps, I walked with purpose toward the staircase. I kept to the side by the wall as I placed each foot gently on the steps, the carpet muffling any sounds. I was as stealthy as I knew how to be and reached the foyer without detection. My rusty-orange tunic and leggings helped me blend into the noxious, ruddy light as I tiptoed across the foyer to the front door.

I paused for a moment, letting the panic settle, talking myself into leaving the relative safety of Argon's house. But I was a different soul than the one who had tried to escape just days before. I knew the streets, knew the souls out there weren't to be trusted, and knew what actions were likely to draw attention. My heart pounded so loudly, I was sure Argon would burst from his library office or Hersh would catch me and haul me back to the cell on the third floor.

Forcing myself to open the door, I peeked out at this foreign world waiting to choke me and slithered through the tiny opening I'd made.

On the other side of the solid mahogany door, I held my breath and waited for pursuit. Waited and watched for movement from inside the house or in the bushes surrounding it. None came. I ventured down the steps and stopped in the shadow of a tall spruce shoving its roots up through the sidewalk in an attempt to find good soil. Sneaking a look at the map I'd drawn, I shoved it deep in the pocket of my tunic, hunched my shoulders against attention from passersby who also hunched as if to ward off mine, and began to walk west.

No one cared. I was not pursued. I was not noticed. I descended into the heart of the city and beyond toward the seedy area I'd memorized earlier. Those same low buildings held the same signs advertising the same wares as before. Scantily clad souls moved among the shadows in alleyways and some even bold enough to venture into the open with their wide-mouthed sloppy kisses and groping hands for all to witness as if they were proud of their behavior.

"Hey! You there! Looking for a good time?" a soul dressed in grass-stained overalls and no shirt grabbed himself between the legs and smiled. He laughed when I turned away from him to run down an alley not on my map.

I kept to the stained bricks on one side of the alley, avoiding souls in various states of consciousness and the trash accumulating next to doorways. I was still headed west, just taking a detour. Fortunately, the alley was short. Catching glimpses of boats on the river between the low buildings reassured me. Now to find a place to hide until I could contact Archeladon or he contacted me.

Chapter Twenty-One

I waited with a throng of pitiful souls on the corner as a cart piled high with wooden barrels barred our way across, hoping Kristoff or Hersh were nowhere near. As a small soul, dressed in garments similar to what others wore, I went unnoticed. I felt their despair rub against my bruised and weary soul. Heard the sighs and grumblings on either side of me as we waited. Nothing in the North was cheerful or uplifting. No bright spots. No pleasing aromas. No soft garments. No kind or happy greetings. Again, I wondered how anyone left, but remembered what the Light-Being had shared about Creator working hard to give these souls opportunities. Realized those around me must be the worst of the worst if they were still here in the North. Realized they were being given opportunities every day but weren't learning.

I convinced myself that I had seized the opportunity to leave the relative safety of Argon's protection, such as it was, to seek out my own destiny. As I crossed the intersection with the others, I chose a softer soul to follow, reasoning that she might lead me to a decent hiding place. There was no logic in the hope, but being a new soul left me with little choice but to trust my instincts.

She walked with head down, carrying a basket filled with wilted flowers. Her steps were confident, even if her posture wasn't. As I followed at a safe distance seeking my hiding place, I scanned each building and doorway to determine what might lay inside. These buildings stood right over the water, some with footings actually in the river. All pretense of decoration was gone, the wood gray with soot from the air and lack of attention. I couldn't avoid the squeaks of rotting wood as I walked, but there was enough foot traffic to hide the noise from my chosen leader.

When she turned into a doorway near the end of the road, I waited in the shadows and pretended to adjust my sandals. It was as I stood to follow her that Archeladon chose to pop into my third-eye sight, blinding me to all but his presence. All I could do is lean against the building and focus my attention on him. I didn't know if I was drawing attention or not as his voice echoed in my ear.

"You're close, Embry. We can feel you. Your blood calls to us, and the crystal. You will need the crystal. Stay where you are and we will come for you." Archeladon's words bounced and ricocheted through my brain, making it hard to reply.

"I have to move from the street. It's not safe." I whispered, not knowing if I spoke aloud or if the conversation was contained inside my head.

"We feel no present danger. Stay close. We're coming." Archeladon's voice faded, leaving me with the feeling I'd been inside of a belltower too close to the bell. As I became aware of my surroundings once more, I realized I was holding my head and moaning slightly, causing a disheveled-looking older couple to pause and stare. I pressed further into the wall and shook my head, hoping they'd move on. They did.

I had to trust Archeladon's words and believe he could sense whether or not I was in danger where I stood. It didn't feel anything like safe, out in the open with souls passing by on their way to do Creator-knew-what. I'd learned one thing from Argon. Don't trust anybody. I didn't. I decided not to follow the girl around the corner. A doorway near the corner of the building caught my attention. Straightening my shoulders and standing as tall as I could, I moved toward it, gripped the doorknob, and turned.

Surprised that the door opened, I almost shut it and turned away, so worried that someone or something sinister lurked inside. Finding nothing to impede my entrance, I stepped in. The room was abandoned and all the furnishings stolen or ruined by vandals. It was probably why the door was unlocked. All I needed was patience while I waited to hear from Archeladon.

As time passed, I worried, another new sensation for my fresh soul. How would I know the dragons were calling me? What would it feel like to go through a portal? I remembered nothing from the first time. Would it be painful? Loud? Colorful or blank? Would others know a portal was opening? How were the dragons able to open one when Creator had forbidden them to do so? Why were they choosing me?

Archeladon had spoken of my blood calling to them. I thought back to what I knew of my origins. My parents must have been descendants of those first souls on Earth. Must have been numerous unions of those bodies within that same bloodline to create me. Had any of those souls gone back to Earth before Creator forbade the dragons to open portals?

The shadows of souls passing by my abandoned room along the river kept me aware of all I had to lose if I was found. It was quite possible Argon would decide I was too much trouble and sell me to Hamisi. I shuddered. Rubbed my wrists where she had touched me with such possession. My skin tingled, chill bumps forming all over my arms and legs and up the back of my neck. Or he might throw me in the cell and forget me again like he had that first day. Forget me and ignore my screaming, forever. Board up the room and leave me to be forgotten by Aunt Katy, Grandma and Grandpa, Dina, Creator, and the friends I'd made in the South.

I dozed, weary of life and filled with despair. Only the glimmer of hope of escape lingered deep within me as I held the crystal in my lap and waited. The buzzing noise had been going for some time before I became aware that it wasn't coming from outside. It was inside me. Inside my third eye, though no color or pattern pierced the dark residing there. The fire opal glowed. I rose, instinct telling me to be ready. Feet spread in a fighter's stance and arms slightly away from my body, I scanned the dusty room. Noticing for the first time that the dust motes swirled in a spiral, I leaned toward the gentle cyclone forming in the middle of the room.

A spot of light in the center of the swirl rose up from the floor, growing large and bright as the swirl increased in size. First red, then orange and yellow, then green, blue and violet pulsed up through the floor, repeating and making me feel as though I were inside of a prism. When the spiral reached the crystal in my hands, every sensation threatened to rip me apart as a cacophony of sounds, smells, colors, and sensations. Even exotic tastes tingled on my tongue though my mouth was closed. I took a step, unable to resist the pull into this source of pure perfect pleasure.

Archeladon's eye filled my third-eye as soon as I reached the center of the spiral. I was swirling then, becoming as light as one of the dust motes caught up in the cyclone.

"Let yourself go, Embry." His glee-filled voice resounded in my being even as I swirled faster.

My last view of the North was of myself as a multi-colored form of dust particles disappearing through the dusty floor of that abandoned and boarded-up building, and then I was falling-floating-flailing-feeling free as I rematerialized on the ground in front of Archeladon.

Part Three
The West

Chapter Twenty-Two

rcheladon bent his wonderful, scaly neck toward me and placed his huge nostrils on my hair, snuffling against me in a gentle laugh. All worry drained out of me into the ground and I would have followed it had he not breathed courage, love, and light into my wounded soul. His breath ruffled my hair and I opened my eyes to see the amazing purples, blues, and violets of his scales so close to me. Even as they formed in my head, my questions for him disappeared. He renewed the purity of my soul with a small lick against my forehead with one of his three tongues.

"Welcome to the West, Embry." His voice was even deeper than it had been in my third-eye's vision of him, more of a rumble with words riding along. "The others are eager to meet you."

"The others?" I asked.

He nudged me with his great head to turn around. I gasped, raising a hand to my cheek as I beheld close to a hundred dragons of every shape and size gathered in a semi-circle around Archeladon and me. I couldn't believe the gathering. Hadn't expected there to be so many. Groupings of fours, sevens, and tens stood waiting to meet me. Each group had its own aura, glowing brightest around their individual outlines and joining and blending into a signature color for the group.

"These are the wisdom dragons, my family." Archeladon nodded toward the group of seven to our left. Their collective aura glowed rich, deep purple nearest their bodies, ebbing and flowing into faintest violet as it swirled into the sky, which was turquoise blue. He named them but the consonants and vowels were too much for my brain and I simply nodded as each one acknowledged his mention of them. His mate stood taller and thinner than Archeladon himself, a sleek, angular body with wings the color of aubergine fluttering almost nervously. The other six were obviously his offspring, the two males thick and heavier scaled than their sisters, who were sharp and angular with promises of their mother's future grace.

Next to them was a group of eleven dragons with a collective indigo aura, their outlines a deep twilight blue. The tallest was shorter than me and I bent down to look in her eyes as Archeladon spoke. Her gaze penetrated deep within, examining each of my experiences since arriving here, making me shy. It was an effort to keep my eyes open against her barrage as she stripped away my walls. When she was done, I felt scrubbed, but not raw. Archeladon snuffled against my neck, restoring my peace.

"Indra's intuitive examinations can be a bit astringent, little one," he rumbled.

"I have never come in contact with a soul without any experience from Earth before," she said. "Your information surprised me." Her voice sounded like a thousand tiny bells with words bouncing off and in between the tinkles. She did not apologize for the examination, but simply blinked her multi-lidded eyes and bowed her head a fraction. "My thunder welcomes you to the West, to the land of the Weyr." She moved her lithe, indigo body along the ground soundlessly as she turned to face the ten female dragons waiting behind her. In unison, they lowered their bodies, which were already only seven or eight inches off the ground. I bowed at the waist, not really knowing how far or how long to hold the bow. It seemed enough as Archeladon moved me toward the next group.

Nine cerulean dragons fluttered their webbed wings as I approached, resettling them against their sleek scaleless bodies. With their mouths open, they looked ready to devour me and it was only later I learned this was what a dragon smile looked like. I couldn't determine whether they were male or female and decided it wasn't polite to ask.

"These are the truth dragons, Embry," Archeladon explained.

They were identical in shape, color, and size except for the range of emotions on their faces. Their auras, every shade of blue, blended with the turquoise sky. If I wasn't looking right at them, they were barely visible, shimmering and fading in and out. When they greeted me, their voices reflected their expressions. The one with the huge, smiling eyes sounded like bubbles popping. The one with a pensive expression sounded like writing on slate. The one with a slight frown and tears in the corners of its eyes spoke slow and soft. Nine different expressions, nine different voices, each shimmering and fluttering as they spoke.

As soon as we moved to the next group, I was surrounded by six iridescent green dragons reaching for me with claws the length of my arm. Just slightly shorter than Archeladon, these dragons moved much more gracefully than he did, as if they didn't really have specific shapes. Even their claws bent and softened when they grasped me in a huge green huddle. I giggled. They giggled. I laughed. They laughed. The ones who couldn't quite reach me rose in the sky, beating their translucent wings to hold them steady as they watched me.

"Want to take a guess as to what these dragons are gifted with?" asked Archeladon.

Before I could respond, they shouted in unison, "Love!" Their voices blended in a perfect six-part harmony as they stretched the word out into a song. We giggled some more and the ones floating in the air did somersaults and acrobatics, creating a windstorm.

"Enough," said Archeladon. "Get your group in order, Cheenta."

The one he spoke to, Cheenta, chittered notes in a high and low melody sounding quite demanding. The other five green-shaded dragons regrouped into a more orderly array and bowed low to me. Once again, I bowed back. As soon as I rose, Cheenta winked his middle of three eyes at me and grinned once more.

The largest group, huge yellow glowing dragons, had decided we were taking too long and had gone to sleep. A collective hum of snorts, whines, and whinnies escaped their mouths as they dreamed. Some even moved their clawed feet in some rhythm only they could hear. Twenty-two behemoths dreaming was a sight. I looked from Archeladon to the largest one, wondering if he found it as amusing as I did. So different from all the others I'd met, these dragons reflected all the light back into the sky with their gold-tipped, yellow scales fluttering. It was like looking at the sun. When

I blinked, my eyes had dark dragon-shaped splotches where the dragons were.

Archeladon didn't speak but began a low rumbling call that all the others picked up and joined in, their unique style of communication creating a symphony. I was tempted to join in, so strong was the urge to make a noise, but I didn't know how without ruining the effect. Archeladon sensed this and nudged me with his nose. It seemed it was his favorite way to get my attention. So, I opened my mouth, curious to see what sound I would make.

I howled. It was the first I'd thought of Anfalmor in days. I howled louder and more sorrowfully as the full weight of where I'd been, what had happened to me flooded my thoughts. The melody switched to join my sorrow and every single dragon wept as they sang. Wept crystals of every hue, amethysts and opals, lapis and sapphire, turquoise and aquamarine, emerald and malachite, carnelian and amber, rubies and garnets.

Twenty-two golden yellow dragons awakened at the sound, their tears falling as diamonds. They stretched their limbs and stood back on their hind legs, using their mighty tails to balance as they gazed down at me. Their previous aura signature while sleeping was nothing compared to the overwhelming brightness and vigor of the shades of yellow pummeling me and blowing the curls out of my hair. I squinted and stumbled back against Archeladon, his great purple forearms bolstering me up.

Archeladon changed his low rumble a bit and the other dragons followed, leading us all back into peace, then happiness, and finally, joy. I had to shut my eyes against the assault of yellow light.

"Zusiden, you're blinding our guest," rumbled Archeladon to the obvious leader of the yellow dragons.

He stood tallest, mighty scales larger than me, fluttering in their own energy. The ground shook when he lowered his front legs.

"Sorry, Archeladon. I forget about the fragility of human souls." He growled at his thunder of dragons behind him and they magically dimmed as I watched in amazement.

Archeladon breathed reassurance on the top of my head as I shrunk against him at the sound of Zusiden's growl. "Don't be alarmed."

With inordinate grace, Zusiden spun to look at his thunder before craning his neck back at me. "We will find a way to return you to the South. You have my word."

He had spoken my heart's desire. A radiant yellow pulsed from back to front of all twenty-two dragons. I took it as a sign that they agreed with their leader. Speechless, I could merely nod at Zusiden as Archeladon stepped away to move to the next group.

Five flaming orange dragons, wide-bodied and multi-legged with chunky spikes striping down their backs, flicked fiery tongues in and out at me as we approached. The tips of their tails resembled fire and the ground underneath them appeared to be scorched. Archeladon's cool scales felt safe and comforting against my hand as we stepped near. The leader cocked her head toward me in order for the lenses of her green eyes to focus. Each eye moved independent of the other, but she trained them both on me.

"Issss thissss the one with the sssstrong origin blood?" she lisped. "I am pleasssed we brought you here." She added without waiting for an answer, "What isss your name, young Sssoul?"

"Embry. I'm Embry." I was mesmerized by her eyes, her voice, her flaming orange colors and that of her thunder.

"I am Fyre, though one of my other namesss issss Ember, much like your name, Embry." She blinked her green eyes separately. I filled with the very best kind of warmth as she spoke, as if she'd kindled a loving blaze inside my heart. Archeladon chuckled. He must have felt it too.

"I am so pleased to meet you, Fyre." I watched her skin flare with flames and her thunder behind her skitter to and fro in approval of our exchange, their skin flaring with flames as well.

At last we came to the final group of dragons glowing red as hot coals. Their bodies, long and lithe and many legged like their orange cousins, rippled with muscles hidden underneath skin that was patterned, as if it had been tattooed with a pen. They had huge ball-shaped heads and enormous lidless yellow eyes bulging from the sockets as if they were about to pop out.

This was the second group to engulf me in their number. Before I knew it, I was bouncing along inside a soft, smushy mound of dragon bodies, unable to see anything other than crimson, cardinal, and scarlet. I wanted to stay there forever in the overwhelming safety of their energy. It was womblike, from what I could remember of those few weeks inside my mother. I pushed against the dragon bodies holding me in their safe embrace.

"Well, now you've met Rosaugus and his thunder of red dragons." As Archeladon spoke, Rosaugus wagged his huge head so that he looked somewhat comical, but I knew it wouldn't be polite to laugh at such wonderful creatures who had joined together into one entity to make me feel so safe.

"And now, dragons!" Archeladon rumble-shouted. "We are charged with finding a way to open a portal to the South to once again restore this soul to her rightful place. We must right the wrong done to her by the selfish soul that used illegal portal magic to shove her into the North. Let us disperse and seek answers. Report to me when you know anything."

Chapter Twenty-Three

Much to my astonishment, the dragons vanished, leaving me to wonder if it had all been a dream. The rainbow colors of their collective auras dissipated more slowly, helping me understand that I had truly seen them. As exhilarating and exhausting as it had been to encounter so many fantastic creatures, I filled with new energy when Archeladon lay his neck along the ground and invited me to climb aboard.

"Are you sure?" I asked.

"It is the fastest way to get anywhere in the West," he replied. "Dragonland is vast."

I reached for the nearest blue spike and scrambled up on to his neck. There was a small scoop just big enough for me to sit at the base of his neck where his huge, scaled body began. It was a saddle-shaped scale with two small spikes that molded to my hands when I grabbed them.

Without warning, he spread his enormous wings and leaped into the air, nearly unseating me. If it hadn't been for his magic somehow sealing his energy around both of us, I'd have fallen. I whooped and he roared a laughing roar.

After the initial, frightened gripping and squeezing my eyes shut against the wind, excitement replaced fear in my heart. I didn't know if Archeladon was working his magic in my soul or whether my experience with him allowed me to trust, but when I finally opened my eyes, we were so far above the crystal-strewn land that all the colored crystals blended together into a crazy kaleidoscope of light-catching gems. His huge shadow cast in perfect relief far below us added to the artistic landscape as we flew toward verdant jagged mountains.

With the tip of his great wing, he pointed to and described sights all around us. I could see all the dragons, places where clear blue rivers reflected the cerulean sky, spectacular forests of strangely shaped trees, their limbs pointing up at Archeladon as if to snag his leathery wings.

"Those are the Abra trees," he said. "The unicorns, peryton, and gryphons live there."

"Where are we going?" I asked.

"To meet the Old Ones," he answered.

Archeladon slowed the beating of his wings, gliding on air currents rising up from the base of a great jagged mountain. We circled over an ever-widening smooth patch of grass as we descended, finally landing in the middle with far more grace than I'd expected from such a large beast. He turned his great face toward me and grinned, his three tongues snaking out as if to taste the air.

"Do you need my help climbing down?" he asked.

Even as he spoke, the spikes that had magically held my hands fast began to loosen and I stood on the scales just below my scaly saddle, shaking a bit but determined to get down on my own. He lowered his neck and allowed me to slide to the ground where I stumbled and fell on my hands and knees. From somewhere near the base of a great Abra tree came a few gentle snickers.

I stood, brushed the grass from my knees while four white-haired souls left the shelter of the trees to walk toward us. Their energy was beyond benevolent, pulsing slow and pink in an ever-widening swath that engulfed me. My own energy signature, purple and vibrating in nervous waves, slowed to their rhythm as they approached. Archeladon seemed to purr like a great cat when the energy reached him. He settled his tail behind and folded his great wings and legs against his sides.

"Who is this young fresh soul, Archeladon?" The soul spoke with an accent different than any I'd heard in the North or South—slow, sweet, and melodic. Her white hair curled down her back into waves tighter than mine and her skin was the color of the bark of the Abra trees, a dark reddish brown like what Aunt Katy had called cinnamon.

The others, two male souls and another female, grouped around us, one placing a hand on Archeladon's side in familiar friendship. Archeladon nuzzled the female's hand.

"She has your blood," he said. "I felt her as soon as she arrived in the South. She was able to take a crystal from our land when using her third-eye vision. As you know, there are only a handful of people who've been able to draw that kind of energy. She was shoved through a portal made in the South. She's been in the North." Archeladon moved his head to wrap his neck around me as if I belonged to him.

"Oh no," gasped the souls.

"Portals opening between the lands?" the cinnamon-skinned woman said, her honey-colored eyes wide and filled with compassion and love. "How? The Light-Beings shouldn't have allowed it." She wrapped her strong arms around me, encircling me in safety. She spoke over my shoulder as she held me in her grasp, her breath tickling the curly hairs around my ears. "Archeladon, you must allow us to care for her while the dragons discover a way to return her to the South."

"That is exactly my plan. I have already sent them out." He rose to a crouch and prepared for flight, waiting until we moved across the grass toward the Abra trees.

After he was gone, the souls led me to a low bench with crystal-beaded, silken cushions upon which each took a seat around me, moving several sleeping cats from their places in the sun.

"Tell us your story," said a wiry male soul who sat on the ground next to the cinnamon-skinned woman. He draped his arm across her knees. She took one of his hands in hers. His skin was darker than hers, his grizzled gray hair pulled back with a green leather strap.

As curious as I was about them, I obeyed and told them my story. The four souls listened in polite silence except for a few sympathetic sighs and gasps as I spoke. The peace, kindness, and compassion only grew stronger and filled me completely. When I was finished with my story, I fell asleep, curled up like one of the cats on the comfy cushions.

Hours later, I awakened with a cat on my head and one on either side of me, but no souls. I lay in the sun, listening to the breeze flow through the branches of the Abra trees and birdsong. I was renewed. No fatigue lingered in my soul. No heavy burdens from what I'd experienced in the North threatened to rob me of the joy growing inside. Though I wanted to leap up from the cushions and run through the forest, I extracted myself from the drowsy cats as slowly as possible. They continued to purr once I stood with my hands on my hips, looking back at them as they resettled without me.

And then I ran. Like the first day I'd arrived in Eternity, I ran as if my legs were brand new. I ran and leaped and shouted and laughed and then I did it some more. I ran through the forest and it seemed to laugh with me. The Abra trees, with their huge trunks and feathery foliage, swayed in rhythm to my movement and released such a delightful aroma of exotic spices and fruits, I almost stopped and licked the bark.

I don't remember the exact moment my feet left the ground, but when the feathery leaves of the Abra trees brushed against my cheeks, I looked down. The discovery only heightened my elation at being free of every encumbrance this life had given me so far. I flew high above the treetops, spinning and flipping with a huge smile on my face. I stopped pumping my legs and allowed the sheer exhilaration of the moment to carry me on the wind. When I wished to drop lower, I did. When I wished to climb into the wispy white clouds, I did.

I discovered that the clouds were filled with rainbows arching every which way as if they were just as happy as me. Small ones, the size of my little toes, smacked into larger ones bigger than Archeladon and every size in between could be seen as I floated among them. When a shadow blocked the light on my left side, I floated toward it, curious.

A flock or pride of winged creatures surrounded me in the clouds, their huge fur-covered wings knocking rainbows into a chaotic jumble before they righted themselves, allowing passage to the newcomers. Knowledge from before I'd gone to Earth helped me recall what they were.

"Hello, gryphons!" I welcomed the creatures with bodies shaped like giant lions and heads and wings like fierce eagles. Their huge eagle beaks opened in wide smiles and sharp whistling noises echoed against the condensation in the clouds. When they cocked their eagle eyes at me, I saw mischief and challenges.

What followed was a wild, rollicking, dare-devilish flight filled with dead drops toward the crystal-strewn ground, races toward jagged mountain peaks where each gryphon took turns winning, and climbing so high I thought we'd fly away from the West altogether. When we tired of these antics, I followed them back to the level of the clouds where they vanished as quickly as they had arrived.

"Bye, gryphons!" I hollered, though I couldn't be sure they were anywhere near. "Thank you!"

When I landed, I was taller. I knew this because my tights no longer reached my ankles, but were now tight against the area just below my knees. Had being in the North caused me to shrink, or had I actually grown? The gryphons had returned me to the clearing.

Only one soul was in the clearing walking toward me with a smile on her face. "Embry, you're radiant. What a difference in your energy and countenance. I'm so glad. Come, sit." She walked to the cushions and chose a bright turquoise and yellow pouf to sit on. With one hand, she lifted her long, gray hair away from her face and looked up at me with wide, green eyes. Her ears were pierced with strands of crystals, her forearms jingled with gold and silver bracelets. Even her ankles were adorned with beaded strands, jingling as she tucked them under her.

"My name is India," she said as I settled myself on the purple pouf. "I am one of the Originals.

"Is that what you all are? Originals?" I asked.

"Yes. Creator made our bodies first."

"Why do you live separate from those in the South?"

Her smile gave her face temporary wrinkles that vanished as soon as I noticed them. For that same split second, her aura completely disappeared, returning to its former white-yellow as her smile faded.

"We are in the West to oversee Creator's most magical and misunderstood creatures." She gestured behind her toward the Abra trees. "You've met a few of them. I imagine we'll introduce you to more before your time with us comes to an end."

We'd only been sitting on the cushions for a few minutes when the sky grew dark and stars began popping out. At first there were only a few large, oscillating spheres. Soon they were joined by hundreds, thousands more, varying in size from pinpricks to massive, multi-colored orbs. I stood, reaching for them with both arms extended. India laughed, joining me.

"What are they?" I asked. "Why did it get dark?"

"They're stars," she answered. "And planets."

"It doesn't get dark in the South, or the North for that matter." I twirled, unable to decide where to look. "The air in the North is tarnished, like it's rusting or something. We get a sort of twilight in the South, but nothing like this."

"Would you like to meet the creatures who come out with the stars?" asked India.

"More than anything," I breathed. I'd met the dragons. Flown with the gryphons. Who would I meet now?

She took my hand and we floated slowly out into the open air of the clearing. Hovering in the middle, she let go of me. Placing two fingers in her mouth, she blew out a short set of sounds, followed by a long shrill note that echoed along on the air. We waited, floating without effort for whatever she had called to appear. When there was no response, she repeated the strange signal, adding another note or two.

"Sometimes they are shy with strangers," India said quietly. "I have let them know they are safe."

Just at the edge of my ability to hear it came tiny, sharp squeaks. A massive flock of birdlike creatures flew toward me, engulfing India and me in a flurry of feathers and huge yellow eyes. It tickled as they landed and took off from my shoulders, my body, my hair. At some point, India found my hand and we drifted toward the soft grass, landing still surrounded by these tiny but excited beings.

"What are they?" I asked. It was difficult to keep them from flying in my mouth as I spoke.

"These are igigi."

Their energy, frenetic and changing from white to black and back again, strobed straight through me. My heart beat to the rhythm, my energy became entwined in theirs. India whistled and several of them landed near our feet, though some chose to land on our heads, shoulders and in my outstretched hands. Standing only four inches high, they had thick, squat bodies covered in almost checkerboard-patterned feathers. Instead of feathers at the ends of their wings, they had tiny hands with three fingers. Their tails, long and agile, wrapped around whatever they landed on. Their eyes were larger than their heads with slitted pupils that widened into ovals when they blinked.

"It looks like that one wants to tell you something," India pointed out.

The one on my right hand hopped as if agreeing with her.

"Come on up," I urged.

It hopped along my arm, straight into my hair, its tail finding a curly strand to grip as it nestled against my ear. I scrunched my shoulders so I wouldn't disturb it, though I very nearly knocked it off with suppressed giggles.

"Pretty," it whispered.

I exchanged a glance with India, questioning its message before it repeated it in my ear more emphatically. "Pretty. New Soul. Shiny."

It swung from my hair into the air and squeaked high to the rest of the flock. They joined it in the air with another flurry of black and white wings and flew toward the stars. My heart returned to its former rhythm. I blinked a few times and looked at India.

"Igigi?" I asked.

"Yes. Creator made them when they were needed to guide lost new souls back to their mothers on Earth." India pointed to the East.

"They aren't needed there anymore?" I couldn't believe mothers never lost track of their new souls anymore.

"Actually, now more than ever, but we had to remove the igigi. Humans who had forgotten where they came from started hunting them for sport. It's taken centuries to restore them to their former numbers." India's voice, sorrow-laden, made me want to call them back and apologize. She took my hand to guide me back to the cushions at the edge of the forest.

Chapter Twenty-Four

I looked toward the forest again as a gentle cloud of mist filled the space between the trees. Peace and wonder filled me, my third-eye vision seeing rainbows in each moist drop.

"There are other creatures in the forest." India had not let go of my hand. "The mists bring even shyer ones out. Come."

I trailed behind her, the dew on the grass tickling my toes as we crossed the clearing opposite the cushions. Before we reached the woods, I saw several creatures with antlers branching up from their graceful fur-covered heads. They grazed on the tall grasses near a small pond I hadn't seen before. When we approached, they paused, turning their heads toward us in unison.

India took something from the pocket of her flowing skirt and held it out for the creature closest to us. It stepped forward on four feathered legs, it's whip-like tail swishing back and forth. Sniffing suspiciously at her open palm, it finally nibbled at the nuts and small fruits it found there.

When its tongue had licked her palm clean, it nudged her as if asking for more.

"Don't get greedy, Pilar." India patted the wide brown forehead between its antlers.

It shook its head and the feathers covering its body and legs puffed for a moment before settling smooth once again. The herd moved closer to us. I wished I'd known to bring treats as I wanted all of them to come near. Their large, brown eyes held depths of wisdom as I looked from one to another in wonder.

"What are you?" I asked.

"Your kind call us peryton," the one who'd nibbled the goodies from India answered in a tranquilizing tone. His feathers, shades of brown, red, and gold, started at the end of his neck. Downy tufts could be seen where fur ended and feathers began. The rest of the herd varied in color from deepest black to lemon yellow, but all of them had brown heads and eyes.

"The dragons told us of a new soul in the West," said Pilar. "We came with the mists to see you."

"Why?" I asked.

The herd snuffled and wagged their great antlered heads at my question.

"New souls don't come to the West often. Your scent is fresh, exotic, renewing." Pilar stepped closer, placing his nose on my forehead.

The touch of his wet nose against my third eye caused it to open and I could see the history of the peryton flash like a living scene inside my head. They, too, had been hunted to near extinction by early souls and had been taken away from

Earth. Tears dripped down my cheeks. Why was my kind so bloodthirsty?

Pilar licked them away. "Don't weep for us, fresh one. No need for weeping anymore. That was long ago."

"Did you have to save them too?" I asked India.

"Nearly all the creatures you will meet in this part of here were rescued by Originals using dragon portals," she answered. Several of the peryton had moved near her and she rubbed behind their large, fur-covered ears, avoiding the sharp ends of their multi-branched antlers.

"Why were the early souls so hateful? I don't understand Earth at all." Not for the first time, I was truly thankful for never having had a chance to live there. I couldn't imagine any reason why killing creatures would have been a reasonable thing to do.

As the peryton bowed their heads and moved away from us toward the far edge of the pond, India guided me into the mists of the forest. It felt like walking through warm, moist breath scented with night-blooming jasmine and honeysuckle. India picked a supple branch from a bush with small pink buds just beginning to bloom and waved it gently in the air as we walked.

"Creator gave souls a will of their own when They placed us there. Though each of us started here with all the knowledge of Creator, our existence on Earth allows us to make choices we didn't have here." India played with the branch in her hands and watched me.

"I don't understand," I said. "If we all come from here, from Creator's perfection, why don't we behave on Earth like we do here? What's in us that makes us kill things and want what others have? Don't we have everything on Earth that we have here?"

"Selfishness," she answered. "Souls have learned what it feels like to have power over other souls. Over the centuries of life on Earth, personalities form through a combination of nature—that which they inherit from their parents through the gene pool—and nurture—the upbringing they receive. Souls learn quickly how to survive on Earth, one way or another."

"Why doesn't Creator fix the brokenness?" I asked. "Why can't they stop people from mating who are going to be bad parents?"

"Well, when you take on your Earth body, you become a free-will being. You are slightly separate from the souls in Eternity. That little difference is where evil sneaks into existence. Creator wants us to choose goodness, compassion, self-control . . . selflessness. If everyone chose to be selfless, learning how big Creator's love really is, there would be no need for a North section anymore." She put her hand on my arm and looked into my eyes, willing me to understand.

I shook my head. I would never understand. "Have you heard from the dragons?" I wanted to change the subject, feeling empty again.

"Actually, I'm needed back in the clearing where I can hear the others gathering," she answered. "Would you like to continue your walk? There are other creatures to meet."

I couldn't hear any gathering, but her ears were probably more in tune with this place than mine. Walking sounded better. I moved slowly and listened, pondering as I walked away from her into the mist.

The foliage grew sparse as I climbed further into the forest, the scents in the mist changing from floral to spicy. I loved it here where there were so few souls like me and so many strange and wonderful creatures. The thought of returning to the South seemed less attractive now that I knew this part of Eternity existed. Maybe I could convince the dragons, the Originals, Creator, to just let me stay. I thought about turning back to join them in the clearing to tell them of my decision but realized too late that I was lost. The mist had drifted up, engulfing the tops of the trees, and grown denser as I walked.

I sat on the forest floor in the middle of the trail, elbows on my drawn-up knees. It had grown darker, moonlight unable to pierce the mist. I could barely see my hands in front of my face, so I shut my eyes, listening. Something scurried past. I listened. Several more somethings scurried past. I didn't move. Didn't open my eyes. Waited.

"Is she asleep?" asked a mischievous voice from somewhere near my feet.

"Sh. I want to sniff her," answered a high voice next to the first one.

"You can't just go around sniffing souls. How do you know it won't hit you?" a third voice piped in.

I felt soft, wet noses against my bare legs. I opened my eyes just enough to see long, red, furry bodies quivering and sniffing. One of them sneezed and I couldn't help snickering. The sniffing stopped.

"She's awake," said the first voice.

"Duh," came the third one.

"Let's go," whispered the second.

When I opened my eyes and shifted my weight to sit cross-legged, the three creatures vanished into the bushes.

"Come back," I called. "I won't hurt you. Promise." I scanned the area, hoping they hadn't gone far.

A pink nose lifted the leaves of the bush nearest me and disappeared again. Moments later, a darker pink nose with little red specks popped out of the middle of the same bush and disappeared after a squeak. I held my breath, watching the bush. Moments later, three furry faces popped out from behind the bush but did not move toward me. Their beady black eyes, wide with curiosity, scrutinized me. Long white whiskers bristled out from pointy snouts and their short v-shaped ears quivered. When I smiled at their adorable faces, they disappeared back into the bush.

"Did you see that?" asked the first voice.

"She's going to eat us," whispered the second voice.

"That was a smile, silly," came the third. "Souls here don't want to eat us."

"He's right," I said. "Please come out."

Not only did the curious three join me on the trail, but about twelve others who apparently took their cue from them scampered from their hiding places in nearby bushes and trees. I was surrounded by creatures with red, furry bodies, white paws and tail tips, who glowed slightly orange as they exhaled. They stood on hind legs, using their multiple fluffy red tails to balance, and stared, waiting for me to speak again. I knew if I moved too quickly or suddenly, they'd scamper away again, possibly forever.

"I'm Embry," I said.

"She's Embry," they repeated to each other.

"I'm a new soul," I said, feeling I needed to explain myself, fill in the silence.

"She's a new soul," they repeated.

"Who are you?"

"Who are we? Who are we? Who are we? We should tell her. Who should tell her? You should tell her." And on it went until finally the little creature who'd spoken first told them to hush.

"We're kitsune." It sounded like a sneeze when he said it. The skulk repeated the word. I started to giggle and couldn't stop before I was laughing so hard, they skittered a few yards away and stared at me in silence.

"I'm sorry." I saw their little confused faces and realized I had either frightened or offended them. "What did you say?"

Another of the shy, furry creatures stepped up to speak. Smaller than the other, its red fur was striped through with blond streaks shaped in odd patterns outlining the curves of legs and body. "We're kitsune. Spirit foxes." She spoke slow and loudly, as if I was hard of hearing. The others nodded their agreement and waited.

"I'm pleased to make your acquaintance," I said.

The skulk moved closer to me and proceeded to chitter at me all at once. I nearly laughed aloud again watching their little animated faces, recognizing only a few words here and there in the cacophony. I think they were each telling me their names and life stories. The urge to touch them was too overwhelming and I moved to my hands and knees. As soon as I moved, they stopped talking but didn't move away. I held eye contact with the one who'd spoken slow enough for me to understand her words.

"Can I touch you?" I asked.

"Why do you want to?" she asked.

"You're so beautiful and you look so soft and I've never met kitsune before." I didn't add that something in their faces and countenance was nearly irresistible. I'd only thought of asking after I'd moved toward her.

The skulk gasped and looked at each other whispering their disbelief. "Never seen us. Never met us. Never touched us. Wants to touch us. Will it hurt us? Do Embrys hurt?"

"Let me come to you," she said.

I held my open hand out and waited. She lowered to all fours; her thick furry tail bristled to twice its original size. She took two steps with her front paws before following with her back ones. Paused. Sniffed. Two more steps. Pause. Sniff. The others watched with wide shiny black eyes. I didn't move. Didn't breathe.

At last, the tip of her nose touched my fingers. We looked at each other. She wriggled her body underneath my hand and tiny flames rippled up out of her fur, surrounding my hand in a fiery glow. It was warm but didn't burn. I imagined she could turn up the heat if she needed to. The skulk moved a step or two closer, as if they couldn't wait to see the outcome of our interaction. She lingered, pressing her little body up into my palm. Ever so slightly, she rubbed her back under my palm and hummed.

No longer able to hold the position or resist the urge to pet her, I wriggled my fingers along her back near her tail. The softness of her fur was exactly as I had expected. I watched the fur on her tail smooth back down as she accepted my touch. I ran my hand along it, feeling its suppleness and structure. She leaped onto my back and chittered at the skulk in their quick language, sounding happy and excited before they attacked me.

Their flaming bodies crawled and writhed up and down my arms and legs, into my hair and across my face as I tumbled to the ground. Some were warmer than others, almost burning me. Several took turns licking my face and investigating my ears, eyes, and nose. They nibbled me from head to toe as if deciding what flavor I was. None of them stayed in one place long enough for me to pet them and I longed to grab one and cuddle it to my chest. I hoped there would be time for that while I was here.

"Embry doesn't hurt," said the first kitsune who had spoken. "Embry is a good soul." He stood on top of my belly as if he'd won a game of king of the hill. The others were sitting or lying across my entire body. Some of them had started to groom themselves and others appeared to have fallen asleep, nestled in my armpits and between my legs. A murmur of agreement rippled through the skulk.

The mists had cleared, allowing me to gaze at the stars and planets through the treetops. When a shadow fell across my face, I assumed it was a larger kitsune adjusting itself in the messy curls of my hair. A few others adjusted themselves and their heated bodies grew uncomfortably warm. I was about to ask them to turn down the flames a little when something heavy stepped near, shaking the ground underneath me.

"So, this is what happened to our new soul."

The voice belonged to one of two glowing white horses standing near my head. The skulk skittered off me as I scrambled to my feet and brushed the dirt from my clothes. A sense of awe filled me as their energy pulsed with the power of thunder and lightning, earthquakes and tsunamis. My third-eye vision told me these creatures were ancient and deserved respect like I'd give Creator.

Chapter Twenty-Five

"The Council of Originals sent us to find you," said the majestic glowing beast.

"They have heard from the dragons," said the other one.

"Is there a portal?" I asked.

"Climb on my back and we will take you to the counsel," replied the first one.

I didn't want to climb on his back. He was too beautiful and terrible at the same time. Power, ancient and knowing, emanated from both of them. Their stark whiteness against the darkness of night nearly blinded me. The skulk of kitsune had scrambled away a safe distance from those mighty hooves. Only when they tossed their flowing manes did I see the long white spikes sprouting from their foreheads. Unicorns. These were unicorns. Of all the creatures I had encountered, these were the hardest to believe existed, yet my memory of all of Creation was returning to me the longer I stayed in the West.

"She wants to run with us, Cryo. Listen to her heart." The second one, standing tall and proud, shone with a slightly different aura, softly tinged with blue.

"Then let us run," he answered.

We left the kitsune behind without a word. Soundlessly we ran side by side, the unicorns moving through the trees like streaks of lightning. Electricity crackled in the air, making the leaves of the Abra trees rustle as if struck by a mighty wind. It filtered through my body, causing my soul to feel as though I would break free from its boundaries. It was frightening and more exhilarating than flying with the gryphons or riding on Archeladon. Under my own power, I was racing with unicorns.

"New souls are so lovely!" shouted Cryo. "I am glad she wanted to run!"

I smiled, feeling proud I'd resisted the temptation to ride on his back, though in truth it had been the other's ability to hear my heart. She glanced at me with her turquoise eyes as we slowed our pace a bit. We neared the clearing where the outlines and glow of the yellow dragons filled the open space with light. Only Zusiden and a few of his lieutenants could fit, and their huge, golden bodies pressed up against the tops of the Abra trees. I worried they'd snap the mighty trunks.

Cryo and his partner, whom I later learned was called Larimar, led me around the dragons on the edge of the woods in order to reach the group of Originals conversing with Zusiden. His yellow glow blinded me, casting everyone in black and white relief when I blinked. Even shielding my eyes with my hand didn't help. I wondered how the unicorns and the Originals could stand it.

"You're blinding the New soul, Zusiden. Turn it down," Larimar said next to me, sounding authoritative.

Zusiden dimmed gently, as did his lieutenants. He touched his mighty nose to my forehead in greeting; my third eye opened and closed as if blinking at the touch.

"Hello, Embry," he said. "We've news for you."

My heart leaped. I looked from him to the Originals and back again. "A portal?" As soon as the words were out of my mouth, I realized I didn't want to leave. Though my dearest wish had been to return to the South as soon as I'd arrived in the West, my time with all the magical creatures here had filled me to the brim with love and wonder. I never wanted to know anything else. The thought of finding out why I'd not been given an opportunity to live on Earth hadn't crossed my mind since arriving. Now it just didn't seem important anymore. Yet, here I was in front of these beautiful Energy dragons who'd worked so hard to find a way of helping me.

"Maybe," he answered.

"Maybe? What does that mean, maybe?" I asked.

"As you know, there are no Light-Beings here in the West," he began.

"No. I didn't know that. What does that have to do with anything?" I frowned.

"Embry, the only souls living in the West are those who no longer need Light-Beings to teach them how to be complete," said a soul with ebony skin and short rows of spiraling gray hair, her rich warm tone wrapping me in velvet. "They—we—have existed so long that we are equal to, though not the same as, Light-Beings."

"And?" I asked.

"The dragons, Zusiden and all the others, have had to travel to the borders of the West to get messages to the Light-Beings They aren't used to hearing from this part of Eternity anymore. Not since the dragons received their punishment. Portals out of here are forbidden," answered India. "We don't know yet if it will be possible to return you to the South without it leading to worse punishment for them."

I considered telling them I wanted to stay, and they could cease their efforts. I thought about how my life in the West was perfect. No one cared that my parents hadn't wanted me, that they'd had me destroyed before I'd even lived. No one sneered or reminded me of all I didn't know and couldn't remember. Magical creatures lived here in the West and I loved every minute of my time with them. I could easily spend Eternity flying with the gryphons, riding the dragons, cuddling with kitsune, and running with unicorns. Really, what other existence could possibly compare? The Originals were wise in all the ways of our kind. They could teach me anything I needed to know. I didn't need to go back to the tutelage of Dina. Even the thought of seeing Aunt Katy, Grandma and Grandpa, or my friends Usan, Isla, and Kenja didn't tempt me enough to want to leave the West.

Yet something tugged at my soul. Something unfinished needled inside near the pit of my stomach. Living here would be perfect, but how did I deserve it when it hadn't been Creator's intention? How did I deserve it when other souls in the South were better, wiser, older? I was here only by virtue of something in my blood that had called to the dragons and the illegal portal Alice had managed to open. Surely there were others with stronger Origin blood ready to be moved from the South to the West. I said nothing of my inner conflict.

"We believe there isn't any way for us to open a portal back to the South from here." Zusiden sounded sad.

"So, she's stuck here?" asked India.

"Would that be so bad?" asked the ebony-skinned man.

"Why don't we ask her, Sandawe?" India looked at me.

"What do you want to do, Embry?" asked Sandawe.

Zusiden and the other yellow dragons shifted slightly to stare at me, their bodies causing the Abra trees around the clearing to groan as their weight placed more pressure against the already-bending trunks. The Originals' energy signature shifted as well and I felt exposed, as if they'd read my mind and heard my inner argument. Even now, the decision was hard.

"I love it here," I finally breathed.

"Of course you do, Embry." Sandawe took a step toward me and placed a hand on my shoulder. His rich, velvet voice reassured me. His deep brown eyes held no judgement.

"I don't deserve it though." I said. "Not yet." I looked down.

"Hm. Interesting." The Original who spoke wore a long, orange cloth tied around his waist and thrown over one shoulder, and a matching turban. A huge multi-faceted opal dangled in the center of the turban. "Why do you feel that way?" He crossed his hands in front of him, waiting for my answer.

"I feel like there are souls, older or wiser or smarter or better equipped to live here in the West. I feel a little guilty at having been brought here." My voice came out in a whisper. The Originals and dragons stepped closer.

"Do you think you will ever deserve to live here?" asked the Original in the orange turban.

"Someday," I answered.

"You realize only those with strong Origin blood ever even get the choice to live in the West, right?" he asked.

"No. I hadn't thought of that. But still, I'm not sure what I should say. Why aren't my Aunt Katy and Grandma and Grandpa here? Isn't it their blood too?" I'd only just realized that I didn't know which of my parents had given me the strong Origin blood. I'd never thought to ask.

He shook his head, the opal in his turban catching the first rays of sun as it rose in the sky.

"Let me tell her, Khoisan," said a woman wearing a multi-layered, floral kimono, addressing me for the first time. Her graying hair was plaited on either side of her wide face, her skin matched mine. "She is most closely descended from my line." She moved in front of Sandawe and Khoisan, taking my hands in hers.

"It is your father who gives you your Origin blood," she said. "His is the same as runs through me."

"Why didn't he want me?" There it was again. All the old feelings of worthlessness crashed down upon me and I fell into her arms sobbing.

Chapter Twenty-Six

She guided me back to the cushions at the edge of the clearing while the discussion continued between the Originals and the dragons. I didn't hear what they decided, but when the dragons took flight, their wings caused a great whirlwind around us. As the wind died down, the other Originals took positions on the surrounding cushions and discussed inconsequential things while they waited for me to stop crying.

The Original, Ainu, brushed my hair away from my eyes and crooned a soothing song in a language I didn't know. I stayed smothered against her as she rocked me, something I'd never known could be so perfect. When the sun was high above the tops of the Abra trees, I lifted my head from her lap to see that several kitsune had joined the circle, as well as the unicorns and some peryton. I guess crying wasn't something done very often in the West. Their energy hit me with sympathy and concern, feeling like warm blankets on a cold night. Two kitsune hopped on to my lap and reached up to lick the remaining tears from my eyes.

"We think the only way you can leave the West is to go to Earth," said Sandawe. "The dragons lost the privilege of opening portals to other parts of here a long time ago. They risked being punished again to bring you out of the North, though Creator sees what they did in the light of Alice's use of illegal magic."

"There has been much discussion between Light-Beings, Creator, and the Elders of the South, but they've reached the conclusion that it's too dangerous to keep opening portals between lands," said Khoisan. "The protective energy keeping the borders secure has been reinforced. There will be no return to the South for you at this time."

"Then I'll stay here." I sat up, displacing the kitsune for a moment before they resettled on my lap and purred. I stroked their soft, red fur. "You can teach me what I need to know, right?" I looked at each of the Originals in turn, noticing sadness in their eyes and in their energy signatures.

"As much as we would love to have you stay with us forever, it is not for us to decide." Ainu put her arm around my waist. "We are under tighter constraints for a time. We are in charge of ensuring that the dragons and other magical creatures don't use their powers to meddle with Creator's plans. It's not been a problem before. You are not an Original. You must not be here."

"Then, where can I go?" I felt anger and despair welling up again. "You say I can't stay here with you. I can't return to the South now. I don't want to go to the North. What's left? And how did Alice and her friends open a portal in the first place? Has anyone disciplined her?"

"Do you know about a book in the archives of Cheshi-phon?" asked Sandawe.

I stared at him for a moment, trying to recall where I'd heard that name. Recent events had erased so much of what I'd experienced in the South. It was as if my brain, so new and unused to thinking beyond instinct, was unable to hold onto things I'd learned in the other lands. The Originals watched and waited while I struggled to retrieve the memories.

I recalled our field trip to Cheshiphon with Dina in the lead. How we'd entered the ancient city filled with marbled columns and wise souls looking important as they walked purposely up and down mountains of steps. How Isla, Usan, Kenja and I talked so casually about inconsequential things. Reliving this moment made me sad. I missed them and my simple, uncomplicated life when I'd first arrived. I missed Anfalmor and our talks up on his mountain at the edge of the tree line.

"My friends and I wandered away from the rest of our group." I began. "We discovered a library." Excitement replaced my melancholy as the memory grew.

"Was there anyone there?" asked India.

"Yes. There was an ancient soul named Parmenides," I answered. "Why isn't he here with you in the West? He surely is an Original, isn't he?"

"No," Sandawe chuckled. "He'd like to think he is, but no. He's just a really wise soul who asked a lot of questions when he first arrived. How many centuries ago was that?"

"I believe he arrived in the South in the middle of the fourteenth century," answered Khoisan. "He was very old when he died there. I think that accounts for how wise he is now. He doesn't like souls much. It's why he's so good at keeping the ancient tomes in order."

"I saw a book about dragons on the shelf while we were there," I said. "It was right after Archeladon spoke to me through my third-eye vision. I remember wanting to look inside to discover how to find them."

"That book should have never been where new souls could find it." India's tone alarmed me. Her energy signature shifted to strong red before resettling into her former blue-violet. "Parmenides must have gotten careless."

"Or someone had borrowed it without him knowing and slipped it back on the nearest shelf." Sandawe's words created a momentary decrease in the energy signature of our little group. Even the unicorns shifted their hooves a bit.

"Alice?" I asked.

"It's possible," answered Sandawe.

"That's got to be it." I scooted away from Ainu on the cushions. "She must have found the book, read about opening portals, and shoved me through. Why does she hate me so much?"

"Embry, it might not have been as personal as you think," Ainu said. "Alice arrived in the South with some issues. I think maybe Creator even debated as to whether she should go to the North first." She looked at the others for confirmation. "Her Light-Being was aware of her past, as all the Light-Being teachers are. Zadkiel must have given her too much freedom too soon."

"So, you're saying I was just the most convenient for her to experiment on?" I asked.

"Something like that, yes," answered Ainu. "Something about you must have reminded her of her life on Earth. It was nothing you did, I'm sure, Embry."

"We need to tell Creator, if They don't already know, that Alice is the one who opened the portal," I said. "Zadkiel needs to know she might be planning to do it again. That she might be planning to try to go through one herself."

"There's no way she can do that, Embry," said Sandawe. "There's no passing through portals allowed in the entire realm right now. Creator has decreed it and eliminated the magic."

"Could there be a dragon or dragons that were in league with her? Helped her of their own accord?" I asked. I couldn't imagine any of those magical creatures doing something so underhanded.

"We can ask, but I doubt it," said Sandawe. "They all seemed quite eager to help in returning you to the South. They must all be present for a portal to open, Embry. It's more likely their power was harnessed somehow by something Alice learned from that book."

Chapter Twenty-Seven

In the end, it was decided. Really the only choice had always been that I would return to Earth to wait until portal magic was returned to those who were authorized to use it, and Alice was disciplined. The discussion turned to whether I should occupy a physical body while I was there or whether I'd simply exist as Spirit. I found it exhausting and since my input mattered little anyway, I leaned against the cushions with my eyes shut, petting the kitsune in my lap.

I was scared. While they discussed the pros and cons of having a body versus only being a Spirit, I thought about my short life here. I was going to get a chance to experience life on Earth and it was the last thing I wanted. I'd seen enough of the North to know awful things awaited me there. Even in the South, there was opportunity to do each other harm, though much less likely.

Animals talked here. Magic was here. I could fly here and take all the time I needed to learn what I'd forgotten from when my soul had first been created. As I sat with eyes closed, I noticed a shift in the light and energy before the others did.

The kitsune under my hands awakened and used my body to prop themselves up, alert to the change as well.

"We think she should have a body." It was Creator's unmistakable voice that shook the ground and brought the conversation to a halt as They appeared. "We have found a circumstance on Earth where souls are making the right choices for her to appear in their lives."

The Originals blinked in the increased brightness of Creator's presence, looking at each other and at me. Nodding at Creator, they waited for Them to continue.

"Why can't you just let me stay here?" I spoke as respectfully as I could, quiet and honest. "Or at least open a portal for me to return to the South. This is all a big mistake, right?"

Creator's unwavering gaze and silence should have made me wither, but it only made me more resolved to get answers. No one else spoke. The kitsune jumped from my lap to Theirs, showing their love and allegiance to Creator. The unicorns tossed their heads before lowering them so their horns were lower than Creator's head.

"Walk with us, Embry," They said.

I rose and joined Them as They walked into the forest. I noticed the kitsune followed a short distance behind us.

"The rules I established, that all Creation must follow, are designed for all of us, Embry," Creator began. "I voluntarily submit to my own rules. In order for the best possible life here, I chose to give souls free will for the time they spend on Earth. You've seen for yourself what that does to souls."

I nodded.

"Eventually, all souls will return here," They continued. "Every single soul will be on their own learning path. My Light-Beings have been charged with the task of endlessly offering choices to the souls in their charge until every single choice is a good one that creates harmony and the greatest and highest good of all. Even the Originals are on a learning path to that end." They gestured back at the four Originals as They spoke.

"Okay," I said. "Let's say that makes sense to me, sort of. I have one more question."

"What is it?"

"Has this ever happened to another soul?"

"Yes." They didn't answer right away and I watched Their energy signature pulse for a second as if They were deciding something.

"Did you have to send them to Earth before they could return here, or am I the first?" I asked. Turns out I had more than just one more question.

"Every case is different, Embry," They answered. "Every soul's story is unique. There have been others."

"Are there any there now?" I thought that if they could place me with souls who had experienced something similar to me, it would make it easier.

"No."

"I'm afraid," I said. "I don't have any experience."

"I know. I've given it some thought and decided I will accompany you."

"What? You? Really?" I put my hand on Their arm, feeling the soft fabric of the rainbow cloth draped over Their body in such a way I couldn't determine Their true shape. "Don't You have more important things to be doing?"

"We are Creator. We can do many things at once." They smiled, kindness and amusement in Their eyes.

"Oh, Creator. That's wonderful news." I threw myself into Their arms and felt every good feeling, every delicious smell, every beautiful color as we hugged. "Thank you."

The Originals must have followed from a safe distance and engulfed us as we hugged. It felt better than flying with gryphons, all joy and love, goodness and kindness, healing and salvation. I couldn't fathom what the circumstances of my return to Earth would be, didn't know how I'd return, or which part of here I'd return to when I finally did. But what I did know was that Creator was going with me. I could face a million bad things with Creator alongside.

The remainder of that day was spent instructing me on things I'd need to know for my return. Creator took Their leave to prepare. The Originals took turns arguing over what I needed to know and whether or not it would be better for me to learn once I was on Earth. My input was minimal, so I spent my time asking the kitsune, the peryton, the gryphons, and the igigi what they thought of the plan. I was greeted with great enthusiasm and I hoped all would turn out for the best.

It was one of the wise igigi who suggested I visit with the kelpies before leaving the West. The entire assemblage of magical creatures moved through the woods toward a large inland sea I had only seen from the air when I flew with the gryphons. I realized my appearance in their lives, the interruption of their routines and patterns, had created quite a bit of excitement and they were curious about what happened next. The Originals weren't asking for their advice, so the creatures adopted me into their ranks.

I smelled the salt in the air before we reached the inland sea. Along with the scent came green and blue energy pulsing in waves in rhythm to the water reaching the shore. The igigi flew around me in excitement and it was the peryton who found a way between two rocky outcrops to a black-sanded beach where we stood still, looking out across the turquoise water.

Without warning, three small human-and-fish-bodied creatures slid onto shore at my feet, slapping their tails in the water to hoist themselves further up. As I watched, their front flippers turned into bluish-green arms. They shook their heads, flinging water at us and smiling mischievously at me, showing rows of sharp, spiked teeth. It was the first time I'd met creatures in the West that I didn't want to immediately hug. It wasn't the scales or the fact that they were wet. It was those sharp teeth I wasn't quite sure about.

When they spoke, it wasn't in language I understood. Even the dragons spoke the language of here. I looked to the igigi for help, but it was Larimar, the female unicorn, who translated their words. The kitsune hopped closer to me on the sand and around us onto the large rocks nearby.

"They ask why you've summoned them," said Larimar.

I shook my head. I hadn't summoned them. They'd just shown up. I said as much and Larimar translated. I waited for their reply.

"They say your voice is new," Larimar explained. "They haven't heard a new voice in so long; it pierced the depths of their underwater city. They knew you were coming to talk to them today."

"The creatures all agreed I should seek you out," I said. "I'm not sure why."

"It is because we were the last to leave Earth when Creator brought us home. We can tell you of the Earth dwellers," they said. They spoke together with three different tones blending in harmony, their language becoming a beautiful song.

All the other creatures fluttered, skittered, and stomped in agreement as if I should have known this was why I'd been brought to the kelpies. Larimar stood next to me while the kitsune settled their multiple tails around their little bodies and the peryton wandered to the sea grasses near the shoreline to nibble. The igigi turned into a giant ball of black and white feathers as they settled on the tallest granite boulder to wait and listen. Cryo stood at my back as a silent sentinel.

"I don't know what to expect," I said.

"Expect cruelty," the kelpies sang. "Expect confusion. Expect lies. Expect selfishness. Expect hatred. Expect discrimination. Expect judgement."

Before Larimar translated their words, I felt the change in energy amongst all the creatures assembled there on the shoreline. The igigi stretched their wings as if to fly off in agitation. The kitsune chittered, standing on their hind legs, using their tails to balance. The peryton stopped nibbling the tall grasses and looked at the kelpies. Cryo whinnied and Larimar shook her head as if trying to shake their words from her ears, her soft white mane throwing sparks of rainbows into the air to stop the flow of darkened and sickly green energy from reaching me.

Dread filled me. I no longer wanted to go. Recalled feeling these things to some degree while I'd been in the North. If Earth was worse than the North, I would never be prepared. I shut my eyes and rubbed my forehead where my third eye was closed. A kitsune skittered up my legs and perched across my shoulders, purring comfort into my ears. Creator's face came into my third-eye vision, reminding me They would be with me. Reminding me that They had created Earth, and it contained good. It contained kind. It contained generous. It contained selflessness. It contained love.

"Creator told me I can find good there," I said.

"Yes. There are souls there who still remember." The kelpies' song was melancholy.

"Why do you tell me to expect such awful things?" I asked.

"Be prepared," they sang.

"I'll have Creator with me," I said.

"They will not be able to make the Others treat you kindly," the kelpies explained. "They can only offer choices because of free will."

"Okay. Thanks for the warning." I wanted to be polite but wished the creatures had spared this part of my education. I turned to go, but the kelpies began singing again. They sang for a long time before stopping so Larimar could translate their words. As soon as they were done with their song, their arms turned back into flippers and they wriggled their way back into the sea. "What did they say?"

"They want you to know they were hunted to near extinction before Creator brought them home," Larimar replied. "Those of us who lived on the land were brought home sooner because Creator saw what Their humans were doing to us, but They thought the kelpies were safer in the sea. They weren't. All the things they just told you to expect are what happened to them. They have told you of these things because of their love for you. You are pure, unsullied by the things they described."

Larimar urged me with her lowered horn to follow her mate back toward the gathering of Originals. I looked at each of the groups of magical creatures, feeling sad and angry at my fellow souls for being so awful with the gift of free will Creator had blessed us with. We walked and flew in silence.

Chapter Twenty-Eight

The Originals were ready for me when I returned. Ainu patted the cushion next to her. The creatures gathered around to listen. I felt a resolute energy emanating from the group. It was time to see what they'd decided. I kept what I'd learned from the kelpies to myself and looked expectantly at each Original, seeing India smile with motherly affection, Sandawe draw his lips together and nod, Khoisan bow his head and lift his hands together toward his third-eye, and Ainu draw me toward her in a gentle embrace.

"You will have a body when you arrive on Earth," said Sandawe. "It doesn't seem appropriate to us to have you there in Spirit when all other souls take physical shape."

"It will be the body you would have had if your parents hadn't sent you here before you were fully developed," added Ainu.

"Will I see my parents?" I asked.

"No," all four Originals said in unison.

"Not if we can help it," added Sandawe. "We're placing you in a situation with souls, people—I guess you'd better get used to that word—who are longing to adopt you."

"How long will I have to stay?" I asked.

"Once Creator has secured portal magic and dealt with Alice, They will bring you home," answered Khoisan.

"But They'll be with me," I reminded them.

"Creator is everywhere, always." India smiled.

"Tell me what I need to know."

"You're being adopted by a couple with strong Origin blood like ours." Ainu squeezed me. "They've been offered other girls from the agency, but they haven't taken one so far. The timing is perfect."

"We're placing you in a thriving country where you will be safe," said Sandawe. "You'll be enrolled in an education system and meet up with other souls your age. You must understand that we've not returned a soul to Earth for a very long time. When the dragons opened a portal that resulted in that soul's second death, they lost the privilege and ended the practice. Creator is allowing it this one time because your circumstances are so unusual."

"Can I die on Earth?" I asked.

"Creator won't allow it," answered Sandawe.

A shadow crossed over us and a strong breeze whipped my hair around as Archeladon landed in the clearing, moving as close to us as the other creatures would let him. He lowered his big head and grinned at me.

"Embry, it's almost time to go," said Ainu. "You won't be long on Earth, we promise. Do you have any more questions?"

Yes, I thought. About a million. But I didn't want to delay any longer. The sooner I allowed this next transition, the sooner I would be reunited with my family, my friends, and my life, here.

Every Creature said goodbye in their own way. The kitsune skittered all over me with their furry, flaming bodies before disappearing into the woods. The igigi fluttered about my head, whispering so many hints about life on Earth I couldn't hear them all. The peryton nuzzled me with their wet, black noses and wished me a quick return, and the gryphons lifted into the air to perform an acrobatic show that made us giggle.

When the Originals took their turn, tears gathered in the corners of my eyes as I realized it would be a long time before I ever saw them again and how lucky I'd been to even get to the West. I thanked each one, receiving final words of wisdom.

"Be kind, even when others are not," said India.

"Remember what you've learned here," said Sandawe.

"Listen to Creator," said Khoisan.

"Stay strong," said Ainu, hugging me the longest of all of them.

And then it was time to join Archeladon. He lowered his head and neck to the ground so I could climb on top of his back and take my seat on the saddle-shaped scale between his giant wings. I took hold of the spikes that wrapped themselves around my hands in order for me to stay on him as he took a giant leap and hoisted himself into the air with great beatings of his wings. I waved a yelled goodbye to the blurry crowd beneath us, tears streaming down my face.

We flew back toward the crystal-strewn landscape where the stark, volcanic mountains rose up out of the ground. The entire cadre of dragons waited for us. The purple dragons of Archeladon's family stood in the center. Flanking them were the indigo dragons on one side and the blue truth dragons on the other. To each side of them stood the green love dragons sitting back on their hind legs and tails, waiting eagerly to hug me as soon as we landed, and the huge group of yellow dragons, almost see-through in the shimmering light of their energy. Closing the circle were the orange dragons and the red dragons sending feelings of safety and calm up into the air as we circled and spiraled to a stop in the middle.

After the love dragons surrounded me in their loving energy, I stood apart from the assembly, feeling happy, sad, determined, and awestruck.

"You're all here," I said.

"It takes all of our energy to open the portal to Earth," replied Archeladon.

"Where is Creator?" I asked.

"We're already there," came a voice from the sky. "We're ready for you."

"Stand in the center, just there," said Archeladon, pointing with his big, scaly snout.

I obeyed him. It began immediately. The entire thunder turned their eyes on me. My third eye opened. Purple light blasted into me from Archeladon's thunder, filling me with their infinite wholeness. Indigo light forced wisdom and intuition into me from Indra's thunder. Crisp, blue light energy pulsed like a tsunami from Saphigos' truth dragons. The green love energy undulating from Cheenta's healing dragons was nearly the hardest to bear as it shot through me with fierce and dangerous love.

When the yellow light energy from Zusiden's thunder of dream dragons, I wanted to shut my eyes against the light but there was no stopping it. It flooded in through my third-eye vision and filled all the spaces I didn't know existed inside. Fyre's orange dragons sent creative energy so strong I wanted to paint and sing, dance, and beat on drums all at the same time. Yet I stood still, unable to separate my soul from the energy becoming my new reality.

Finally, it was Rosaugus's turn to join his red dragons to the mix of infinite energy. They overwhelmed all the others with feelings of safety, of instinct, of perfection. Just when I thought I would shatter into a million pieces, each color exploded into the others. Tearing me. Shredding me. At the same time, calming me, reassuring me. It was unbearably loud. It was silent. It was prisms of rainbow colors. It was completely dark. It was painful. Pleasurable. It was delicious. It was nauseating. I lost consciousness.

Part Four

Earth

Chapter Twenty-Nine

I woke up to sounds coming from somewhere on the other side of a closed door. Soft salmon-pink sheets felt a bit like the down on a peryton's neck as I shifted my new body to look at my surroundings. Three paper lanterns in turquoise, salmon pink, and one with an arrow pattern dropped down from the sloped, slatted ceiling above my head. A comforter as soft as the clouds I'd flown through with the gryphons brushed my cheek, the chevron patterns making me think of my dear igigi.

What had I done? Why had I agreed to come here? I lifted the covers to look at my body. I looked the same as I had before, but I felt heavy. Felt the blood pulsing through my veins. Lifted my hands to look at my fingers bending. Marveled at my fingernails. Put my hand on my belly to feel it rise and fall with each breath. I didn't like any of it; the reality of flesh and blood wasn't anything like I'd expected. I began to panic.

What was on the other side of that door? What if they rejected me like my parents had? What if Creator had lied?

"I'm here, Embry." Their voice echoed inside my head, blotting out all other thoughts.

"Oh, Creator. What have I done? Can I go back now? I'll be good. I'll make friends with Alice, no matter how hard it is."

"Embry, I'll bring you back as soon as the portals are healed and safe." Creator's soothing energy eased the panic away.

"What do I do now?" I asked.

"Your adoptive parents are waiting for you," Creator replied.

"Are they nice?" I asked.

"They're dying to meet you," They answered.

"Why?" I asked. "They don't know anything about me."

"In their minds, you're exactly what they've been hoping for." Creator said. "They've wanted to adopt for a long time. They passed on girls they could've adopted for nearly three years without knowing why. The bed you sleep in, the decorations, clothes, books, everything has been prepared for you as they waited. When you popped up in the system, they called right away. You're going to be happy."

"Really?" I asked.

"As happy as one can be in this part of our Creation," They answered.

I rose from the bed and, feeling a bit self-conscious, wrapped the white chenille robe I found hanging from a hook on the back of the door around my body. Creator hummed a soothing melody in my head as I opened the door.

The scent of coffee wafted onto the landing where I stood looking out on a rainy morning through the high windows of a large family room below me. My new parents spoke softly to each other from a brightly lit room off of the main one. I tiptoed to the railing and peeked over. A young boy looked up at me from where he sat on the large sofa and grinned.

Startled, I stepped back to the safety of my doorway and listened.

"She's up, Mom," said the boy on the sofa. I heard excitement tinged with nervousness in his voice.

The voices stopped. I waited. Creator changed the tune in my head to one that filled me with happy anticipation. I took a step toward the railing. Heard whispers, excited and hesitant. They reflected exactly how I felt about meeting them. It gave me courage. They were possibly as nervous as me. I didn't wonder for a moment why this was so. I took another step and reached the railing again but I didn't look down. I felt like I'd made time stand still, lingering on the landing as they lingered downstairs. All of us not knowing what our next move should be. Was it up to me to go down to them? Was it up to them to come up to me? Should we meet in the middle?

"Would you like to come down and have something to eat, Embry?" said the male from the bottom of the staircase.

I leaned over the railing again, saw the boy still grinning at me, and looked at the man standing there. His skin was slightly darker than mine, his hair curlier and cut very short. He wore circular, wire-rimmed glasses that made him look distinguished and intelligent. Kindness in the form of gentle, grass-green energy emanated from him. Creator urged me to answer.

Instead, I took a step along the hallway, passing a bathroom and another bedroom before I reached the top of the stairs without replying. I stared down at the man, the woman standing just behind him. He was still grinning, his straight, white teeth like those inside the peryton's mouths. He nodded encouragement.

After the first step down on the soft, carpeted stairs, I held on to the railing and descended to the step two away from my new parents. The boy on the sofa had joined them to stare at me.

"Hi, Embry," said the boy. "My name's Toma. I'm your little brother. I'm eleven and in the fifth grade. I got to stay home from school today to meet you."

"Slow down, Speed Ball," said the woman. "You're too much for her, maybe."

"We made pancakes," said the man. "We don't eat meat, so you'll have to let us know if you want some."

"There's fresh raspberries," added Toma. "But you can have them with just syrup if you want."

His mom gave him a look and a shush.

"Sounds great." When I finally spoke, my voice sounded quite different to my ears than it had before. I followed them into the brightly lit room from where the delicious smells had wafted upstairs and took a seat at the table so I could look out at the rain beating down on the tall oaks and cedars standing in groups around a wide lawn.

The woman placed a stack of pancakes in front of me, steaming and smelling of vanilla. "Coffee?" she asked.

"Please," I replied.

The man, my new father, set a tall mug of the hot dark liquid in front of me before they both sat down. We were joined by Toma at the table. It appeared I was the only one eating and they took turns shoving things at me: syrup, berries, coconut milk, and sugar. I took a little of each, not wanting to offend.

"I'm Jomon," offered my new father. "You can call me Joe, if you don't want to call me Dad," he added.

"And I'm Imeka," said my new mother. "Most people call me Meeks, though."

I ate the pancakes while we studied each other. Meeks's hair was cropped short near her chin and had no curl at all but was thick and shiny black. I kept wanting to stare at her wide, dark eyes but shied away from being too openly curious. Their depths held sorrow I'd not seen before. The short sleeves of her dainty floral blouse showed slender arms covered with short dark hair. As I ate, she picked at a loose thread on the placemat in front of her. I wanted to place my hand over hers and stop the fidgeting. She had nothing to worry about from me. I planned on being the perfect daughter to these two generous humans.

"Dad makes amazing pancakes, doesn't he, Embry?" asked Toma. He bounced a bit in his chair. His energy radiated a warm, red glow that burst into yellow flames where his body touched any surface. He reminded me of a kitsune. I smiled at him.

"Just one of my many talents," said Joe.

"How did you sleep?" asked Meeks. "Do you like your room?"

I swallowed before replying. "Great. My room is lovely. Thank you."

"Was it awful?" asked Toma.

I couldn't imagine what he was talking about. Had no ready answer. The only awful things I could think of was waking up in the North after Alice opened an illegal portal, and the physical pain caused when Argon hit me. I was pretty sure he wasn't referring to either of those incidents. My expression must have shown my confusion.

"Toma." Meek admonished. "Embry might not want to talk about staying in the detention center. We talked about this."

"It's okay, Toma." I realized I didn't really have a cover story for my past, how I'd landed in the middle of their family. Panic welled up from my stomach, making the pancakes feel like weights. I grabbed my stomach, realizing they were going to come back up. Was I dying? It felt like it. From deep within my head, I heard Creator urging me to leave the table.

I made it as far as the sink and vomited violently. Physically, mentally, and emotionally raw, I rushed out of the room, up the stairs, and slammed the door to my room.

"Creator, what do I tell them?" I whispered. "What just happened? I don't know what to do, what to say." I hated the taste in my mouth, hated the weight of my physical body, hated the thought of disappointing my new family.

Chapter Thirty

Creator described Their plan for me to tell my new family. They explained what was happening in the country I was in and where I lived now. After a quick trip to the bathroom to rinse my mouth out and wash my face, I was ready to try again.

Meeks was just climbing the stairs as I opened my bedroom door. Her countenance and energy were wounded and worried, alternating red, yellow, and orange. Her wide eyes, framed by lifted eyebrows, asked permission to come closer to me and I nodded.

"Are you okay?" she asked. "You don't have to talk about your past, ever."

"Okay." I opened the door to my bedroom wide enough for her to enter and we sat down on my bed.

She took my hand in hers. Her touch, the first human touch of my life, bonded us immediately. My shoulders relaxed from where they'd been hovering up around my ears. I breathed fully for the first time, the air filling my lungs a wonder in itself. When I smiled, her energy settled into a clear red that grew out around her to encompass me. Safe. I was safe. Meeks wanted me. She wanted me as her daughter. I could read it in every part of her.

"What is it about me that made you want to adopt me?" I asked.

Joe came in. I realized he'd been standing in the hallway, listening. His energy was larger, the emerald green and sapphire blue taking turns as they pulsated with the beat of his heart. "How's our girl?" He sat in the turquoise-cushioned chair near a small, white desk, moving throw pillows of different shapes and sizes to accommodate his large frame.

"She wants to know why we adopted her," explained Meeks. She squeezed my hand.

"Guess we should tell her, then," replied Joe. "We've always wanted a daughter. Meeks lost a baby, a girl, just after we were married, and I almost lost her. She's not really built for babies, as you can see." He pointed to the small woman holding my hand as if I'd understand his words, as if it was evident that she wouldn't be good at being pregnant.

I just nodded.

"After that, we just gave up our dream of having kids," Meeks continued. "When Toma came along five years later, we were surprised."

"We were ecstatic," said Joe. "He really is a miracle kid."

"When Toma was about seven, we started to hear about immigrants coming to this country being detained at our borders and something just snapped inside of us," Meeks continued. "I'm from an ancient tribe of Ainu, originally occupying Japan. For some reason, it became important to us to seek out anyone who might be of my line. I can't explain it, but we just didn't want anyone else. If we couldn't help an immigrant with our ancestry, we weren't interested."

"We agreed to take any age, but we were hoping for a *younger* sister for Toma," said Joe. "It's taken four years. We could've taken at least ten other girls, but none with our bloodline, so we said no."

"We gave up," said Meeks. "I think the agency working with Immigration got a little tired of us saying no. I can't tell you how excited we were when we got the call last week that you were being processed through."

"A week ago?" I asked. They'd said yes to adopting me before I'd even known I was coming here.

"Last Tuesday, they called Joe at work with the news. The agency determined you had no living relatives and that you were ready to be adopted," explained Meeks. "They asked for a trial period before we agreed, but"—she looked at Joe with shining eyes—"we signed the paperwork that afternoon and here you are. You're ours."

Inside my head, Creator whispered, "You are wanted." Inside my heart, love grew, green and nourished like a new water lily fresh from the depths of the pond.

"Thank you." Unable to hide my tears or gratitude, I hugged Meeks, and Joe kneeled at my feet to embrace both of us.

"I want in on that." Toma rushed in and landed in the middle, making us tumble back on my bed in a heap of humanity.

Family. I had a family. I was wanted. Creator surrounded the four of us in a rainbow energy bubble. I never wanted to leave. I couldn't imagine this life containing anything like what the kelpies had told me to expect. I was wanted. These three humans held me in their hearts before they'd even met me, before I'd even known I would come here. Parents of my own, and a little brother—I felt whole. I felt safe.

They took turns showing me the house, Toma interrupting Joe and Meeks with his own brand of commentary. My room was the smallest bedroom, but I was thankful for the view of the trees out of the corner windows. I had a small desk with a computer they said I would need for school.

School. Oh goody. I'd have to attend school here too. How was I to navigate that without ever having lived here before? Seeing my questioning look, Meeks reassured me that they'd informed my teachers I might be a bit behind coming from another culture.

"I teach at your high school, Embry," she said. "You can come to me any time you're feeling overwhelmed. You're not the only immigrant to attend JFK High."

I nodded, sucking on my bottom lip.

"Mom teaches physics," said Toma. "I'm going to be on the swim team," he added. "Go Fighting Irish!" He ran to his room down the hall and returned with a pennant in the shape of a sideways *V*, slightly dog-eared from handling. "You need this now, since you go there."

"Let's get her one of her own," said Meeks.

Toma withdrew his from in front of my face, looking crestfallen.

"Thanks, Toma," I said. "This one's perfect till I get one too. Then we can wave them together, cool?" I tacked it to the bulletin board behind my desk. His smile returned with his pulsing energy. "What's a Fighting Irish?"

Toma's mouth opened, his eyes wide in disbelief. "How can you not know who the Fighting Irish are? Mom, she doesn't know who the Fighting Irish are." Before she could reply, he launched into an explanation of a college called Notre Dame, football, and who John F. Kennedy was, and how cool it was that my high school was named after him, and how lucky I was to go there before him, and was I going to go out for a sport, and was I good at sports, and what was my favorite subject, and that his was math.

He bewildered me and delighted me at the same time. Nobody I'd met before compared to Toma. The kitsune came close, but even their energy couldn't match his. When he asked if I wanted to walk to the lake nearby, I agreed, letting him take my hand and drag me toward the stairs.

"Hold on there, Speedo." Joe took his arm and pulled him back into my room. "Let's let Embry change out of her pajamas and into something a little more appropriate for outside. Then we'll *all* go down to the lake. This is a family day, remember?"

Meeks showed me some clothes hanging in the closet, their price tags still on. "We're going to go shopping, but this is what the kids are wearing at school, so I picked up a few things to get you started. Dress warm. It's a brisk day."

They pulled the door shut behind them and left me to choose some clothes.

Chapter Thirty-One

We spent the day in glorious warmth and love, discovering each other and the wonders of my new home. Migrating geese occupied the small lake down from their house and Toma showed me how to sneak up on them from behind the tall cattails without disturbing them as they scuttled in the mud for snacks and preened their feathers. He showed me how to put a flat blade of grass between my thumbs and blow, making a sound similar to a squawking duck. He took off his shoes before Joe and Meeks could stop him and waded into the shallows, catching tadpoles in his hands to show me. He could name many of the plants growing around the lake, checking with his mom to be sure he had it right.

There wasn't much need for me to speak, and so much for me to discover. Scrunching through piles of maple, oak, and alder leaves, we rounded the lake on a wide paved path with only a few joggers and cyclists for company. Crisp fall air nipped at my ears and an occasional gust blew my curly hair around my face.

"I love your hair," said Toma. "It's like a combination of Mom and Dad's. Like, curly but long. I want long hair, but mine just goes out from my head like a scrub brush, so I have to keep it short."

He was only slightly shorter than me, though I had arrived as a sixteen-year-old. My physical body was in every way identical to how I'd looked in my afterlife. I wondered how Creator had done it, made my adopted parents look so much like a blend of me. It gave me insight into what my natural parents must have looked like and a pang of sadness filled my heart. I turned from Toma's adoring little brother gaze for a moment so I could compose myself. He didn't notice, and when I turned back, I took his hand and skipped ahead of Joe and Meeks.

We skipped all the way back to the house, a two-story with gray wood siding, similar to every other house on the block. Toma ran ahead. By the time I entered the sliding glass doors from the back porch, he'd turned the television on and was engaged in some kind of game, the controller in his hands. I declined his offer to play and returned to my bedroom. Creator's voice, or rather, Their energy, ran through me, soothing and reminding me of Their presence.

My closet doors were mirrored. I looked at myself, seeing my brown eyes and skin. For the first time I could compare myself with actual human bodies, not eternal bodies. Wondered for the thousandth time what my real parents looked like. Were they still alive? Was time the same here as Eternity? Were they close, or on the other side of the planet? It didn't matter, I reminded myself. Creator had chosen Joe and Imeka for me and how could life get any better? If I was to stay until the magic in the portals was restored, I was confident I would be fine.

I showered and changed into another set of comfortable clothes—sweats, they called them when I descended the stairs. They were also in sweats and seated around the living room, watching a movie. Delicious smells wafted from the kitchen. When Joe noticed my interest, he smiled.

"We put vegetable stew in the Instapot," he said. "I hope I didn't season it too much. We don't want a repeat of this morning's reaction."

At first, I was appalled, recalling the pancake incident, but relaxed when he gently punched my arm.

"Kidding," he added.

We spent the evening enjoying each other, eating in front of the television, watching a family comedy. I laughed when they laughed, not really getting some of the humor. At nine, they switched the television off. Meeks ordered Toma upstairs for a shower and turned to me with a serious face and countenance.

"Let's talk about what to expect tomorrow," she said. "I'll take you to school in the morning. I've arranged a student guide to help you since it's your first time at school here. Each teacher will probably give you an entrance test to determine what you know. Don't worry. We expect gaps in your knowledge."

I pictured Dina and my friends sitting in the clearing relearning what they needed to live in Eternity. Wondered if they'd moved on to pursue their own interests or whether they were still under Dina's care. Melancholy drained my energy. I listened through a fog of dread as Meeks described what my day would probably be like. Creator whispered, "We're here."

After Meeks blew me a kiss and left my room, door ajar just in case, she disappeared down the hall. My body vibrated with emotions I couldn't name, leaving me confused and jittery. "I love my new family, but there's so much to learn about being human—with a body and a heart, and a stomach, and having to pee, and sweating, and—"

Creator interrupted me with Their laugh. "Oh, Embry. Yes, there's a lot more to having a body than being an ethereal being. We couldn't have described any of it. You had to experience it yourself." Their voice soothed my jitters, reset my emotional balance. "We're happy you're doing so well. You barely need Us."

"Yeah, we'll see how that holds up tomorrow when I go to school," I said. "Meeks said there are hundreds of kids my school. Hundreds. One of them is going to figure out that I'm not really one of them."

"But you are," They answered. "You are human. You always have been. Your soul has taken a backseat to your physical human body, but it's still really you. Same as all the others at school."

"Hmmm. We'll see."

They went silent.

I slept in fits and starts, dreaming of being thrown off cliffs and unable to fly, thrown into deep water and unable to swim, thrown into a teeming mass of people all yelling and clamoring at me to do something but I couldn't understand what. When I finally reached the deepest sleep of the night,

Meeks had to shake me and say my name many times before I was conscious.

"Someone's a deep sleeper," she said. "Joe has coffee on. Get up and ready. We leave in about forty-five minutes."

"Have a good day!" Joe's voice echoed up the stairs.

"Love you!" answered Meeks.

I got ready to face whatever awaited me at JFK High School. After my fitful night, my curly hair was in tangles I didn't have time to comb out, so I threw it on top of my head in a messy knot. As we backed out of the driveway, Toma waved from the corner where he waited for his bus, lunch pail firmly gripped in one hand and skateboard in the other.

We didn't talk to each other. I couldn't think of what to say and Meeks was busy talking to someone at school on the car's speaker. The sky, filled with gray clouds threatening rain, seemed ominous to me. Humans walked on sidewalks, drove looking straight ahead in cars of every shape and size, waited at stoplights, and generally looked half-dead. Too many signs begged to be read. Too many noises begged to be attended to. Too much unhappiness threatened to swallow me up. The effort to hide my emotions from Meeks took all my energy. Only Creator's continued soothing hum kept me from screaming at the top of my lungs. They crooned, "Soon, soon, soon." It gave me enough hope to watch as we pulled into the teacher parking lot, gathered our things, and walked through the glass front doors into the office.

Chapter Thirty-Two

"Is this her?" asked the front-office clerk as we neared the massive wooden counter.

"This is her." Meeks voice held so much pride, I stopped holding my breath.

"Hi, Embry. Welcome to JFK, home of the Fighting Irish." The lady looked over short glasses when she talked. Her white skin was freckled with red dots large and small all over her bare arms and face. Small pearls dotted each of her earlobes and a pen perched behind one ear, disappearing into her curly, graying, red hair.

"I need to get to my room, Ms. Dewar." Meeks pushed through the swinging door at the end of the counter, held it for me, and stopped to embrace me in a hug so tight I couldn't breathe. "You're going to be fine," she whispered before disappearing toward the back of the office.

"I've got it, Ms. Falade," replied Ms. Dewar. "We'll take good care of her. Come on, then, Embry." Ms. Dewar patted my arm. "Follow me." She was already walking purposefully toward a door marked *Vice Principal*. "Your student guide is waiting in here with Mr. Hart. Ms. Valenzuela wanted to be here to meet you but there's a meeting at the district office. Here she is." She preceded me into the office, turned, and gestured toward me like she was showing off a prized pet.

Mr. Hart and a tall blond boy stood as I entered. They both held out their hands and I didn't know what to do. Mr. Hart was thin and bald and a bit frightening, his dress shirt and tie fitting loosely as if he were starving. The blond boy was at least a foot taller than me, with blue eyes like the sky in the West. He wore a jacket with the school's mascot emblazoned on the front and he smiled, showing a row of straight, white teeth. He too, was nearly too much human for me. Too big, too friendly, too blond.

When they realized I wasn't going to shake their hands, they lowered them and chuckled to each other.

"Right. I've got work to do, people." Ms. Dewar left me standing in the doorway.

"Come in, Embry," said Mr. Hart. He gestured to a chair next to the too tall and blond boy. "Have a seat. We'll go through the itinerary and get you two off and running. This is Craig, your student guide today and all week if you need him."

I was feeling far too shy and uncomfortable to look at Craig, so I just nodded in his direction. I could barely hear Mr. Hart describe my schedule over the pounding of my heart in my chest. Short shallow breaths left me feeling a bit dizzy. When he asked me to sign a few papers, I surprised myself by knowing how to write. I'd never learned, so Creator's quiet chuckle inside my head made sense.

"Embry Falade," said Mr. Hart. "Has a nice ring to it, eh, Craig?"

Craig nodded and smiled at me. His energy, green and blue mixed with a bit of red, communicated friendliness and yet I couldn't allow myself to relax.

"So, do you have any questions, Embry?" asked Mr. Hart. When I didn't reply, he stood and reached across his desk to shake my hand, remembered what I'd done before and lowered it, looking slightly nonplussed. "Ready, Craig?"

"It's all cool, Mr. Hart," replied Craig. "Let's go, Embry."

The same feelings I'd had during my dreams, of falling and not being able to fly, of being underwater without knowing how to swim, of entering a point of no return blackened my vision for a moment, but Creator crooned in my head. I took one step, another, and found the courage to follow Craig out of the office, across the blue carpet and out into the corridor of JFK High School. Wished I'd thought to ask Creator for a kitsune or an igigi to accompany me. Imagining a kitsune or two scrambling down the corridor made me smile.

"Hey, that's a good look on you," Craig said. "I think you're even breathing again."

"You noticed that?" I asked.

"Yeah. I thought I might have to use my first-aid training on you back there," he replied. "Everybody is really curious about you coming from the detention facility and all. Expect uncomfortable stupid questions." He paused, gesturing left for me to follow him toward a blue door. "It's one of the reasons they chose me to be your student guide. That and I'm your Mom's favorite." His smile disarmed me, the twinkle in his blue eyes enhanced by his friendly energy.

"Why's that?" I asked. Creator had stopped crooning in my head, allowing me to fully concentrate on Craig and my surroundings and the newness of the situation.

"For one, I'm not intimidated by anybody." He held up his hands to count off reasons. "Two, I'm an immigrant too. And three, I'm amazing in physics." There was that grin again. I was growing accustomed to it. It was losing its power to make me breathless. I could see why Meeks liked him.

Before we entered the classroom, Craig described what I should expect. "Everyone is going to stop and look at you. It's the end of first period, so Ms. Finch will look perturbed. Ready?"

It was exactly as he described. What he hadn't mentioned was the effect the bright, fluorescent lights buzzing overhead would have on my ability to focus. He hadn't mentioned the smell of so much humanity in one place. Neglected to remind me that the collective energy of individuals in the classroom would pummel me with conflicting emotions. Of course, he couldn't have known of these effects on me.

"Finally," said Ms. Finch. "Here you are, then. Take those seats in the back, Craig, and write down the homework assignment. You'll be able to text me with questions, Embry. I don't have time to test you to find out what you know. We'll do that tomorrow."

We did as she said, sharing a look of raised brows and rolled eyes. A loud bell startled me from copying notes from the screen and I let out an involuntary squeak. The other students chuckled.

"Not used to bells, or do they just remind you of Asia?" asked a shorter, black-haired guy in front of me as we gathered our things to leave.

"Yeah, the bell startled me a bit," I admitted.

He shook his head and lifted his backpack to his shoulders. Craig and I followed him out and all the way to Trig, the other students going in all directions. Craig received a few high fives and fist bumps as we walked through the crowded corridor. Several groups of girls smiled the same kind of white-toothed smiles I was getting used to at him, frowning slightly as they saw who he was with. Me.

Mr. Chan, the trigonometry teacher, was ready for me, handing over a stack of papers as soon as Craig introduced me. Seated at a desk near the front of the class, I flipped through them to find I knew how to do almost everything on the test. Again, I heard Creator chuckle inside my head. "This is knowledge you had before, from the beginning. All knowledge is within you when you arrive in your physical body and We provide ways for you to know it. We just made sure you had what you would need for your stay."

Nothing else was expected of me besides taking the test, so I looked up every now and then at the students, the classroom, my surroundings. As I worked out algebra problems, a few geometry problems, and a lot of basic math stuff, I felt the curious stares and energy from the other students in the room. A few students pulsed with darkened reddish energy, making me feel unsafe. From the middle of the class came a noxious green and orange energy similar to that of the sky in the North. Two girls and one boy took turns looking at me and whispering to each other. Craig looked at me and winked a few times.

In Meeks's class, nobody whispered about me. She had a test ready too, so I spent that hour watching, listening, and answering the questions with ease and more chuckles from Creator.

Chapter Thirty-Three

Sitting at a table with Craig at lunch, I was overwhelmed again by the noise, the smells, the lights, the chaos. Several of his friends joined us. I nibbled at my salad while trying to focus just on those seated at our table. I laughed when the others laughed, not really sure what was funny. I couldn't think of anything interesting to add to the conversation, not having really ever lived, answering questions with one or two words and noticing glances exchanged when I stopped talking. They were trying very hard to be nice to me. I could feel it and see it in their energy.

From out of nowhere, I got hit in the back of the head with a spoonful of something wet. Craig and his friends were on their feet instantly, ready to accuse and defend. Those around us at other tables stopped talking, waiting to see what would happen next. I pulled the green glob of spinach from my hair, untangling the curly strands as best I could.

"What the heck, man?" asked Craig over the quieted crowd.

"I was aiming for you, man," a voice from across the cafeteria taunted.

"Yeah, well you have shit for aim, Conner." Craig walked toward the windows where Conner sat with the two girls who had whispered and giggled in trig. His friends followed, except for one girl who stayed behind and scooted next to me.

"It's okay, Craig," I said, turning around and speaking loudly enough for the entire cafeteria to hear. "Really. It's just spinach." I didn't need this. Didn't need to be noticed on my first day of high school, bullied, or made fun of. I just wanted to do my time and return to the South.

"Hear that, Craig?" called Conner. "Girl says she's cool."

"She might be, but I'm not." Craig continued to weave around tables of silent students.

The girl next to me took my hand. "Sorry about this," she whispered. "Conner and Craig have been at it since third grade when Mr. Ames liked Craig's drawings better than Conner's. It's so stupid. So caveman. They used to get in fights at recess. Craig never starts it, but he always finishes it. Conner's so stupid to pick a fight with him. He knows how it will go."

I saw her roll her eyes and shake her head. Such a petty rivalry made me think of Alice. I wondered if her life here had been filled with situations similar to this one. If she arrived in the South with habits and patterns where she always came out in the wrong, it could explain why she'd hated me. My arrival had made her remember. Made sense.

While Conner and Craig continued to throw barbs and taunts at each other, Creator said inside my head, "Stop this." I argued with Them, shaking my head slightly. The girl holding my hand noticed but didn't say anything. "Trust me," They said. "Walk over there. We promise to guide you."

The girl tugged at my hand as I stood up.

"It's okay. I'm going to handle it."

As I walked toward the windows of the cafeteria, heads turned. Cafeteria attendants were beginning to move in on the two boys. I had a very small window of opportunity to follow Creator's instructions. When I stopped next to Craig, he went silent, as did Conner. The only sounds in the room were footsteps of cafeteria attendants and an occasional fork scraping across a plate.

"Look, Craig," started Conner. "Your girlfriend is here to defend you. Better listen up."

"I'm not his girlfriend." I crossed my arms, sending adrenaline-filled energy toward him like a fist. "I'm new here. This is my first day in high school in a new country. I'm an immigrant from North Africa and I've been in a holding facility for the past two years, and if you think a little spinach in my hair is going to intimidate me, then you are a special kind of stupid, aren't you?" I paused, watching the full brunt of my words and energy ripple through the room. Even the cafeteria attendants had stopped walking toward us.

"My real parents are dead. My adopted parents are Mr. and Ms. Falade. If you have an issue with me or anyone I choose to hang out with from now on, you take it up with me." I turned away while whispers of who my new mom vied with approving comments. I ignored everything and returned to my seat just as the bell rang, signaling the end of lunch. I breathed a sigh of relief, thanked Creator in my mind, and received a hug from the girl who had held my hand.

"Way to go, Embry," she said next to my ear. "Respect, girl. Respect."

Craig escorted me to my last classes without much conversation, though I did ask him if there was still any spinach in my hair. I caught him looking at me with new eyes, his energy showing me how his opinion changed with rings of purple flowing through his orange and reddish glow. I smiled inwardly at the change.

As soon as I entered Meeks's classroom after school, she looked up from her desk where she sat grading papers and rushed to hug me. "I heard all about what happened at lunch. Everyone is talking about the badass new girl." She held me away from her for a moment, pride in her deep brown eyes. "Guess I'm not going to need to worry quite so much about you."

"Guess not," I replied.

"Do you have homework?" she asked. "I've got papers to grade, so I thought we could stay here for a bit. That okay?"

"Sounds cool," I said.

I looked through all the papers I'd received, organizing them, highlighting due dates, and learning how to maneuver around the school-assigned iPad. The analog clock on the wall ticked. The heater cycled on and off and the fluorescent lights buzzed. Meeks shook her head a few times, making marks with a green felt-tip pen on students' papers.

"Hate to interrupt this study session."

Meeks and I looked up, startled at the intrusion into our silent school sanctuary. Conner stood in the doorway, half in and half out. His sullen stance hinted at a desire to be anywhere else. I noticed his brown hair needed trimmed, his black jeans needed a good washing, and his backpack was frayed beyond what was fashionable. Creator infused me with sympathy as I stared at the spinach-throwing boy.

"What do you want, Conner?" Meeks asked. "Come in or go out, but decide."

"Yeah, so about lunch," he began. The door bumped against his backpack as it closed. "I'm sorry, Ms. Falade."

"Don't apologize to me, Conner." Meeks nodded toward where I sat near the heater along the windows. "She probably needs it more than I do."

I studied Conner. He hesitated before sitting down two desks away.

"Yeah, so, sorry," he said.

I wanted to tell him it was okay, but Creator held my tongue. "Let him say more. Let him explain. This is a moment We have created for his good." As I filled with compassionate energy, glowing green and changing to blue and back again, his tough and indifferent expression morphed. I saw him with Creator's eyes, a downtrodden and wounded human. As much as he tried to hide it, the facade of indifference melted.

"I didn't know." Conner looked from me to Meeks and back. She ignored us.

This was our moment. I continued to stare at him as if I didn't understand. Took a deep breath and bit my lower lip, thinking.

"Didn't know what?" I asked. "That I was new? That I wouldn't care? Or that I would call you out? Or is it that if you'd known I was Ms. Falade's adopted daughter you'd have perfected your aim to your original target?"

He didn't answer. Just opened his mouth to answer but nothing came out.

"I just didn't—didn't think," he finally said.

"Well, there you go," I said. "Obviously." Creator whispered a warning to give him grace and I felt a rebellion in my heart. It felt good to have the upper hand. I wanted to keep it.

"My parents were immigrants. From Mexico." His words had the desired effect. I softened. Creator had known. Had wanted Conner to admit this to me. Not for me. For himself. He moved to a desk right in front of me, putting his feet in the chair and setting his backpack on the floor.

"Yeah?" I asked. Letting go of control and allowing him into my sphere was much harder here. I began to understand the power behind selfishness. Began to see how souls ended up in the North when they first arrived. A life spent seeking that feeling, that power, that control was certainly a powerful motivator. It felt almost better than Creator's love.

Conner told me about his journey with his parents from Mexico when he was five years old. How they'd ridden in the back of an old mail truck packed with others seeking a better life. How he'd been separated from his parents and had to stay in a facility at the border. It was similar to the story Creator had given me as my own. The difference between us was that I'd lost my parents and he'd been reunited with his.

"So, I don't know," he continued. "Anyway. I'm really sorry. I'm glad you said all those things in the cafeteria. You won't get teased like I did when I started school here." He stood, gathering his backpack, unburdened by guilt and glowing a brighter and stronger yellow and orange. "So, I'll see you around."

I watched him leave, thinking about Craig in a new light. Maybe he had done a bit of teasing back in third grade.

"All good?" asked Meeks. "Ready to go?"

"Yeah," I said. "All good."

Creator hummed.

Chapter Thirty-Four

Toma bounded in from school, curious to hear how my day had gone and we sat at the kitchen counter, swapping stories while Meeks threw chickpeas and some herbs in a food processor for fresh hummus. We snacked on hummus and naan, waiting for Joe to get home. With no clouds in the sky, we sat on the back porch, eating grilled vegetable kabobs dipped in spicy reduced balsamic and watched the stars pop out, accompanied by a crescent moon.

Meeks described what she'd heard about the lunchtime encounter. She made me out to be some kind of superhero, cape and all. I added details from what really occurred, but she was determined to hold on to the image of caped crusader. Joe puffed up with concern for a moment, making me feel as though he would have punched Conner in the stomach. When I related his story to them while eating s'mores we made over the hot coals of the grill, he calmed down, nodding with new understanding.

The next few days went in a similar way. I learned names, made a few friends, and got used to whispers in the hallway still centered around my performance in the cafeteria. Guys fist-bumping me mouthing, 'Respect,' as if they'd never seen a strong girl. Girls seeking me out for advice handling other bullying situations. Suddenly I was the sage of my class. Having the Creator of the Universe inside my head didn't hurt anything.

Classwork was easy, thanks to the knowledge of all creation at my disposal. I asked Creator daily for news of the portals and each day They replied, "Not yet." I began to worry that I was doing so well in my made-up life that They might have decided to just leave me in it, but They assured me this wasn't the case.

I no longer needed Craig to guide me, but he sought me out to check in at the beginning of each day, his girlfriend Olivia by his side. I worried about the jealousy I felt through her expressions and energy, but Creator assured me not to. Everyone here was a project. Everyone here was monitored by Creator. Everyone here was learning what they needed to before dying. It was difficult to comprehend, and even harder to navigate. Sometimes I wished Creator out of my head so I could ponder my opinions without guidance, but They'd promised to stay with me and more often than not, I was glad for that.

Much to my surprise, it was Conner who waved for me to eat at his table at lunch. Each section of the cafeteria had its own energy, the top students and upper-class members emanating a slightly stronger indigo glow over their individual signatures. Students less able to find their niche by getting good grades or performing well in sports took on other energy signatures from each end of the rainbow spectrum. Conner's group radiated strongly red and I didn't know if this was why it felt safer with him than at Craig's table, but I soon understood the girls he hung out with, Tina and Janelle, felt like outcasts too.

Janelle was blond and shy, often not speaking or eating at lunch except in soft, short answers. Conner held her hand under the table as if he was holding a bird egg, the feelings they shared for each other expressed in the soft flames of green that shot from their hearts when they looked at each other. Her wounded energy, soot-tinged yellow, made me instinctively want to protect her too, though I barely knew her.

Tina was harsh and brassy in comparison. Multiple piercings in her ears ended in large gold hoops that reached her shoulders. I could tell she was naturally dark-haired, but the blond tips of her spiked hair flamed with orange energy like a kitsune. Her affection for us was evident in the strong, red safety net she spun around our group. She'd only whispered about me in the beginning because of some misplaced jealousy. She thought I'd be shallow and snobby.

After school on Friday, I waited in the parklike atmosphere of the quad area for Meeks to finish paperwork. Without a cloud in the sky, the cold air felt good against my skin after a grueling session of running miles in PE and I had shed my navy-blue peacoat. Piles of red, orange, and purple leaves littered the ground where the janitors had raked them. Conner and Tina appeared from around the brick building without noticing me. Snippets of a heated argument reached my ears.

"Her family . . ." said Tina.

"I thought she was . . ." said Conner.

"Well, she wasn't . . ." said Tina. "You guys shouldn't . . ."

I wanted to wave at them, let them know I was there, but Creator held me in check, whispering for me to keep quiet and listen. I did. As I'd guessed, they were discussing

Janelle. Tina was animated, hands flying as she spoke, getting in Conner's face. They stopped in the center of the quad.

"Listen, Conner. You guys have to get rid of it," Tina said.

"I'd be a good dad," Conner replied.

"That's not the point, stupid." Tina placed her hands in the pockets of her black leather jacket and continued gesticulating. She looked like a bat ready to take off. "Think about her. I mean, Janelle's, like, crazy talented and she has a chance at art school. The baby would end that dream. Is that what you want for her?"

Conner shook his head, looking a lot like he had the day he'd come to apologize. Had that been just four short days ago? I couldn't believe how quickly I'd adapted to life here, how quickly I'd come to love the people in my life. Creator hummed inside my head.

"No. No, Tina. I don't know what to do." Conner looked down at the rusty red bricks under his feet. "I love her."

"Well, duh, you stupid idiot." Tina sassed her head. "This has nothing to do with love. This has to do with your future." She took her hands out of her pockets and held them out from her head. "Picture the two choices. Number one, Janelle gets a scholarship to art school, gets a job doing her art, whatever that looks like, and you guys live in a high-rise apartment in some major city. You take business classes at Community so you can manage her career. That's choice number one."

Conner shook his head and opened his mouth.

"Just shut it." Tina held a finger in front of his face. "Number two, Janelle has to tell her parents she's pregnant. You're the father, she has the baby and either you guys are forced to get married or they forbid you to see her again. They really don't like you, Conner. To them, you're a loser." She shifted her weight, hands on hips. "Either way, in that scenario, Janelle loses. See? She is stuck with a baby, your baby. You have no way of really helping her right now, and she ends up working at a shit-heap job while raising your baby. Without you. What the fuck, Conner? That's got nothing to do with love and everything to do with selfishness."

As soon as she said that word, I stopped listening. They moved on out of the quad and I remembered what the kelpies had told me. Remembered Creator's greatest challenge here in this life was to present each soul with opportunities to overcome selfishness. It resulted in the horrifying choices people made to hurt others, to want everything for themselves, to stop caring if their actions hurt others. Self was the voice they listened to instead of Creator's.

"Now you know," said Creator inside my head. "It's far worse in some people, but this is how it begins for others."

"What should I do?" I asked, speaking aloud to the cold air as I drew my peacoat close.

"Trust yourself. And trust Us."

I nodded as Meeks entered the quad.

"Ready? Why didn't you come to my classroom? Janelle was in the hallway and said you were out here. Kind of cold, isn't it?" She didn't wait for me to respond and we walked to the car.

Chapter Thirty-Five

We went to the football game that night, dressed warmly in blue and gold. Joe kept a running commentary on the game as I admitted to not knowing what football was all about. I cheered when we scored. I worried about the hard hits each player took, wondering how Creator allowed Their creation to smack each other so hard while playing a game. I heard Their explanation in my head, but Toma provided better running commentary.

"They're wearing pads everywhere, Embry," explained Toma. "It doesn't hurt them. I'm too small or I'd be playing. It's why I'm a good swimmer though." He was exuberant as always, cheeks glowing red in the cold.

Fall, with its warm vibrant colors and crisp frosty air, created the perfect backdrop for the experience. New friends waved; many greeted Meeks with respect in their voices. Even Joe got a few acknowledgements by students and staff as we sat on a JFK "Fighting Irish" blanket covering the wooden bleachers. The cheerleaders fascinated me with their leaping and urgent requests to join them in chants. Frenetic energy across the spectrum emanated from the group, no energy signature standing out from the others. It was as if they were all one person.

Above us and to the left sat Conner, Janelle, and Tina. I wondered why they'd come to the game knowing their disdain for crowds and general indifference toward traditional school events. As often as I could, I glanced over my shoulder, but Creator spoke clearly about leaving them alone. I yearned to disobey but couldn't bring myself to do it so contented myself with bonding with Toma.

"I feel like some cocoa, Embry," said Joe. "Want to take Toma up to the snack bar and get some for your mom and me?"

"Yeah, Dad. Good idea." Toma was already out of his seat.

"They have soymilk right, hun?" asked Joe.

Meeks nodded, concentrating on the game. "Gotta ask for it."

Joe handed me a twenty-dollar bill. "Bring me the change, kiddo."

I looked at the money without comprehension, but Toma grabbed my hand and we were climbing the stairs before I had a chance to ask what it was. The line was more of a mob, so I allowed him to guide me along while I looked at the selections written across a board above our heads.

"Don't forget to ask for soy." Toma pointed at the small letters at the bottom of the sign.

"Why do we ask for soy?" I asked.

"We're vegetarians, remember?" Toma tugged me forward as the line moved ahead. When he saw my confused expression, he shook his head and rolled his eyes. "So, we don't eat meat—like from animals. We don't eat anything from animals either. Sometimes we eat eggs, but only because the ones in the stores are already sterilized and we're not really eating a life that could have been a life, right?"

I was no more enlightened.

"You do know that milk comes from animals, right?" He squinted his eyes.

I realized it was something I should know. Creator painted a picture of several species in my head: cows, horses, goats, all nursing their young. "Yes, of course. Everyone knows that."

Toma had already shuffled forward again without waiting for my reply. To add to the picture, Creator showed me a human mom nursing her infant. The rush of emotions was so unexpected, I had no time to stop the tears from flowing down my cheeks.

"Oh," I said aloud.

"You okay?" asked an older gentleman standing next to me in line.

"Hey, Embry. What's up? What happened?" Toma was by my side, looking up into my face as I worked to stay standing.

"I need to go to the bathroom, Toma." I nodded at the gentleman and skirted through the crowd. Inside the last stall, I doubled over, sobbing. The picture of the nursing mom lingered in my head long after Creator had shown it to me. Their words and feelings of calm had no effect as the extreme grief I felt could not be contained. Could not be gotten rid of. The purest light of love—unselfish, complete, all-encompassing—glowed around mother and child, surpassing anything I'd felt or experienced in Eternity.

"Why, Creator, why?" I sobbed.

They engulfed me in a barrier of love and protection as I leaned on the wall and finally sunk to the floor to rock back and forth, holding myself. Thankfully no one heard.

Thankfully no one interfered. I was allowed to feel it, the physical pain of a broken heart.

"I hate this body. I hate it here. I hate being human. Why? Why? Why? Why must it hurt so bad to have never been suckled by my mother? Adored by my father?" I hated Creator for creating me and wanted to end my life. To feel nothing at all, to cease to exist. That was better than this pain.

I lost track of time sitting and rocking behind the gray door of the bathroom stall. Creator sent orange energy from every source on earth toward me, allowing, listening, understanding. They were there. They were with me. They reached inside to my deepest soul self and comforted. My rocking stopped. My tears dried. I stared with unseeing eyes at the gray barriers of the stall while people entered and exited the bathroom, chittering away about inconsequential things.

It was Meeks who found me. "Embry? Embry, are you in here?" Footsteps on the concrete floor drew near before I saw her face peek under the door. "Oh, Embry. Open the door, honey. Come on. Whatever happened, you're okay. Toma's worried sick about you."

Seeing her concern and love caused a fresh flood of tears, but I stood and unlocked the door. Meeks rushed in to embrace me in a fierce crushing hug. "Oh, Embry. What's wrong? Was someone mean to you? Tell me who it is, and I'll make sure they suffer."

"Is she in there?" Joe hollered from outside the door. "Is she okay? I'm coming in."

"No, Joe, you'll freak everybody else out." Meeks looked at the others in the bathroom with reassurance as they looked toward the door where Joe stood just out of sight. "She's fine. I think."

Her energy pounded and pulsed red with anger and protection, matching the beating of my heart. Much to the consternation of the others in the bathroom, she guided me outside while continuing her bear hug. I could feel her hair brush against my face as she shook her head at any requests for information.

Toma stood next to Joe just outside the door and joined Meeks hugging me. "What happened, Embry?"

"Leave her alone, guys." Meeks brushed him away. "Let's go home."

Joe hugged us to him and together they parted the crowd as we walked to the parking lot. Silence descended inside the darkened cab of Joe's SUV. Even Toma, usually so exuberant, sat quietly in the glow of the game on his cell phone.

It was comforting to press my head against the cold glass of my window, thinking nothing. Not even the thought of returning to the South intruded on the numbness in my soul. I didn't care anymore. Meeks and Joe and Toma were wonderful people. They deserved a daughter who wasn't this complicated on the inside. For the first time, I wondered what would happen to them when portal magic was fixed and I could return to where I was supposed to be. Would I die and they have to mourn? That wasn't fair. Was that part of their story? Creator, in the background of my thoughts, let me ponder without answering, though I sensed They had a reply to every single question flowing through me.

Joe pulled into the garage and we sat for a moment before seatbelts unfastened and we climbed out of the car. Toma ran ahead upstairs, eager to get to his room and continue the video battle he was fighting on a larger screen.

"Toma," Joe called, "we need to sit together as a family for a minute. It can wait."

I watched him descend, his energy shifting from self to concern for me again. Once Joe had turned on the fire and adjusted the lights in the living room, he settled on the couch next to Meeks and looked at me.

"Tell us what happened, honey." He placed a hand on my knee as I sat down on the footstool in front of them, Toma bouncing next to me with anticipation.

"Everything is still really new," I started.

They nodded. "We know."

I didn't know what else to say. All I could do was feel. Tears threatened again. I sniffed. Breathed. Clouded up with all the emotions flowing around the room. Joe and Meeks scooted toward me and pulled me to them, which made me feel even more despair at the thought of what would happen when I left them. They just wanted a daughter. They'd chosen me because of my bloodline. The dragons had chosen me for the same reason. I felt like I was letting everyone down. Toma completed the circle of warmth and love while Joe rocked us all and my tears flowed.

Chapter Thirty-Six

"Feel better?" asked Joe.

I nodded.

"I guess we don't need to know what happened right now." Joe wiped the tears on my cheeks with his thumb. "Whatever it was, tomorrow's Saturday, and we're going to have pancakes, and rake leaves. Meeks might take you to yoga if you want." He patted me on the back as we all stood up, looking awkwardly at each other, the moment of caring intimacy replaced by our tired energy trying to untangle itself.

After a shower, my fuzzy pajamas and soft sheets erased some of my hopelessness. Alone in the dark with light from a half moon shining through open curtains, I allowed Creator to completely engulf my thoughts.

"Oh Embry," They said. "We're sorry." Peace and grounding pushed against the raw sorrow of my broken heart. "Humanity is broken. It is not what We intended. It is why We accompanied you here. Choosing to allow you to arrive as a fully formed human was difficult but your presence here will not have a negative effect."

"What will my new family experience when I'm gone?" I asked.

"We are in all places making things happen for them," Creator replied.

"Yeah, that answer really sucks, so You need to tell me something," I said. "I mean, here I am with You in my head helping me make choices for my own greatest and highest good and some of them are creating situations that don't resemble anything like the greatest and highest good for everybody around me. What's up with that? I'm starting to feel the power of selfishness."

"Exactly why some souls arrive in the South and some in the North," They said.

"I figured that out on my own."

"Have you figured out where you are?"

"On Earth?"

"Yes and no."

"Here we go." I shook my head against the pillow. "Nothing is ever straight forward with You is it?"

They chuckled but I didn't feel any amusement fill my heart. "You're in the East."

"The eastern part of Earth?" I asked. "I thought I was in the west. That's what's on the maps at school."

"Earth is in the East," They replied. "Hadn't you noticed that the three other places you've been were South, North, and West? Those are all places of the kingdom."

"No way," I said. "Do the portals work here? Can they be opened by anyone here?" My heart raced at the thought.

"No," They said.

"No? Then how do souls get from Earth, the East, to where they need to go after they die?"

"There are thousands of Spirit Guides accompanying them to the North or South at every moment."

"Can they be seen by us?" I looked around the room before realizing nobody was likely to need a Spirit Guide in this house at the moment.

"There are occasions where they are seen," answered Creator. "Souls most connected to their origins see them the most. And children. Children see them all the time."

"So if I died here, a Spirit Guide would take me home, to the South?" It seemed the simplest answer. I didn't need to wait for portal magic to be restored. Didn't need to stay here any longer, screwing up Meeks and Joe and Toma's lives. They'd mourn, sure. But better now than when we got super attached to each other. The pangs of loss already tugged on my tender heart. But the yearning to be done with this whole mess overrode any other emotions.

"What are we waiting for?" I said. "Kill me." I sat up in bed, expecting to be slain immediately.

Creator was silent.

"Well? I'm ready."

"Embry. You've already died. Doing so again would kill your soul forever." Creator's voice in my head was filled with more loss than I could imagine. Hope died. There would be no easy solutions for me. My birth parents' decision probably hadn't been an easy one, so why would I think I could take the easy way out. Alice's selfishness, even in the afterlife, had doomed me to walk this path.

I thought again to the conversation I'd overheard before my kidnappers sent me to the North. When I'd first regained consciousness they'd talked about someone's monument. We'd been inside someone's crypt. It hadn't dawned on me that there shouldn't be anything like that in Eternity. Everything finally clicked into a clear picture of how the dragons had lost their portal magic. They'd let someone die a second death. I lay my head back down on the pillow, silent tears trickling down my cheeks and into my ears.

"If you die here, your soul will be gone forever and that is a situation We cannot allow to happen. Again." Creator surrounded me with glowing green love energy.

Now I knew what They meant. The toll of such an emotional day made me yawn. I'd wake tomorrow in this bed, on Earth, which was in the East of there, or here, or . . . I didn't know what to think anymore. I just wanted to go home.

Creator gave me beautiful dreams and I slept deeply. I toured the Earth, the East, and saw its borders where North, South, and West met. I saw waterfalls and lakes, snowy peaks, and bare deserts where the wind reshaped sand into mountains and valleys. Saw people living simply in huts who looked a lot like me, and people living in high-rise buildings. Their voice narrated each part of the dream, reassuring me that They knew each and every soul and that all were part of the plan for everyone's greatest and highest good.

It wasn't until the smell of sweet syrup blended with the rich deep scent of coffee in the French press that I stirred from sleep. Rain spattered the windows and a breeze helped detach more leaves from the trees. Before I could stir from the covers, Toma bounded in and landed with a bounce at the end of my bed.

"Get up, Embry." He patted the bottoms of my feet. "Meeks wants to know if you want to go to yoga."

"Toma," called Meeks. "You didn't go up there and wake her, did you? That is not what I asked you to do."

Footsteps on the stairs told me Meeks was coming to deal with Toma, but I was already awake and didn't mind the intrusion.

"It's okay, Meeks," I called. "I was awake."

"See, Mom?" Toma had moved to the window and was toying with the stuffed unicorn they'd bought in anticipation of my arrival in their lives. I couldn't avoid the pang of guilt at the thought I'd come with no intention of staying. Selfishness, it seemed, was something we could still experience in the afterlife.

Chapter Thirty-Seven

The weekend passed too quickly as we spent time doing normal family things, laughing while jumping in piles of leaves Joe was happy to rake up again and again. Toma gave me a few bruises in his exuberance to jump on me before I had a chance to move aside, and though he was reprimanded, I really didn't mind. The external bruises kept me from thinking of the internal ache in my heart.

Meeks and I drove in silence on our way to school, our moods subdued by our return to classes. Before I could enter my English classroom, Conner grabbed my arm and drew me aside. I felt his worry, his energy exuded alarming red fear.

"Janelle isn't returning any of my texts, have you talked to her?" His face was inches from mine, his voice almost sinister with concern.

I shook my head, wondering why he wasn't talking to Tina instead of me, but Tina brushed past us into class without stopping. Her aura was also red but spotted with a dirty yellow. Conner looked from me to her and back before widening his eyes, needing answers.

"Conner, I don't even think Janelle has my number or knows where I live." I stepped back so his face was at least in focus. "What's going on? Did you guys fight? I saw you at the game Friday. Sorry I didn't come over and say hi."

"Yeah, well, that's just it," he said. "I thought we'd decided on something." He hesitated, finding words. "There's something I need to tell you. For some reason, I can't shake the feeling you need to know. I don't know what that's all about."

The bell sounded in the corridor and Mrs. Finch waved us in before I could respond. Creator sent electricity through my brain, indicating They were responsible for Conner's decision to confide in me. Unfortunately, we had to focus our attention on Mrs. Finch's lecture on Ray Bradbury's *Fahrenheit 451* and its implications for today. Forty-five minutes later, when it was time to move to trigonometry, Conner walked toward a different math class and I had to suffer through not knowing what the hell was going on.

Tina focused on taking notes, never allowing me to make eye contact with her. Craig, sitting between us, must have thought I was flirting with him as I missed no opportunity to try for Tina's attention. Olivia noticed, of course. As we exited the classroom on our way to physics, she shoved me behind her, and I bumped into the wall.

"Bitch," Tina said under her breath. At least she was paying attention to me, even if we weren't talking. Her comment had been aimed at Olivia. Splotchy, red and yellow energy still swirled around her. It basically screamed for others to leave her the hell alone.

I followed Tina to physics, where Meeks greeted me with a smile as I took my seat next to Craig again, avoiding Olivia's jealous stare. I couldn't wait to track Conner down at lunch. Olivia walked between Craig and me while he asked me how it was going and how I was adjusting to life outside of the detention center. She steered him toward the student store before I could fully answer, claiming he owed her a soda.

Conner sat across from Tina, Janelle noticeably missing from the table. Tina wielded her fork at him as if it were a weapon, talking with such vehemence, I stopped in front of other students loaded with food trays, nearly causing them to fall.

"Yo, watch it Embry." It was one of the guys who had fist-bumped me in the corridor after I'd told Conner off. "Just 'cause you're Ms. Falade's daughter, doesn't mean you won't get your ass kicked if I spill my spaghetti."

I stepped out of the way, apologizing. He smiled.

Tina stopped talking as I sat on the bench between her and Conner. Her stare should have made me change my mind and find another table, but with Creator in my mind, I knew I was supposed to stay.

"I'm going to tell her," said Conner.

"Let me tell you all the reasons why that's a fucked-up idea, shithead." Tina waved her fork again. "First, Janelle doesn't want her to know. Second, she's Ms. Falade's daughter and she'll slip up and tell her."

I opened my mouth to protest, but got the fork waved in my face so stayed silent.

"You just want to tell her because you didn't like what we decided Friday night," she continued. "You want someone to side with you. God, Conner, you're such a dick. How can you be so selfish? Besides, it might not matter. She's not feeling well."

"Someone tell me what the hell is going on." I sounded so authoritarian that I surprised myself. My own violet and white aura caught my attention, assaulting and surrounding Conner and Tina without any consideration to theirs. I was flooding the space around us, using Creator's energy to affect the mood.

"Janelle's pregnant," blurted Conner.

"What the fuck, Conner? Seriously?" Tina looked murderous. I didn't know whether she wanted to kill him or me, or both of us.

"Oh my God, what?" I asked.

"Tell her." Tina stood. "I'm going to go get some more soda. I can't even believe this."

My lunch sat cold and forgotten as I listened to Conner.

"Janelle's pregnant," Conner said softer this time, sorrow filling the air.

"So you said."

Creator reminded me how that happened, a visual of loving intercourse filling my mind for a moment. New and strange feelings bounced from my heart toward my vagina and back again. But I couldn't dwell on myself. Not when Conner needed my full attention.

"I thought she was on the pill," he continued. "Turns out she hadn't told her parents she was taking it so when they found them, they threw them away and forbade her to go back to the Health Center for more. She didn't tell me."

I leaned forward, curly hair making a shield wall between me and the rest of the students in the cafeteria, watching the tears leak from the sides of his eyes.

"Embry, I didn't know. Would never have had sex without protection, or just stopped altogether. Seriously. I love her. I never forced her. At least, I don't think I did." He looked down at his clenched fists, unable to continue. When he finally met my eyes, he looked completely panicked.

"So, he's an asshole, right, Embry?" Tina returned holding a soda that could have quenched the thirst of a small army.

"God, Tina. You're not making it better," said Conner. "What should we do?"

"We? We? Seriously? We? You're not pregnant." Without a fork to point, Tina used her finger. "And we"—she paused to gesture at our little group--"are not going to do anything. You, Embry, are going to keep your mouth shut. Janelle has enough to handle without getting you or your mom or the whole fucking school involved."

"You said she's sick, right?" I asked. "Is it the baby?"

"I don't know. She didn't tell me anything this morning." Tina's anger-filled energy changed to green compassion for her friend. "She's even afraid to text anything about the pregnancy in case her parents—they're such assholes—find out."

"Maybe we should go see her after school," I offered.

"Were you not listening?" asked Tina. "We, and you, are not getting involved with what she decides to do. We're just going to be there no matter what. That's what friends do." She pointed at Conner's chest to emphasize her point.

I knew about abortion. I knew exactly what that soul faced if that was what Janelle decided. It took all of my own effort as well as Creator's not to blurt out my truth. Realized with increasing clarity that They had, once again, planned for this exact moment in time and space. Janelle, Conner, and Tina were walking through a situation in which their decisions would affect their afterlife in ways they could never imagine. My interference at this important moment in their lives could force them into making a selfish decision. I quite literally bit the end of my tongue inside my mouth. Not hard enough to draw blood, but hard enough to keep it from moving into speech.

Tina opened her mouth to admonish Conner some more, but the obnoxious school bell cut her off. She hoisted herself off our bench, flipped a bird at the bell and walked toward the exit, holding her now-half-empty soda. I didn't need to read her aura to understand her body language. She was angry and afraid, but not for herself.

Chapter Thirty-Eight

I sent a quick text to Janelle on my way to history, asking if I could stop by after school on the pretext of giving her homework. She agreed. I promised myself, and Creator, that I wouldn't interfere. I just wanted to hear what she was thinking and maybe, just maybe, connect with the soul inside. Creator couldn't argue with my desire to bring Their presence into the situation. Normally, They weren't as close to anyone as They were right now, occupying a space in my head. I was unique. Though everyone heard Them on a daily basis, helping, reminding, comforting, and so on, I carried Them with me. It was kind of a surreal realization, and slightly frightening.

Convincing Meeks to drop me off at Janelle's on the way home was easy. She was delighted I was making friends. She liked Janelle.

"We'll have to get you into driver's training, Embry," said Meeks. "You're old enough. I'll make some calls when I get home."

"Thanks, Meeks," I said. "I love you."

Her look of surprise made me laugh.

"Love you too." She waved and drove away. I was surprised at the pang of slight regret at keeping Conner's secret from her.

I texted Janelle that I was here. She had asked me to warn her as she wasn't sure how her parents would react to me. She'd said she would explain when I arrived. Creator showed me the difference in my skin color compared to hers and I realized we were different. I didn't know how or why that should make a difference in how I was treated.

Compared to the house I lived in, Janelle's was modest. Manicured hedges bordered a small, immaculate lawn. Two windows with tiered curtains were perfectly spaced on either side of the white door. No flowers or adornments gave any indication as to the personalities living inside. I knew nothing about Janelle aside from what I'd learned from Tina and Conner, so I was not prepared for the downtrodden, mousy spirit of the woman who answered the door. She was shorter than me, with dry tawny hair done up in a braid and lashed to her head with numerous bobby pins. A brown, plaid blouse, buttoned all the way up, was tucked into ill-fitting corduroy pants that were too short and showed short, white socks.

"What do you want?" She scanned the street before looking me up and down as if I was dirt needing to be swept off her front porch. Her frown made her small, squinty eyes even less readable. Her aura, pea green, told me of her unhealthy soul.

"I brought Janelle's homework from today." I reached inside my backpack while the woman watched with suspicion.

"Do you have a gun in there? Are you going to shoot me?"

"What?" I said, shock making my voice squeak. "No." I managed to free the papers from the depths of my backpack and show them to her as if surrendering.

"Thanks," she said. "But you didn't need to bother. She told me this morning she can get all of her missing assignments online or something." She started to close the door.

"Right, but there's a few things I need to explain to her. We've got a new assignment in history she'd probably like to get started on." I was grasping at any reason to get past this woman to see Janelle. I was beginning to see why Tina hadn't wanted me involved and it didn't have anything to do with who my mom was.

"Let her in, Mom." It wasn't Janelle, but some other small child's voice coming from within the house.

"You shush, Jeremy." The woman looked behind her, narrowing the gap in the door. "Nobody's talking to you."

"Jeremy, can you tell your sister I'm here?" I knew if that door shut, I'd never get her to open it again. Wondered how in the world Janelle was able to have a friend like Tina, with piercings and her tough exterior, or a boyfriend for that matter. Maybe this woman didn't know about them? That was most likely the case. This home held poisonous energy.

I was surprised when the door was pulled open and Janelle stood next to her mom. I could see the resemblance. But Janelle had somehow escaped whatever toxicity had stripped her mom of health. The soul inside her, bitter and downtrodden, must have been shrinking by the minute.

"Is she your friend?" asked the mom. "Her kind? Wait till your father hears you've got someone like her for a friend."

"She's new at school, Mom." Janelle sounded tired. "Mr. and Ms. Falade adopted her. She lived in a detention facility."

The last sentence didn't help. Janelle's mom wrinkled her nose further as if I'd taken on a disgusting smell. "Oh. Really. Hmm." Her lips disappeared.

"Can I come in for a minute?" I did my best to ignore the woman, giving Janelle a pleading look. "I need to explain about the history assignment." I held it up as a visual, hoping to increase my credibility.

The door opened enough to allow me in and was quickly closed by a still-suspicious mother standing in the entryway to the dingy interior of the house. Everything was brown. Floor, walls, furniture, and curtains varied little from the shade of brown high-rise corduroys the Mom wore. Janelle's younger brother Jeremy stood staring at me as if he'd seen his worst nightmare, not daring to speak. Fear, the color of burnt peas, emanated from his heart.

"You can sit at the table, Janelle." Her mom pointed toward a small room off the kitchen containing a cheap copy of a formal dining set, the sides chipped to reveal it was made of plywood. "I don't want her kind upstairs."

Creator gave me a picture of a white-skinned person handcuffing a dark-skinned innocent, speaking harsh words and shoving the person to the ground. Prejudice.

With new understanding, I followed Janelle to the table and sat near the window as far away from the woman as I could get. Was she going to join us? Listen in? Would I be able to have a real conversation with Janelle? I fought the instinct to get out of the house, away from the poison I felt here. It reminded me of the energy of the North, but harsher, less tempered by the presence of Light Beings. The words of the kelpies warning me of cruelty, selfishness, and hatred echoed again through my brain.

The woman did not follow us into the dining room but puttered nearby in the kitchen. For a moment, Janelle silently communicated her apology for her mom's bad behavior. A tear slipped from the corner of her eye and she unconsciously rested her hands on her belly for a split second before remembering herself and placing them folded on top of the lace placemat.

"Are you feeling better?" I asked.

"A little." She glanced toward the kitchen, knowing her Mom was most likely listening.

We needed to establish a normal friendship tone, so I continued as if my only purpose to visit was to discuss our assignments. A small, outdated computer sat in the corner next to a sideboard where an ancient set of china was displayed as if it was worth far more than it probably was. Faded yellow Post-its curled against the side with anti-technology sentiments written with a jagged hand lined the sides of the screen.

"Dad doesn't like technology," she explained. "We only have that because they want me and Jeremy to get good grades."

I nodded, wanting to place a hand on her folded hands to show how much I understood but refrained from doing so. There was a huge barrier of blood-red protective energy surrounding her and breaking into it now would cause her emotional harm. Creator whispered for me to go slowly, be gentle. I showed Janelle each assignment as if it was the most important of her school career. The puttering in the kitchen was a constant reminder of the eavesdropping, so I delayed asking the mounting list of questions in my head.

It was half an hour later I noticed silence from the kitchen. Janelle noticed too, leaning closer. "Why are you really here?"

"I know about . . ." I nodded toward her belly.

"They weren't supposed to tell you." She placed her hands over the area once more, her energy brightening to a clear garnet color shot through with sparkling apple green.

"Is it okay?" I asked. "Are you okay?"

"I'm bleeding," she answered. "Just spots, but I'm cramping too."

"God, Janelle. We need to get you to the doctor. That's serious stuff." I placed a hand on her arm.

"I don't know, Embry. If my parents found out, they'd freak."

"Let's go somewhere so we can talk without her hearing," I suggested. "Is that possible?"

"Mom's pretty strict when we've been sick. She doesn't let us do anything until we prove we're better." She shook her head, long tawny hair falling between us for a moment.

"Try." I was desperate to find out what she planned to do about the pregnancy.

"Okay." Her look held new determination. "Hey, Mom?" she called.

"How many times have I told you not to shout for me from another room?" Mom came bursting in from the hallway. "If you want me, come find me first." She paused to give me an evil look as if I was the cause of this transgression. Perhaps I was. "Well, anyway. I'm here. What do you need?" She exhibited no concern over how pale and miserable her daughter was.

"We need to go upstairs for a minute so I can look through my backpack for something. Is that okay?" Janelle's tone was of a supplicant, a servant to her master. It made me feel nauseous. Made me want to smack her mom and scream at her for being such a succubus on Janelle's soul. Only Creator's reminder that there was a miserable soul inside stayed my hand.

"She stays here," her mom replied, pointing at me. "Better yet, she stays out on the porch while you go get what you need."

"No, Mom. Really. She's fine. She's a good person." Janelle sounded mortified.

"You're lucky I let her in. Maybe she should just leave. You can't be that dumb that you need things explained over and over again, are you?"

"Mom, really. I just need to double check something, and the paper is upstairs. Please?" Janelle appeared to actually shrink in stature. I noticed she fought to keep her hands from her belly as she spoke.

"It's okay. I'll wait outside." I moved to the hallway before Janelle could say anything. Letting myself out, I immediately felt better, even though toxicity still circled this oppressed home.

"I'll be out in a minute," called Janelle.

I heard her hurrying on the stairs, then a window above me opened. I stepped forward on the porch and looked up. Janelle's face popped out and she mouthed 'Hold on.' She disappeared and I checked the window on my level for signs her mom might be watching me. I sensed she was hiding behind the curtains to make sure I didn't steal something, though there was nothing on the porch to take had I felt the inclination.

Janelle popped out of her window again, holding a sign scribbled on the back of her notepad. 'I want to go to the Health Center. Can you take me?'

I nodded, "Yeah, sure."

She disappeared for a moment and reappeared with a new sign: 'Give me half an hour. Wait at the corner.'

I gave her a thumb's up and walked down the steps leading to the sidewalk. Resisting a glance over my shoulder, I walked toward the corner.

Chapter Thirty-Nine

"Hurry. Mom will check on me soon." Janelle looked horrible wrapped in a brown plaid coat with Sherpa lining that looked as if it belonged to several others before her. A bluish tone underneath both eyes stood out against her pale skin. Her unsteady breathing showed me how much pain she was in.

"How did you . . . ?" I began.

"No time to explain," she interrupted. "Let's go. There's a four-thirty bus that goes by the Health Center. If we hurry, we can get there before they close."

I grabbed her hand, squeezing it tight so she'd know I was all in. Creator surrounded us in a ruby-red safety aura. We were untouchable. Even Janelle's breathing steadied. With quarters Meeks had given me for snacks at school, I paid for Janelle and me to ride into the city. She stared out the window still holding my hand. I managed to text Conner with one hand before she noticed.

'Meet me at the Health Center.'

When I realized how late it was getting, I texted Meeks to let her know I was staying at Janelle's to study and received a thumbs up. She was probably grading papers or busy with Toma. The feeling of deception tweaked something inside, but it also felt as though Creator approved of my actions, so I forced the feelings to the back of my head to deal with later. It was only when They said something about portals and portal magic that I remembered I didn't really belong here in the first place. I shoved that thought aside as well. Janelle was pregnant and we were on the way to the Health Center. This was reality and happening now. It was for me to ignore my own needs and be there for this terrified soul.

We exited the bus in front of a boutique coffee shop, and I offered to buy Janelle a drink, but she shook her head, doubled over now with pain and holding her belly while she walked. Though she didn't really have much of a bump, there must have been something going on inside that was causing her to throw caution to the wind. She didn't care who saw her holding herself. She was determined to get to the Health Center before collapsing.

About halfway down the block, I saw Conner, hands in pockets and a worried aura of green shielding him from passersby. When he saw us, he rushed toward Janelle and she allowed him to pull her close, leaning on him and moaning a bit.

"Come on, boo. It's going to be okay." Conner's aura brightened and blended with the safety bubble Creator surrounded us with.

As soon as we entered the Health Center, the receptionist discerned our emergency and took over. She rushed around the desk and called for assistance from someone down the hall. Conner helped Janelle to a wheelchair in the corner, kneeling in front of her and whispering soothing words.

"What the fuck is going on!" Tina whispered, shoving the door hard as she entered.

As soon as she saw Janelle bent over in the wheelchair, I grabbed her before she could curse too loudly again. I quickly explained the situation and we joined Conner hovering over Janelle.

"We need to get her to the examination room immediately," said a curvy woman dressed in white scrubs and a stethoscope around her neck. Others dressed in green scrubs fussed over Janelle, brushing us aside.

When the three of us started down the hall after them, the curvy woman turned with a hand up. "It will just be a minute. You need to let us take care of her."

We protested, but she was adamant that we needed to stay behind, so we watched as they wheeled her around the corner. Tina and I kept Conner from following.

"Come on, shithead. Let's go sit down. Maybe they'll even give us some stale coffee. Yum." Tina steered Conner back to the sitting room near the receptionist's desk. "So, which one of you knows what's going on?"

I described my visit to Janelle's house and they nodded knowingly as I mentioned her mom's behavior.

"How did you even spend enough time with her to become friends?" I asked.

"Church," they replied at the same time.

"Church? Seriously? How?"

"They go to church every night," said Conner. "I found out it was the only way I could see her when I first noticed her in class last year, so . . ." He lifted his hands and shrugged.

"We're both projects for their little youth group," added Tina. "You should see them, sphincters shrinking every time we walk in." She snorted. "He's the baddie from the wrong side of the tracks they're trying to save, and I'm the one with too many piercings and not enough fucks to give that they think they can fix. It's hilarious." She made air quotes. "Jesus saves."

"So, Janelle and I would sneak away from youth group and just hang out," added Conner. "At first she wouldn't even hold my hand. It was Tina that told her the facts of life."

"Seriously, her parents have given her some fucked up beliefs about sex and men and all that shit." Tina shook her head, angry.

I was angry too. The kelpies' words echoed in my brain. Here was evidence of selfishness, of hate, of humans taking a beautiful expression of intimate love and making it into something dirty. I excused myself to visit the restroom where I could be alone with my thoughts and Creator's voice.

"Why are humans so stupid?" I asked. "You created us with everything, right? Why don't we enjoy it? Why don't we live in peace and harmony, sharing everything and showing love to everyone? How did we get so fucked up? People like Janelle's parents shouldn't even be able to have kids. This is so messed up. And what should I tell Janelle to do? Should she keep this kid and ruin her life? Should she get rid of it and deny the soul inside a chance to live?" I paced in the small room as I railed against Creator.

"I'm sort of leaning toward telling her to get rid of it," I continued. "This world sucks. I don't think much of this free will stuff, frankly."

"We've been trying to tell you something, Embry," They answered.

"Yeah, well, I've been a little busy dealing with this situation I find myself in." I crossed my arms.

"Portal magic is restored. Whenever you're ready."

Chapter Forty

"Are you kidding me? Now?" I punched the towel dispenser, hurting my hand, and shoved it in my mouth.

"Embry? Is someone in there with you? You okay? Unlock the door." Tina pounded the door as she shouted at me.

"I'm okay." I opened the door, still sucking on my wounded hand.

"What did you punch?" Tina asked.

"The towel dispenser," I said.

"Yeah. Been there, done that. Hurts." She led me back toward the sitting area where a nurse stood talking to Conner.

"...should be okay." The doctor, a woman well into her sixties with cropped gray hair and tiny diamonds running down both sides of her ears looked up as we joined them. "I was just telling the father that Janelle's bleeding is most likely from a harmless cervical polyp, though the cramping worries me. Does she normally have cramping during her menses? Her period?" She looked at the three of us, not sure who might know the answer.

I shrugged, not really sure what she was talking about, though Creator helped me out with a visual. Except for my eyes narrowing, my reaction went unnoticed.

Tina and Conner exchanged glances. "She's miserable every month," said Tina. "Her mom tells her it's her curse for being a woman and won't let her take anything for the pain. Sometimes I let her stay at my pad during the day. She can't even walk sometimes."

"Her increased levels of estrogen can cause these polyps to bleed, or..." She looked at Conner. "Have you two had sexual intercourse since she knew she was pregnant?"

"Yeah." He nodded, shrinking into a ball of yellow guilt.

"It's okay, and normally pretty safe," said the doctor. "It just might have aggravated the polyp." She scrutinized us for a moment as if making a decision. "Look, I have to ask, do her parents know she's pregnant?"

We shook our heads.

"It's okay. Really." She exuded reassurance. "I just need to know who is going to make sure she takes care of herself. She needs to be off her feet for a day or so, stay hydrated, and no heavy lifting for the rest of her pregnancy, unless..."

"Her parents won't let her slack off," said Tina.

"They'll make her go to church tonight, too," Conner added.

A woman approached us as we discussed our options and placed a hand on the doctor's arm. She was about Meeks's age and wore her hair in a million tiny braids gathered together behind her neck in a loose scrunchie. She looked as if she was ready to go for a run. "Hey, Kirsten. They said you had some clients out here that might need to talk to me? I've just been to see Janelle."

"These are her friends." She paused while we introduced ourselves and how we knew Janelle. "I think there might be a problem with the family."

"I'm Carmella, one of the counselors here on staff." She shook each of our hands. "Janelle's lucky to have three friends who care so much. She's getting dressed. Would you like to join us in my office so we can talk about options?"

We followed her, feeling a mixture of relief and fear. Creator reminded me I didn't have to do this. Didn't have to follow through. They were ready with a portal. I could be back in the South immediately. I did my best to shut Them out. I needed to see this through. It was important for me to understand how decisions to end a pregnancy on purpose were made. Plus, these were my friends. My very own friends made not because we were souls arriving in the South at the same time and going to the same classes. We were friends because we'd chosen each other.

Carmella pulled a chair in from another office as Janelle joined us, looking a little less pale and with a clearer, green tint to her energy. Conner moved to take her hand and guided her to the chair next to his. Carmella closed the door to her cozy office furnished with pictures of her winning triathlons next to inspirational sayings and African art. There was even a framed child's drawing depicting two women holding a small girl by the hand as they picked flowers.

"I need to go over a few things before we get started." Carmella looked each of us in the eye before focusing on Janelle. "You are in complete control of your body, and any decision about this pregnancy is ultimately yours. Your friends are here, and you're welcome to listen to their advice, but I'm here only as your advocate and to assist you with whatever you choose."

"Okay," said Janelle.

"Now, the law is very clear," Carmella said. "If you choose to end this pregnancy, it is legal and this Health Center can help you. Another option is to carry to term and put the baby up for adoption. The third option is to keep the baby and raise it." She paused. "This Health Center can help you with all three, but you are under no obligation to use our facility or services. Do you have any questions?" She pushed some papers across her desk for Janelle with everything she'd just said spelled out in detail.

"Yeah, how soon does she have to decide if she's going to get rid of it?" Tina asked.

"God, Tina, really?" asked Conner.

"Well, it's the question on all of our minds, right?" asked Tina.

I was beginning to understand the complexity of such a decision, even as Creator continued to urge me to get out of the situation. I couldn't understand why They were so adamant about keeping me from seeing this through. I felt like this one life lesson would change me for Eternity and I wasn't about to miss it. I barely kept from shaking my head and shouting no.

"Why don't we let Janelle guide the discussion, Tina?" said Carmella. "Janelle, have you given it much thought?"

"It's all I think about." Janelle looked at Conner as he squeezed her hand. "My parents, oh my God, my parents would kill me if they knew. Conner wants me to keep it and we'll raise it. Tina obviously wants me to have an abortion, and I don't know what Embry wants."

I simply shrugged. I just wanted what was best for everybody that would make it all go away. I felt Creator send soothing energy into the office, surrounding us in a peaceful atmosphere. It helped. I watched Janelle's shoulders drop from where they'd been hovering near her ears, Tina relax and scoot back in her chair, and Conner loosen his death grip on Janelle's hand. I thanked Them.

"What do you want?" asked Carmella.

Only the analog clock on the wall ticking the seconds made any noise. Janelle wasn't used to all the attention. She dropped her head into her hands and sobbed. "I just want it all to go away. I don't want to be pregnant. I don't want to carry it or kill it. I don't want to give it away, either. I want to go to art school." Her voice broke as great, heaving sobs took over.

Carmella slid the tissues toward her and we waited, allowing the moment. Though Janelle apologized several times as she sniffled, wiping her eyes and nose, nobody spoke. Only when she looked up at Carmella did we know that she'd regained control.

"More than anything, I want to go to art school," she said. "It's the only thing that I'm good at that my parents allow. They've taken everything I've ever loved away except for art. Dad said that if I could get a scholarship, I could go. If I don't, I have to get a job here and never escape. That's just not an option. I hate it here. I have to get away." She looked at Conner. "And I love you, but I don't want to end up like Mom in a marriage I resent."

Conner opened his mouth to protest, but Janelle continued.

"I know. I know. You're nothing like Dad. And you're going to be an awesome husband, and father. But, really? Right now?" Janelle shook her head. "No. No way."

"Now she's making some fucking sense," said Tina. "Isn't that what we decided last Friday night?"

"What did you decide last Friday night, Tina?" asked Carmella.

"That she'd come here and have an abortion," said Tina.

Carmella leaned back in her office chair. "Okay, well, I feel like we're going in one direction, so let me give you some details about the procedure."

Creator burst into my thoughts and insisted on being listened to. Their voice blocked Carmella's as she described what Janelle would experience.

"Embry, Archeladon is waiting and has arranged for Dina and Aunt Katy to receive you," They said. "We would prefer you to choose to come with Us rather than stay and hear this. It is, however, your choice. As it has always been."

Chapter Forty-One

"My choice? Nothing really has been my choice since leaving the South, has it, Creator?" I excused myself to the bathroom again, claiming a personal emergency. My timing was horrible, but so was Creator's. Instead of going to the bathroom, I went back outside.

A small gathering of anti-abortion protestors had gathered on the sidewalk in front of the Health Center. Some held signs showing what babies looked like inside the womb, others held hands and prayed. A man appearing to be in his twenties looked up from the praying group to glare at me. I gasped. He looked almost exactly like Tay, Alice's boyfriend in the South. Same athletic build, same long ringlets of curly black hair. Though his eyes were a dark brown instead of green and gold, they held the same ability to take my breath away. Creator's voice grew louder in my head, but I didn't hear a word They said.

He stared back, as shocked as me. There wasn't any way he could have known me, yet recognition filled his confused face and he stepped away from his group of prayer warriors. Frozen, watching him walk toward me, I filled with adrenaline for fight or flight. How was Tay here? It wasn't possible.

Creator continued to knock on the doors of my conscious mind. I ignored Them.

"Kamuy? Is that you? It can't be you," Tay's lookalike inquired. He stopped about three feet in front of me, waiting for an answer.

"You are not supposed to be out here!" Creator finally broke down the walls of my thoughts to shout at me. "Get away from him!"

I grabbed my head in my hands, unable to handle the volume and urgency of Their voice contained in my head.

The young man rushed to my side, "Are you okay, Kamuy? Do you need to sit down?" He was already guiding me to a bench outside the center. His gentle hand on my back jarred me back to the reality of the situation and I shrugged away. "Sorry, I was just trying to…"

We sat, him being careful to sit far away enough not to touch me again, but near enough if I needed him.

"Who are you?" I finally asked when the pounding inside my head subsided a bit. Creator tried to soothe the pain They'd caused, but I held on, wanting to feel it so I could more easily block Them out.

"I don't understand," answered the man. "How can you not know me?"

"Who do you think I am?" I asked.

"You're Kamuy," he urged. "We—you and I…God, don't you remember? Is there something wrong with your head? Is that why you don't remember me?"

"I've never seen you before in my life," I answered. "And no, there's nothing wrong with my head. Just a sudden headache. Lots going on in there." I pointed toward the center.

"Come on, Kamuy," said the man. "It's me, Bryan."

I finished wiping the tears from my eyes with my sleeve and looked up at him for the first time. Clearly, he thought I was someone who should know him, and clearly, he was mistaken. He wasn't Tay. I knew that for sure. He didn't have the same sneering or judging aura that I'd seen around Tay when he was with Alice. This man's aura, though circled with a tinge of judging, ice blue on the outer edges, emanated a forest green of love. He was a confusion, if anything. And an unwanted interruption as I remembered the conversation going on inside the center. I had to get back. Had to hear the decision.

"I have to go." I stood and took a few steps toward the entrance.

"Please don't go," he pleaded, almost touching my shoulder with his outstretched hand. "Tell me your name first."

"I'm Embry," I answered. "I have to go." Creator flooded my head with insistent words of portals and magic and people waiting for me in the South. "Shut UP!" I shouted just before pushing the doors to the Center open. They went silent.

The man followed me inside. I ignored him and walked back to Carmella's office, closing the door behind me.

Chapter Forty-Two

"You look like shit," said Tina.

"Thanks. Yeah, bit of a headache," I answered.

"So, anyway, that's what you're looking at, Janelle," continued Carmella.

Janelle looked at Conner before she spoke. "My choice, right?"

He nodded.

"You won't get all freaked out and hold it against me forever if I decide to have an abortion, right?"

"I love you, Janelle. No matter what." He pulled her hand to his mouth and kissed it.

"Okay." She looked at Carmella. "Then that's what I want to do."

The pain in my head amped up to excruciating. I gasped, grabbing it in both hands.

"I'll take her outside," said Tina. "You guys do whatever you gotta do now."

The air in the corridor didn't help much. I was still

keeping Creator at bay somehow. Tina walked me to the waiting room windows and chose a blue pleather couch to sit on. "What the fuck, Embry? You're a real lightweight, aren't you?"

I couldn't answer.

"We've got to go now, Embry!" Creator kept shouting with increasing frequency and volume. Sparks flew from outside my third eye into my brain as if They were using a welding torch to burn Their way in.

"She was like that outside." It was the Tay lookalike. "Maybe we should get her some help?"

"Who the hell are you?" asked Tina.

"My name's Bryan," he answered. "Kamuy doesn't remember me."

"What the fuck are you on? This isn't Kamu-ee or whatever you just said. This is Embry and she has a headache." Tina shuffled through her backpack, finding a bottle of pills and shaking them in front of Bryan. "All she needs is a little ibuprofen. "Get the fuck away from us, you hypocrite."

"I was just trying—"

"I don't care what the fuck you're trying to do," Tina said. "Leave or I'll have to cave your head in. Go back out there with your fucking friends."

I heard all of this above the pounding and shouting in my head. Watched with half-open eyes as Tina stood, taking a fighter's stance. There was no doubt in my mind she could cave his head in with her Doc Martins. "S'okay," I croaked, my mouth dry all of a sudden.

The pleather couch squeaked as I shoved myself up from where I'd been lying. "Go get me some water, please, someone."

"Did you hear her?" asked Tina. "You want to help? Go get us both a bottle of water. I'll think about whether you get to stay when you come back."

I watched him head toward the vending machine and hung my head in my hands again.

"Do you know him?" Tina asked.

"Never seen him before in my life," I said. "He thinks I'm someone else."

Yeah, I got that," Tina said. "Doesn't give him the right to hang around though. Want me to get rid of him?"

I smiled. Tina's aura was glowing so brightly red with protective energy it was hard to see anyone else's. "No. I'm curious about who he thinks I am. Let him stay for a minute."

He returned with ice-cold bottles of water and sat across from us.

"This should be interesting," said Tina. She poured some small orange pills into my hand and watched me gulp them down with about half of the bottle.

The two of them watched me in silence, waiting as if they expected the pills to take immediate effect. I was happy for the silence. Creator still called my name, but They were ebbing into the background. I felt proud of my defiance. I was standing on my own here on Earth and if that was what selfishness was, then I decided it was okay. I didn't want to leave yet. I wanted to live here on Earth a little longer. I said as much to Them in my head. They left me alone then, though I felt Their disapproval and frustration with my decision. As a final word, I reminded Them of Their decision to create us with free will and to honor those decisions. Why would I be any different?

"Better?" asked Tina. I nodded as she stood. "Then I'm going to go see if Janelle's going to have it today. Scream if this moron tries anything."

"Is someone you know having an abortion today?" asked Bryan. "Can I pray with her?"

"No, you cannot fucking pray with her and it's none of your fucking business," Tina said. "Who do you and your little group of friends out there think you are anyway? Like, who died and made you the morality police? Jesus? Yeah, I know all about fucking Jesus. He was all about healing the sick and forgiving people and helping the fucking poor. Which part of what Jesus did looks like you? Huh? Shut the fuck up."

Once Tina gave Bryan a last hateful look and disappeared down the hall, Bryan looked at me, then out the window toward his friends, and sighed.

"Why are you here?" I asked. "Are those people out there your friends?"

"Not really," Bryan answered.

"Then why?" I repeated. "Out of all the things you could be doing with your time, you're here trying to make people feel bad for getting the medical help they need?" I watched his aura change as cloudy blue energy showed me his shame.

"You look just like a girl I knew," he said.

"Didn't answer my question," I said.

He ignored me. "She went away with her family after she and I"—he hesitated—"I cheated on my girlfriend with her." The cloud of blue shame engulfed him.

"Cheated?" I asked. "Did you love this girl who looked like me?"

"No. No, she and Alice were best friends," he said.

"Wait, what? Alice? Did you say your girlfriend's name was Alice?" I couldn't breathe again. Pulse racing, headache returning, fists clenching, I wanted to pummel him. She really had a type, didn't she? This guy and Tay could be brothers, twins even.

The sound of a wolf howling from my back pocket jolted me back from my inward spiral. I'd picked the ringtone with Toma's help and approval. There were few numbers in my phone, and I knew before I looked that it was Meeks. "Hi," I said, trying for cheerful, though it sounded too high and breathless.

"Hey, hon," said Meeks. "Joe and I were wondering when you're coming home. We'll hold dinner for you if you need a few minutes. Also, is Janelle's mom bringing you home or should we come get you?"

I looked at the time on the big clock on the wall across from me, realizing I'd lost track. Bryan watched as I searched for a way to stay here with Janelle, interview him about his Alice, and make it home in time for dinner with my family. I was coming up empty. And the last thing I wanted was Joe or Meeks coming to the Health Center to pick me up. That idea was too much to contemplate. There'd be too much to explain.

"You there, Embry? You sound a little off." Meeks prodded.

"Yeah, no, I'm good," I said. "It's all good. Janelle and I were just taking a study break. I don't think her mom's keen on the idea of bringing me home. I was just going to walk if that's okay."

"No way," answered Meeks. "Not after dark and with you so new to the area. Joe's already pulling his coat on."

I had to think fast. Think of another lie, so I told her Conner and Tina had joined the study session and I'd ask one of them to drive me. Meeks finally agreed and we hung up.

"I gotta go find my friends," I said. "Looks like your friends are disbanding for the day. You'd better go with them." I felt his eyes on my back as I walked down the hall. Wanted to turn around and insist he tell me his story. But it wasn't my business. He was a stranger. It was simply a coincidence that he looked like someone I knew from the South, that had a girlfriend named Alice, that was hanging out at a Health Center where abortions were performed. Yeah, that was it. Coincidence.

Chapter Forty-Three

J anelle was smiling when I found the room they used to prep patients for surgery.

"They gave her the good stuff," said Tina. "Wish they'd give it to all of us." When she saw my expression, she paused. "What's up with you?"

"Meeks called and wants me home," I answered. "She still thinks I'm at Janelle's house and was sending Joe to pick me up. I told her one of you could. Sorry."

"I can't leave Janelle," said Conner.

"What's the plan after she's out?" I asked.

"Tina called my mom," answered Janelle in a dreamy voice. "She's the only one of us brave enough to face her down, in person or on the phone."

"Man, was she pissed at you," said Tina. "I let you take the blame for Janelle's sudden disappearance so you are *persona non grata* around that house from now on." She shrugged like it was no big deal, but I felt the hate settle deep inside my heart. Now I had enemies here, too. "I told her you'd convinced Janelle to come with you to my apartment. You should have heard her yell."

"How did you explain she wasn't coming home?" I asked.

"That's the best part," said Conner.

"I told her that I was glad you had come by because I wanted to talk to Janelle about Jesus and that you did too," Tina's smile lit her face like I'd never seen before.

"You didn't," I said.

"She so did," grinned Conner. "It was the perfect thing to say to get Mrs. Ogden to calm down."

"Yeah, she calmed right the fuck down," chuckled Tina. "I asked her if she would please let Janelle spend the night so we could get all of our questions answered. God, I'm good."

"Tina, can you take me home?" I asked. "I don't want to leave, but I feel like it's best for all of us if I do."

"Yeah, explaining to Ms. Falade is not what any of us want to do right now, or ever," said Tina.

We said our goodbyes to Janelle and Conner, Tina promising to be back soon. When we got to the darkened parking lot, Tina led me to her motorcycle. As she snugged the straps on her extra helmet, I noticed a car several spaces over with its parking lights on.

"Hold on to my waist, but not too tight," instructed Tina. "And don't lean when I do. Just sit there like a sack of potatoes or you'll throw my balance off, even though you weigh about as much as a sack of potatoes."

I couldn't see much from inside my helmet sitting behind her and concentrated on not leaning. She revved and raced through the streets toward my neighborhood. Riding a motorcycle almost felt like flying with the gryphons. It didn't take as long as I'd thought it would and I was a bit sad when she stopped outside my house. My house. That was a warming thought.

Tina grabbed her helmet, said some quick instructions about keeping my damned mouth shut, and was gone before I saw Toma peek out the window from his bedroom window.

The motion lights along the pathway up to our house lit the landscape and Joe was at the door before I could fish my key out. "Hey, kiddo, missed you." He pulled me into a bear hug, suffocating me. Made me feel safe, loved, sad.

"Suffocating me," I managed to squeak.

Meeks was getting my plate warmed up and Toma slid-skipped down the stairs and grabbed me in a replica of Joe's hug. I shook my head. This family. This family was making me want to stay.

I managed to dodge specific questions about Janelle, hinting of female problems Joe and Toma didn't want to know more about. Meeks winked at me when they got squeamish. Just before dinner ended, our doorbell rang. Joe answered as we began to clear the table. Creator urged me to go upstairs.

"Embry, We don't want you to see who's at the door. He isn't making a good choice right now and if you're not around, he'll leave and make a different choice. If you go upstairs, We can extract you now and wipe everyone's memory. Your family will just think the man has the wrong house."

"I choose to stay," I said.

Joe followed the stranger inside, emanating the strong red of safety and protection into the entire room. "Embry, this man says he knows you."

Creator nudged the gut feelings of warning. I ignored them. I had to think of a new lie to tell my family about where I'd met this man. I nearly blurted out that he'd been at the Health Center but caught myself. Instead I just nodded.

"How do you know him, Embry, honey?" asked Meeks. "If it's a bad experience, tell us. He doesn't need to stay."

"I just met him once," I said. "At the detention center. He was there for a friend." I looked at Bryan with pleading eyes, hoping he'd pick up on the subtle lie. Either he did or he was too keyed up himself to notice it, his aura a whirlwind of mixed and dirtied blues.

"Why don't you sit down?" asked Joe, motioning to the dining table.

Meeks, Joe, and Toma sat too.

"Um, can I speak to him alone?" I asked. "His name's Bryan and he was nice to me at the center. It's okay."

"Are you sure?" asked Meeks.

"You know what? I trust you, Embry," said Joe. "We'll be in the study with the door open, okay? Toma, go upstairs and shut your door. You can play a few minutes of Super Mario."

Toma didn't argue and raced upstairs, slamming his door. Meeks took Joe's hand and they gave me one last look before entering the study. Even then, I waited a few moments before settling into my chair at the table.

"Did you follow me here?" I asked. "What kind of pervert are you? Seriously?"

"I couldn't get you out of my mind, Kamuy—I mean Embry," said Bryan.

"Okay, Bryan," I said. "Spill it. Tell me about her, about Kamuy."

"I had a girlfriend named Alice," he began.

"Had?" I asked. "As in past tense? Gone? What happened."

"She died in a car accident a few months ago, with my twin brother, Tay," he said. "We'd just patched things up after the incident."

"The incident with this Kamuy, or something else?" I asked.

"Yeah, when I cheated on her," he replied. "We were doing really good, talking marriage and family. When I saw you today, it brought it all back. Especially since I was at the Health Center."

"What does that have to do with anything?" I asked. "Did you two come to protests together there or something?"

"No, nothing like that," he said. "She wasn't interested in causes. I only started protesting after, after . . ."

"After what?" I decided he was the worst storyteller in the world, or maybe I was just the worst listener. Maybe it was Creator's voice in my head telling me I should end this conversation now. They certainly weren't getting any quieter as Bryan talked.

"Kamuy got pregnant," he said. "When she found out, she panicked and came to me. I got the money and paid for her to have an abortion. I couldn't have a kid with someone I didn't love and Kamuy's parents would have disowned her. She'd have been homeless. It was the best decision."

The nuclear explosion inside my heart blinded me. I was sitting across from my dad. My. Real. Dad. He hadn't wanted me, hadn't loved my mother, had been in love with Alice! The Alice that sent me through the portal. Creator surrounded me then with rainbow circles of universal healing energy. Somewhere inside, a tiny voice reminded me of my human body, my human family, my very human situation, but all I could do was take in short, shallow breaths until my vision cleared somewhat.

Bryan sat watching me, concern in his eyes and countenance, leaning forward across the table, trying to put his hand on mine.

"Where is Kamuy now?" I asked. Where was my mom? My real mom? Alice was dead and in the South, and apparently in love with Bryan's twin brother, Tay. Bryan, my dad, sat here in my living room. My adoptive parents sat just out of earshot and Janelle was at this very moment having an abortion.

"She's moved back to Hokkaido with her family," Bryan said.

"I need you to leave," I whispered.

"But I need to know how you can look so much like her and not know anything about her," he said.

"Well, I don't know the answer to that, and I really need you to leave." I stood. "Now. And don't ever come here again. How you could join those protestors after you actually paid to get one for your friend is beyond my comprehension. Get outta here."

"Everything okay in there?" Joe appeared in the doorway of the study, a cloud of safety blasting toward me.

"Bryan's leaving," I said.

He had no choice but to stand and precede me to the front door, Joe and Meeks following.

"It's been interesting catching up with you." I opened the door and stood to the side, daring him to say anything else. Closing the door behind him, I grabbed Joe and Meeks and held on as if my life depended on it. I loved them so much.

Chapter Forty-Four

In my room after a shower and a short conversation with Tina to check on Janelle, I lay on top of my comforter, listening fully to Creator's plan. They'd confirmed Bryan's story, answered all of my questions and soothed my soul. I knew They were right. I knew I needed to leave this life and go through the portal. I ached all over from the emotional toll of the day.

"I'm not going unless you tell me what will happen to everyone when I'm gone," I declared. "Everyone in this realm is going to be affected by my departure. What are You going to do about that, hmm? Did You even have a plan or am I just going to disappear and leave Meeks, Joe, and Toma wondering what happened and grieve and be heartbroken? You suck as a Creator."

"It's not the first time We've been told that," They replied. "We told you we'd chosen when to insert you into this world. Everyone's going to be fine."

"I'm not sure I believe You, really," I said.

The room felt suddenly soundproof as They filled it with loving green energy, a tinge of red urgency around the edges and in the corners.

"They're going to forget you, forget you ever existed," They said.

I took a breath, allowing Their words to sink in. "Nobody will remember me?"

"If We allow anyone to remember you, your parents' decision to end your life will be affected," They said. "We are aware of every soul all the time as they are a part of Us. By allowing anyone to have a lingering memory of you, it will ripple into their lives and We can't let that happen. You came here to wait until portal magic was restored. It's restored and we must go. You must go. We will give much attention to these souls after your departure."

"Not even a nugget somewhere deep down in their hearts can remind them of me?" I asked.

"Not even a nugget."

"This is so fucked up."

"Your parents said the same thing when they were deciding to end your life."

"Can I say goodbye? To anyone?"

"It's better for everyone if you don't, but again, it's your choice," They said. "We can smooth everything over no matter what you decide. Now is the time to go."

It always came down to my choice. Everything always came back to that.

Aunt Katy's worried face, Archeladon's huge back with its saddle-shaped scale just behind his head, Dina's beautiful way of teaching me, the kitsune cuddling against my skin, the Originals, even Argon and Kristoff wandered through my mind as I turned my thoughts to Home.

Home. I was going Home. After all the adventures of my short life I was returning Home.

Chapter Forty-Five

I hadn't expected to feel my body disappear. Hadn't expected the sheer joy at seeing Archeladon's huge violet eye at the end of a long funnel-shaped whirlwind of rainbow energy as Creator whisked me away from Earth, from the East, toward Home. Hadn't known which part of Home I would arrive in, but as the crystal-strewn landscape became clearer, I knew I was in the West, the land of mythical creatures, the Originals, and the place in all of my travels I'd loved the best.

Creator's presence left my head as Archeladon nudged and snuffled me with his great, scaly nose and fiery breath. It tickled. Before I could properly hug him, the love dragons surrounded me with hugs and dragon-squeaks of sheer delight. I was tumbled between them as if I were in a rugby match but felt nothing but happiness, forgetting the broken heart I'd left behind.

When Ainu cleared her throat, I looked to where she stood with India, Sandawe, and Khoisan, waiting for the dragons to relinquish me. The same rainbow from the portal shimmered around the four souls, reflecting the peace in their eyes at my safe return. Home.

"We are overjoyed at your safe return, Embry." Ainu stepped forward, holding out her arms for me to step into. She hugged me harder than I'd expected, a small sob escaping from her.

"Why do you cry, Ainu?" I asked.

"Those are happy tears, little one," replied Sandawe. "Happy tears."

"Will I be allowed to stay with you?" I asked Ainu. I felt her shake her head, her sobs increasing.

"I'm to take you through to the South," Archeladon said. "It is only because portal magic has been restored completely and you've safely returned that we allowed you to come here first. The Originals wanted to see you again. It will be a long time before you can join them. Perhaps the newly restored portal magic will allow a visit from time to time. We've changed some things because of you." His dragon smile would have been terrifying to anyone who didn't know him.

I hugged each Original before climbing up his great foreleg and into the saddle-shaped scale just behind his head. It was if it had been made for me. I wondered if it had been. If Creator had known all along that I would someday ride this great beast between worlds. It didn't matter.

"Aunt Katy and your Grandparents await your arrival," said Archeladon. "Dina is there as well."

"So, I'm returning to the South?" I asked. I'd surmised that was where I would end up, though the momentary selfishness and power I'd felt while in my human body made me wonder if I'd earned a place in the North for a time.

"You have much to catch up on and much to share, little one." Archeladon leaped into the air and the love dragons joined us, flying on either side like escorts. Once in the sky, we were joined by all the dragons I'd met as well as the gryphons, igigi, and peryton. Even before I could wish to see the kitsune, I saw them riding on the backs of the gryphons, their tails and fiery fur sending sparks into the air.

Archeladon dipped his great body toward one of the crystal mountains where Cryo and Larimar stood whinnying loud enough to be heard over the wind. I waved and they dipped their great, pointed horns. One by one, the creatures dropped back to return to their land, their lives in the West. Only Archeladon and I continued toward the South.

We passed through the rainbow energy filled with lightning and ethereal sounds from the stars and planets, landing in the clearing where I'd spent my mornings learning from Dina. Aunt Katy raced toward Archeladon but before she reached us, he disappeared beyond her reach, leaving me bouncing in the soft grass. Only I heard him whisper, "Goodbye, dearest Embry. We will see each other soon."

"Oh, Embry, I've missed you like crazy." She fell to the ground and hugged me while other souls joined us, surrounding us in a semicircle of concerned and elated energy.

My homecoming appeared to be a cause for everyone in the South to celebrate and I didn't have much of a chance to think during the next few days. In those moments, I wondered how Janelle was doing, what Conner thought about things, and how my human family was doing. I chose to believe Creator had erased all memory of me from the East. It was harder to deal with thoughts of Argon and the North. How was he doing? Would his behavior change as a result of our encounter? Was he making good choices? Enough to someday come South? I hoped so.

When I had a moment to myself, I thought of Alice. The cause of my entire journey had not been anywhere during the celebrations. I understood her actions, but it would be a long time before I forgave her. Though I wouldn't want to repeat it, the knowledge of all of Creation filled me with a far larger capacity for giving and receiving love in this life. I knew my parents' story. My connection with Alice was clear. I understood the deep scars of her heart, how she needed Tay to fill the hole left by my father. Even in the South, with Creator near all the time, and Light-Beings available, Alice needed a boyfriend. Made me wonder about Tay's story.

"Embry, there's someone here to see you." Aunt Katy stood in my doorway, a shadow behind her.

Before I could answer, Anfalmor shoved past her and bounded onto my bed, knocking brightly colored pillows about like confetti. I hadn't seen him since my return, and I hugged his furry neck as soon as I could corral him into holding still.

"You're alive!" I felt a little piece of my heart slip back into place. "Oh, thank Creator, you're alive!"

Anfalmor licked my face with his great wet tongue. "Of course, I am. Remember where you are young one."

"I was sure you were dying when I was kidnapped." I burrowed my hands deeper into the thick fur around his neck. I could find no evidence of injury except a small scar near his snout, just under his eye. I leaned my face against the side of his and closed my eyes.

"We need to talk about Alice," he said. "Walk with me."

I followed him outside and across the small creek running behind my cottage. Gypsy, our tortoiseshell cat, greeted Anfalmor with a touch to his nose and purred loudly as we climbed up the small hillock on the other side, away from other souls. Into the forest we strode. A feeling of heaviness increased with each step. I'd hoped I was done, yet I still wondered if she'd been punished. She'd not only disrupted my life, but a great many others, including the humans now living with perhaps a nugget of a memory of me.

When we reached the rock where it had all begun, Anfalmor led me around to the north side and there she was. Alice stood with Zadkiel and Dina, the Light-Beings in charge of us. Visions of slapping her, yelling at her, shoving her off a cliff, and other equally mean and selfish reactions flowed as quick as the shifting sands of the desert. I refrained from acting on any of them. I waited, breathing and seeking appropriate energy.

"I'm sorry," said Alice. "I'm so, so, so, so, sorry." She looked at Anfalmor, remorse filling her eyes with tears. She looked at me and shook her head as if shaking away a bad memory.

"Anything else?" He sat almost on my foot, like a protector.

Zadkiel and Dina stood nearby, urging Alice to move closer to us with a gentle nudge against her back.

I crossed my arms, a behavior I'd seen Tina do a million times. I was tempted to cock my head like hers and stand as if ready to fight but thought it might be too much and backed off. I wasn't going to make it easy for her. She'd put me through hell. Probably not the nicest way to show I'd forgiven her, but then again, I guess I hadn't.

"I hate you," Alice started.

Anfalmor growled.

"I mean, I did." She looked back at Zadkiel and Dina. "I was jealous. When you arrived, I saw her. Kamuy. I saw their child and I was angry all over again."

Anfalmor leaned against me, growling louder, his hair standing on end. "This story better change soon. I won't be responsible for my actions if it doesn't."

"You?" I said. "You were jealous of me? Seriously? I don't get it."

"I was happy again in the East. I'd patched things up with Bryan, my boyfriend there, and then boom, car wreck and I end up here—in the South, thankfully." She motioned around her, pointing at the crystal-clear pink sky, the talking wolf sitting on my foot, and the forest in the background. "I stole the book from Parmenides, the one Zeno wrote about dragons and found out how to open a portal."

I'd felt anger. Fear. Lots of fear. I'd felt despair and impossibly lost because of her. Wanted to send her through a portal to a worse place than the North if it existed. Now, I felt pity. My eternity was going to be richer for the experiences she'd forced me to have. Hers was going to be poorer. I don't know what Creator was going to do with her and it wasn't for me to punish her or put her in her place. It was for me to speak the words she needed to hear and allow fresh, green, loving energy to fill the void left by the hate I'd harbored for her.

"I forgive you," I said.

Anfalmor stopped growling.

THE END

Acknowledgements

Without the unwavering support of my husband, Peter Wonderly, I would not have written Embry's story. He has been my biggest fan as I learned how to move from elementary school teacher to writer. Reading every word, listening to every pondering, allowing entire rooms to be overtaken by writing paraphernalia, sketches of characters, and talismans from Doctor Who, Hunger Games, Harry Potter, etc., he has enriched every moment. Thank you for being the best Doggy-Daddy ever.

When Rebecca Erwin urged me to join her at The Random Writers Workshop, little did she know she was creating a writing monster. Thank you, Rebecca, for recognizing my passion, even before I saw it in myself.

It was at the first Random Writers' meeting I met one of the most influential people of my life, Jeannie Hart. First a friend and sometimes editor of those early attempts at writing, Jeannie Hart has mentored me through the technical side of writing and publishing. Jeannie is my guide to all things creative, taking me to Rose City Comic Con as a booth babe and introducing me to Cre8Con in Portland, Oregon, she sees all of my possibilities when I cannot. Her latest contributions to this project were to design the beautiful cover and format the book for self-publishing and I'm sure you, dear reader, are thankful it flows so beautifully.

The invaluable feedback from my Beta Readers, Kathleen Bulloch, Matt Garbell, Susan Schreiber, and Timothy Swanson helped carve away a lot of the dross and helped me look at the story from different perspectives. I listened and valued their frank critiques of the first few drafts.

I'm grateful for Daja Terry at Sphinxediting for her strong technical editing, and for urging me to be careful with capitalization.

Karen Dionne, bestselling author of The Marsh King's Daughter and The Wicked Sister, was always available to answer questions about agents and contracts. Jonathan Evison, bestselling author of All About Lulu, West of Here, The Revised Fundamentals of Caregiving, and This Is Your Life, Harriet Chance!, helped with questions about editing and self-publishing. Knowing these two authors were willing to help this newbie gave me the courage to persevere through those hard moments of self-doubt. Jen Violi, author of Putting Makeup on Dead People, helped me see that asking the important questions about my story makes a huge difference.

The two people on this earth that have known me the longest are my sisters, Linda Hillis and Kathy Hayes. I had a perfect childhood with two older sisters providing me with so much love and support, teasing and teaching. From those summers playing 'school' to those phone calls about our students when we were all teaching elementary school and swapping crazy student stories, these two women have helped define me and I am crazy-in-love with both of them.

Forty years ago, I found myself faced with making the hardest decision of my life. I chose to have a safe and legal abortion. The choice, hidden for nearly a decade from my family, was the best decision I could make at that time given the facts as I knew them. Who would've thought my journey would lead me to the story of Embry.

About the Author

Patty Renfro-Wonderly is a playwright, yoga instructor, and author of the new novel Child Lost, Child Found. A retired elementary school teacher, Patty has spent over a decade writing New and Young Adult Fantasy novels, one-act plays, and scriptural studies for a high school audience. Her debut novel combines her love of fantasy with her strong political views concerning Women's Rights. Patty is a founding member of The Random Writers Workshop, has attended writing conferences in Los Angeles, San Francisco, and Seattle, and her one-act play So Damned Heavenly Bound was produced in Hollywood. Patty writes from her home in Vancouver, Washington, often with one of two terriers or the tortoiseshell cat on her lap or writing desk. When not writing, she can be found in her home yoga studio teaching or practicing, hiking with her husband, or honing her paleo/keto cooking skills.